EXTRAORDINARY ACCLAIM
FOR THE WORK OF DOROTHY UHNAK

CODES OF BETRAYAL

"This work effectively portrays one man's agony with life gone wrong ... Police procedural and mafia readers will love this well-paced, well-written tale."—*Library Journal*

"A super plot, great characters, and a satisfying conclusion could re-establish Uhnak in the upper echelons of crime writers. A good choice for Joseph Wambaugh fans."—*Booklist*

"Uhnak is skilled at sketching the diverse cultures of New York's boroughs."—*Publishers Weekly*

THE RYER AVENUE STORY

"Detail, complexity, and old-fashioned storytelling ... Ms. Uhnak demonstrates that she has lost none of her skill."—*The New York Times Book Review*

"Dorothy Uhnak has written several excellent crime novels, but this [work] signals her return as a serious novelist ... One spellbinding novel."—*San Gabriel Valley News*

"Compulsive reading ... Chock-full of unrelenting and addictive scandal ... Uhnak is on target."
—*Booklist*

"Dorothy Uhnak could well be the Fannie Hurst of modern crime novelists."—*Chicago Tribune*

Also by Dorothy Uhnak

Police Woman
The Bait
The Witness
The Ledger
Law and Order
The Investigation
False Witness
The Ryer Avenue Story

CODES
OF
BETRAYAL

DOROTHY UHNAK

St. Martin's Paperbacks

CODES OF BETRAYAL

Copyright © 1997 by Dorothy Uhnak.

Cover photograph by Don Banks.

Library of Congress Catalog Card Number: 97-23598

ISBN: 0-312-96531-1

Printed in the United States of America

St. Martin's hardcover edition / November 1997
St. Martin's Paperbacks edition / January 1999

10 9 8 7 6 5 4 3 2 1

To Dr. Kishore R. Saraf,
who has brought light to my dark places
for more than twenty years.

To the Tuesday night artists' group, who have
given me more support and encouragement
than they realize.
All of you, but especially Janet Culbertson,
Marnie Hutchinson, Rose Slivka,
Mary Jane Meaker, and Marggy Kerr.

Again, always, to my husband, Tony,
and daughter, Tracy.
They know why.

CODES
OF
BETRAYAL

1964

There was a hard, cold wind blowing from the Hudson River, with Thirty-fourth Street acting as a corridor. The steelworkers, braced on the open skeleton of the twentieth floor of what would eventually be a forty-two-story condominium, were used to the weather. The tension among them was prompted by the presence of three men in suits, obviously not construction men. The tallest, Vincent Ventura, was one of the owners of Ventura Construction, Incorporated. The two men with him were common, ordinary, run-of-the-mill thugs.

Ventura stood back and watched as his two henchmen talked, quietly at first, to a workman. They moved in closer, and in response he moved back a little. They began to shove the man back and forth between them as Ventura watched without expression. The steelmen glanced at each other but no one made a move until Danny O'Hara, the crew chief, arrived on the scene.

"Hey, what the hell's the matter with you guys? This is open work up here. Vincent, your guys have no right to be up here. You got a beef, you take it down to ground level."

As long as Danny O'Hara was there, nothing could

happen. After all, he was Vincent's brother-in-law.

But something did happen. The thugs got a little louder, a little rougher. It was about an unpaid debt, and although the construction guy pleaded for more time, they ignored his words. One of them shoved him a little too hard and the usually surefooted man slipped, or maybe twisted an ankle. He went flying off the temporary flooring, smashed into a beam, and disappeared into space. It was so windy that his cry was muffled almost immediately, although it could be assumed that he yelled all the way down.

The two thugs turned to Vincent Ventura, whose face had gone pale. He licked his thin lips, then motioned his men toward him. The other workers moved in a semicircle; but suddenly guns were pointed at them, and they froze.

Only Danny O'Hara made a move—toward the field telephone. Vincent intercepted him, and within seconds his men held Danny firmly by the arms.

Vincent Ventura picked up the phone, dialed a number. His eyes stayed fixed on Danny as he spoke and then listened. He replaced the receiver, took a deep breath, and turned his thumb down. In response, the two thugs shoved Danny O'Hara, husband of his sister, father of his nephew, over the side.

The three men then turned slowly and confronted the other workmen.

Vincent spoke in a quiet voice that seemed to shake just slightly. "This is a terrible day, right? Two men swept off by a strong wind."

There was absolute silence as Vincent and his men boarded the open-air elevator. "Remember," he told them, "you all tell the cops the same story. Danny reached out, to try to save Charley, and instead of saving him, he got caught in the wind too. We all got that? I'm sorry I wasn't here when it happened, but how could I have helped? I'm not a high-rise man, right?"

Before he pushed the "down" button, he told them, "One more thing. Please remember this. Accidents can happen anywhere. Anywhere at all. At a man's home, with his family sleeping, or watching TV or eating. In his car; his wife's car. Jesus, even his kid's school bus, right? Terrible things can happen."

They watched as the open elevator slid down with a loud humming noise.

No one could meet the eyes of any of the others.

Accidents do happen. Anywhere. At any time.

To anyone.

PART 1

THE TRUTH

CHAPTER 1

1991

Eddie Manganaro pushed his sunglasses to the top of his head and held the newspaper to the light coming through the passenger window of the unmarked, beat-up Chevy surveillance car. He held his finger under the tiny print.

"Nick, listen. This has got to be the best. What they call a saver. I gotta keep this one."

His partner, Nick O'Hara, rubbed his eyes. Every time they had a fixed surveillance, Eddie distracted himself by trying to find the craziest memoriam printed on the obit page of the *New York Daily News*. It seemed that every single person being remembered— on a birthday, or death date, or significant anniversary— had been too good for this earth. A saint with a smile the angels envied. Nick wondered how many of the relatives ever told the poor bastard how terrific he was when he was alive.

"Lemme ask you something, Ed. Do these people being remembered have a subscription to the *News* up in heaven? Who delivers the papers to them?"

Eddie ignored him. He narrowed his eyes. "This is great. Jesus, it's signed 'Grandma.' Listen—listen up. 'Michael, it's two years since they did that to you. Don't worry. Every day since then, they pay and pay. They never get off the hook and they know why and their mothers will cry when they rot in hell. Rest in heaven remembering my promise to you. Love, Grandma.' Wadda ya think about that?"

Nick was impressed. "I think Grandma is some tough cookie."

"Sometimes I think these messages are coded. Y'know, not what they seem to be. Coupla years ago, I used to read the personals in the *Times* and—"

Nick turned to his partner. "The *New York Times*? *You* read the *New York Times*?"

Manganaro shrugged. "I worked with a better class of partner then. Anyway, there was a message, like four times a year, to some guy named Paul. Very cryptic. Like: 'We waited for the phone call. Michigan was cold. What happened?' Then, a few months later: 'Paul, like clockwork. How are the classes going? Don't call.' "

Despite himself, Nick was curious. "Any messages from Paul?"

Manganaro shook his head. There were strange things in the world, if only you looked for them.

Nick chewed on a pencil; consulted his watch; tried to conjure up an eight-letter word for "doubled consonant" that would fit the three letters he already worked out on the down words. What he did to kill time was to work out crossword puzzles. He had stored away an endless number of esoteric, totally unusable words. He wondered when the hell he'd ever get a chance to use "acrolect." Someday maybe he'd have an investigation that took him to New Orleans, so he could impress the hell out of the cops there: ask if any of them spoke that particular variety of Creole that approximates most closely standard language. That'd make him popular down south.

These were a couple of ways the two detectives from

the Seventeenth Precinct Detective Squad Unit passed the heavy time of waiting. Not that they weren't watching the comings and goings of various people in and out of the three-story brownstone across the street and a few houses down from where they sat slumped in the Chevy.

What they were watching was an upscale whorehouse. The clientele included movie stars, in New York on a promotional jaunt; athletes, celebrating or lamenting after a basketball or baseball or hockey game; even high-level diplomats taking a quickie on a lunch break from their duties at the UN or their desk at the embassy. These bastards even had the balls to park illegally. There were a lot of familiar, public faces coming in and out of the elegant building—which housed, according to a small, neat, brass nameplate, something called the Whalen Institute. It was supposed to be a center for new age, new wave, relaxation, rejuvenation, or stimulation, all for two hundred bucks an hour. That was what they reported as income to the IRS. What the institute forgot to mention were the services over and above steamy massages, herbal wraps, weird music: the charges for lithe young women doing lithe interesting things.

Nick and Eddie were on a fill-in assignment, as a favor to a couple of guys who had court appearances. They didn't actually know too much about the operation, or who specifically was interested in the Institute. There were allegations of heavy drug turnover, money laundering, illegal meetings—or, rather, indiscreet get-togethers between foreign nationals. There were probably enough scandalous things going on to take up a hundred hours of TV talk showtime, not to mention pages in the sleaze press. As well as the so-called straight press—it was hard to draw a distinction nowadays.

Nick and Ed weren't the only people on alert. There were probably a couple of guys monitoring what was going on via camera surveillance. Wires may or may not have been tapped. When you are on a temporary basis, just doing a favor you hope will one day be returned, you do what's asked of you. Nick and Ed wrote down the arrival and departure times of various vehicles and their license plates; descriptions of persons entering and leaving. It was boring work; they were glad they weren't too involved.

Eddie Manganaro, thirty-five, son of two immigrants from Sicily, looked like a poster boy for the Irish Tourist Board. He was a green-eyed, redheaded, snub-nosed, pale guy with the face of an altar boy. He had a punch like a sledgehammer, developed as a result of being the fourth in a five-boy family. Many a culprit was surprised to learn a skinny boy-face like Eddie, with his sweet smile, could be so rough. And calm about it.

Nick O'Hara, a couple of years older, inches and pounds larger, also looked like a guy with the wrong name. He was a swarthy man with a strong face, black eyebrows, and unruly black hair; he had startlingly blue eyes, unexpected against his complexion. The dark coloring came from the Ventura side of his family; but so did the blue eyes. Whatever was Irish about him didn't show, but his father's ethnicity made him a member of the Irish fraternal organization. And his mother's family qualified him as a member of the Italian organization. Of course, all ethnic and fraternal and religious organizations were more political than fraternal. It was essential to belong to one or another—or more than one, if you could, in order to give you some solid backing when promotions or assignments came up. Or if you were in trouble, and needed some friends with clout.

Nick was eight years old when his father died in a

construction accident. His mother died of a heart attack just six months later. He had been adopted by his uncle, Frank O'Hara, a New York City Police Department lieutenant. He had known, without ever asking for reasons, that the O'Haras and the Venturas had nothing to do with each other. Routinely, he had spent time with his grandfather on birthdays, some holidays, anniversaries. Both sides of his family loved him; neither side talked about the other. After two years in the army, Nick took and passed the police exam. His uncle, Frank, then a captain, was very pleased. When he spoke to his grandfather, Papa Ventura listened quietly and asked only if this was his idea, or had the O'Haras influenced him? It was the only time he ever asked such a thing. Assured that Nick had made his own decisions, his grandfather nodded, kissed his cheek, then looked directly into his eyes.

"Whatever you do in your life, Nicholas, do it honorably. It is all a man has at the very center of himself. His *honor.*"

Through his fifteen years on the job, the question arose many times in Nick's experience: What, exactly, is an honorable man?

Two hours before the relief team would arrive, both partners spotted the van at exactly the same instant. It was large, light tan, driven slowly by a young black guy. Another black guy walked stealthily behind a well-dressed woman, carrying a Bonwit's shopping bag, a pocketbook dangling from her right arm. The van practically crept down the street, pacing the mugger. The woman was in a world of her own, totally oblivious of her dangerous situation. And she was in danger: Nick and Ed both recognized the van, knew who was inside. This team had not only robbed, but beaten, more than eight or nine women on the Upper East Side in the last month. And were suspected of ten or more similar hits in midtown earlier and in Queens before that.

The detectives couldn't leap out to scare off these mutts; someone from the brownstone might spot them. There was no way they could just sit and watch what was about to happen. Nick grabbed the car phone, hesitated a split second. He couldn't hit nine-one-one; that would send a couple of squad cars racing, sirens blasting. Nick squinted at the brass plate outside the brownstone: The Whalen Institute. He punched out the phone number engraved on the plaque.

A woman's soft voice answered. "Whalen Institute. Linda speaking."

In a hoarse distortion of his own voice, Nick said, "I'm a neighbor. There are two guys right outside your place—gettin' ready to mug a woman. Black guy, right behind her, another in a van following. I don't wanna call the police any more than you do." He hung up; let them wonder later who the hell called.

The message must have been relayed instantaneously. Both of the Institute doors burst open and two very large men in gray maintenance uniforms barreled down the steps, each carrying a baseball bat.

The intended victim turned, startled; before she could make a sound the bat-men had turned her toward the corner, told her to *Get the hell outta here.* She didn't stop to ask questions.

The stalker froze for a moment, then tried to react—but was stopped mid-motion by a blow to the back of his skull so loud that both Nick and Ed gasped and sunk deeper into their seats. They heard the sound of glass breaking; watched as the bat wielders not only broke every window on the van but smashed the headlights, taillights, and, for good measure, took a few swings at the van's body.

The passenger's side of the van was yanked open and

the stalker was shoved in next to the driver, who was wiping a bloody eye with smashed fingertips. Apparently acting on instructions, he put the van in gear and raced down the street, swerving as he went.

The two gray-clad maintenance men, having preserved the peaceful condition of their community, stood, hands on hips. They glanced around at the two- and three-story brownstones, as though expecting applause or at least a nod of thanks. New Yorkers, being by nature very private and discreet citizens, did not appear at any window. Both lit cigarettes, took quick drags, then regretfully stamped them underfoot.

Apparently, no smoking was permitted within the walls of the Whalen Institute. Obviously: It was a health facility.

Neither Nick nor Ed would mention the incident in their notes or reports. What for? A few more limos dropped off somewhat stealthy, though expensively dressed, "health seekers." Finally, they received the phone call they had hoped for, earlier than expected. Relief was on its way. Nick kicked the motor on just as a gray-blue Toyota pulled alongside. The driver, grinning and nodding, ecstatic at his good luck—how about that? he'd been anticipating an hour's search—backed up so Nick could pull out. Nick pulled down his window and shook his head.

"Sorry, partner," he called out politely. Rolled up the window so he didn't have to hear the wails of indignation, disappointment, and despair. Hey, he had to save the spot for the next team.

Which arrived about two minutes later. Nick pulled out, the new team pulled in. When Nick reached the corner, the guy with the Toyota, double-parked, was standing outside his car, looking around wildly, when he spotted Nick.

"You bastard," he screamed. "You bastard! You selfish rotten bastard!"

Eddie looked at Nick. "Friend of yours? He seems to know you."

Nick shrugged and pulled away without acknowledging the hysterical man. "He must think I'm someone else. Happens all the time."

They dropped the car in the police garage, prepared the necessary forms. They were both tall men and cramped by the hours of inactivity. In the squad room, Nick checked his mailbox, pulled out a sheaf of papers. A report had been returned.

He glanced at the notes, written in red ink. "Oh shit! The lieutenant wants more information on the Sobelman killing. Jesus, looka this. He's correcting our grammar, for God's sake. Hell with it—it'll keep until next week."

Detective Johnson, a huge man with a florid complexion and a very small voice, looked at them and shook his head. "Well, looka the Bobbsey twins. How come you guys aren't in court bookin' all the bad guys? Ya fallin' down on the job or what?"

Eddie waved the report at him. "We been doing some research. You know, for our *book*. Very hush-hush, don't ask, okay?"

For three years, Johnson had claimed to be working on the next "big cop book," and the best way to needle him was to say you were working on *your* book. He believed everyone.

The team of Hoffman and Smith came into the squad office, dragging a frightened, bone-skinny woman by the arm.

"Tried to pick my damn pocket, can you beat it? I'm on the subway; just as I get off, there's this hand reaching . . ." He held up the thin hand. The lightweight sleeve of a torn coat slid down the woman's arm, revealing needle tracks. "Sit here," he instructed her. He leaned to Nick. "She's in a helluva bad way. Four months' pregnant. Gonna try to get her into detox."

Hoffman only looked like a monstrous uncaring bastard. He was really softhearted under certain circumstances. It was known that he had a drug addict son doing time in a rehab somewhere in Minnesota. He had taken it very hard; hadn't been able to follow the edicts of the "tough love" group his wife insisted they join. Against all advice, he had hugged his kid and told him that he loved him and would love him forever. He didn't let anyone know that he would take the kid back over and over again, no matter what.

Hoffman poured a mug of hot coffee from a sticky pot and thrust it at the woman, who jumped. Not realizing how loud and threatening his voice sounded, he bellowed at her, "I'm gonna give ya this cuppa, now promise not to boff on me, okay?"

Nick told him, "Hoff, she don't know what the hell you're talking about. Look at her—you're scaring the hell outta her."

Hoffman shrugged and backed off, then remembered something. "Hey, Nicholas, my man. You goin' to that big seventy-fifth birthday party for your grandfather, right? Waddya gotta do, kiss the ring before you kiss his cheek?"

"You'll never know, Hoff."

A new member of the squad, a skinny Puerto Rican named Silvio but called Slick, listened in. He didn't know if he resented the nickname or not. He walked over to Nick.

"Hey, no kiddin', O'Hara—your grandfather is that guy Ventura, the big mob guy?"

Only certain guys are permitted to joke about someone's family. Slick was not one of them.

Nick stiffened and looked down at the smaller man.

"Something you want to discuss with me about my family, Slick? 'Cause if there is, there's a coupla things I wanna talk to you about your mother."

Eddie grabbed Nick by the arm and tugged him to the door, waving Slick off. He whispered to Nick, "Christ, Nickie, c'mon, don't be mean. You know how those PRs are about their mothers."

As they walked down the stairs, Nick said loudly, "Sure, because they don't know who their fathers are!"

A furious voice called after them, "I heard that. I heard that."

There was laughter coming from the ready room, as the eight-to-four guys were being relieved by the four-to-one A.M. men.

"C'mon, that's Del White in there," Nick said. They entered the room, anticipating. He was the squad's storyteller.

"Nick, my man, lemme tell y'all about what happened to me on my watch through the night. You notice I'm still here at what? Four P.M. Had to collar a guy, damned if I didn't, just as I went off last night."

Detective Second Grade Delaware White's skin glistened ebony pure. He was handsome, meticulous, a regular GQ dandy.

"So I stop off at Healy's for a quick one and walk into the middle of a real ongoing brawl—fists and beer flying."

He had a magnetic voice, and he seemed to disappear into the scene he was depicting. Guys paused in their paperwork—those on the telephone only paid half attention to the voices coming from the receiver.

"So I tried to keep out of it—hell, I'd done my job of work, but wouldn't you know it? Right in front of my face, this stupid-looking little Irishman, I mean a right off of the boat donkey," he glanced at the Irish guys who waited him out, "no offense, honest, but this man, he even had those little pointy ears your Irish fairies have."

McFyphe looked up from his typing. "We Irish don't *have* fairies, so be careful what you say, Mr. White."

Nick called out, "Leprechauns."

"Ah, that's it, that's what he looked like, one of those. Those little guys you haul out for the St. Patrick's Parade. Anyway, this dumb dude holds off and slams Magee the barkeep right in the chops, and Magee grabs onto me and yells, 'Arrest this bastard before I kill him.' So I had to take the man into custody. By now, we've got a coupla off-duty guys trying to straighten things out, but my little friend lands one on *me*. So I cuffed the culprit and begin to read him his rights."

White covered his eyes with his hand and shook his head.

"I check with my little card, to make sure I say everything in the right order. Then I look at the guy and he has a really nutty look on his face, so I go, 'What? What's up? Do you understand what I'm tellin' you?' And he looks at me and says, 'Jesus, I thought you was supposed to read that to *you people*. Why you readin' this shit to me?'"

McFyphe, without looking up from his report, asked, "Well, isn't it just for *you people*?"

White ignored him. "So I ask him, nice, y'know. And just *which* people are you referring to, m'man? I can see this little . . . guy . . . is working hard now. He gotta be careful, so he says, 'the Negro people?' I glare at him. He tries again—'the black people.' I tell him to try again. 'Okay, I mean the *Afro-American . . . African Americans* . . . Jesus Christ, you people keep changing who you are every other day, how the hell are we supposed to know what to call ya?'"

The detective had a contagious laugh, and in the pause, McFyphe asked, "So how come, Del-a-ware, you people call each other 'nigger'—hell, I hear it all the time on the street and in that rap music and all—so how come *we* can't? Use the word, I mean?"

White smiled, put his heavy hand on McFyphe's shoulder, and said softly, "Just don't try, brother, just don't try. I tell you this as a friend."

He turned back to his audience. He hadn't finished. "So I book the guy and I tell him: listen, my man, I want you to know something. You have just been arrested by the best goddamn cop in New York City, and I want you to remember my name, okay? The guy nods. So I straighten up, look him right into his beady, shifty little eyes, and I tell him: *I am White!* Talk about a confused Irishman!"

CHAPTER 2

As he turned off the parkway and headed up the winding road that lead to his home, Nick regretted that he hadn't touched base with Kathy. He hadn't been home in two days. He and Ed had to work around the clock chasing down an elusive informant, whom they hadn't found until the very early hours of the morning. By then it was too late to head for home, or even call. What was the point of waking his wife up at four in the morning to tell her what she already knew: that he was stuck? Three hours later she'd just be getting up again, to head out for her teaching job at the high school.

And he hadn't called today because, well, he'd see her soon.

That of course was rationalization. He hadn't touched base with her in more than forty hours because he didn't want to hear the sound of her voice. The pained *Okay; I understand; sure.*

There had been a time when she did understand. And when he did call, no matter what the time, day or night. When they were young and newly married, she worked for her teaching degree at Queens College and he worked round the clock in uniform. They were

happy in the small two-room apartment in an old building in Forest Hills; they couldn't wait to see, talk, touch
each other. She'd come wide awake at the sound of his
key in the door. They'd make love even if he was tired
and bored from a long uneventful eight hours on patrol,
or overly excited by the unexpected, wildly implausible
events every cop encounters.

She'd tell him about her student teaching classes:
how much she liked the kids, how guilty she felt when
she really couldn't warm up to a particular student.
He'd tell her about his amazement when he watched a
group of women in their mid-thirties being booked for
prostitution. All housewives from a community in Long
Island, working the motels for some extra cash, for
mortgage payments, clothes, an extra car. One even was
sending her kid to a private school to protect her from
the riffraff in the public school.

They talked about the odd things people did, the
peculiar way lives were lived. He couldn't get over the
way total strangers confided in him: men and women
both, telling him their deepest thoughts and hopes,
their sex lives, some of their darkest deeds and regrets.
Nick had a sympathetic manner, but he was often uneasy about what was told to him. But he could tell Kathy anything. Actually, whatever he saw or encountered
didn't seem complete until he shared it with her.

Some of the mounting tension between them began
as he became more and more involved in the criminal
justice system. He couldn't believe the way the law, as
written and practiced, bent over backward to favor the
criminal. The bad guys walked free while citizens
started to live behind expensive, decorative bars and
triple locks and signal devices. He'd lock a guy up and
meet him hours later on the street, bailed out or d.o.r.

When Kathy argued that some bad guys were bound
to benefit from laws that were necessary to protect the

innocent, Nick gave up arguing. Her government classes taught her one thing; his reality showed him another. Nick had never seen an innocent guy stay locked up. He sure as hell saw plenty of guilty perps walk free, grinning at their victims. The randomness of the system was overwhelming. A guy walked on the whim of a judge; on a technicality because someone was careless; or because the DA just couldn't be bothered, and agreed to a deal without really knowing what was involved. He watched vicious, violent crimes bargained down and adjudicated for time served. And, on occasion, he'd seen the bad guys walk because of something much more sinister: outside interference. Manipulation. Corruption.

Kathy maintained her schoolgirl innocence and confidence. In one bitter argument, he told her he was glad she hadn't become a lawyer. She'd have that revolving door spinning.

She had influenced him, though, to continue college—and he had to admit he loved his classes at John Jay College of Criminal Justice. The courses were repeated, day and night, to accommodate the working tours for the cops going for their degrees. The civilians in the classes didn't know the way the criminal justice system really worked. They just read the books and the learned opinions. No one told them about the deals cops had to make with the scum of the earth, who would become your informant-partner in order to reach even lower scum. No one taught them the difference between theory and practice.

The kids Kathy taught in her senior high school government classes were suburban kids—mostly from intact families, with an average share of drug, alcohol, and sex abuse in their backgrounds. What she didn't experience, on a day-to-day basis, was the kind of charged atmosphere in which a mob of high school kids would be ready to kill a best friend or casual acquaintance over a dirty look, an unintentional jostle, an offhand remark. Nick knew those kids—knew where they were coming from. He even knew the sociology behind it all. What he didn't know was what the fuck was the solution.

The slow decline of their marriage was caused by so many things: his long, irregular hours. His growing inability to discuss his work. Too many disagreements, too much theorizing. Cops tended to socialize with each other, and he admitted that he could be prone to their us-against-them attitude.

But it wasn't that either. Not really. Partly, it was women. It was a given, on the job, in uniform or out: A cop represented power and authority, and there was a wide and strange contingent of women who were turned on by the idea of a gun, handcuffs, and the absolute power to deprive someone of their liberty, even of their life. Not only submissive women; some very strong, dominant women just wanted, for a brief period of time, not to be the one making the moves and the decisions. It was a form of play, except cops' wives wouldn't see it that way.

Nick hadn't gotten into anything serious; nothing important, anyway. Hell, in this day of AIDS and other diseases, it wasn't like the days he heard about from the old-timers. There were one or two women he'd met in the course of investigations. One complainant asked him to come over one evening to discuss the case she was involved in as a victim; her businessman husband was out of town and she was alone in her Park Avenue apartment and maybe he could just tell her about one thing or another? Nick would call home: he got stuck on an interview, not to worry.

A whiff of perfume as he stripped off his clothes for his shower gave him away. The feeble explanation—

some dweeb of a hooker went around spraying the crap on everyone in the squad room—was met with a cold stare. "They don't make Chanel in a spray," his wife observed through tight lips.

After a while, whenever he stayed away from home, whether it was for a legitimate reason or not, he felt guilty. And so of course he acted guilty, and that made him mad. And Kathy madder.

And another problem: Nick's love of gambling. It started when he was in the service. What the hell else did a young single guy have to do with his time and money? It was fun, recreational. The betting never got too heavy. Sure, a few guys lived from payday to payday wiped out, but sometimes they hit on the numbers; made the point in a dice game; beat the odds in a tight horse race. Played their cards right.

When he was a young cop, he'd pick up a tip—there was always a tip or two floating around the house. Third race at Hialeah, horse named Blame Me—that was irresistible—twenty-to-one and you wouldn't swear a fix was in, but shit, a fix was in. Sometimes there was a big payoff. Sometimes not. Most times not, but what the hell, you play your walking-around money, not the rent.

He made a lot of excuses to Kathy about short money on pay days: some guy's kid had a terrible illness that insurance wouldn't cover, so we all kicked in. There was a big drive for starving kids somewhere in some starving country. A coupla orphans at the scene of a double homicide were dressed in rags; been abused; no food, no toys, nothing. He went a little overboard— fifty bucks—but Christ, Kathy, those kids needed everything and they had nothing.

They spoke about gambling and he tried to explain. Yes, he lost most of the time, but there was always that chance. Someone always wins. He agreed to set a max-

imum for betting money—not more than she spent on
cosmetics, haircuts. Not important money, just walking-
around money. But when an absolutely sure thing came
along at Aqueduct and he laid down a heavy bet and it
paid off—a coupla thousand bucks, for Christ's sake—
how the hell could he not play?

After Peter was born, there was just enough money
around—at least until Kathy went back to teaching—
to cover necessities. He didn't stop cold—he'd still get
into the squad baseball, basketball pools—but he doled
out his bets very carefully. Avoided getting into bad
situations, which he had done a few times in the past.

As he pulled into his driveway, Peter came toward him,
followed by a couple of dogs. The oldest, Woof, was
Peter's. The others were temporary residents. Peter
helped out at the local humane society, baby-sitting
strays until they were permanently placed.

Nick thumped the dogs one by one, while studying
his son. Peter, at twelve, was at the tall and lanky stage.
His face was not yet firmly defined; Nick could still see
traces of a child's softness around his mouth. But his
eyes, amazingly black and thick-fringed, like his
mother's, no longer held their look of complete innocence and surprise at the world around him.

By the time he worked his way into the house, Nick
had managed a quick, hard hug for his son, a jostle
with a few of the dogs.

"Mom's in the kitchen. Dinner's almost ready."

There was that worried look on the boy's face. It was
hard to reassure him that everything was okay when he
knew nothing was okay anymore.

"Take care of these beasts, okay? See you later."

Kathy was pulling a roast chicken from the oven, and
even with her back to him Nick knew exactly what to
expect. Her body language was familiar. He moved

aside as she put the pan on the counter. She turned to him, waiting.

Her face was so familiar, too, with its traces of the young girl he had married. Slight lines from the corners of her eyes—laugh lines, although he couldn't seem to make her laugh much anymore. She had her dark brown hair pulled back from her face in a ponytail. She wiped sweat from her forehead with the back of her hand as her large dark eyes narrowed and her mouth tightened. She was still as slim as a girl, and as conditioned as one of her high school students. She had always been considered "cute": button nose, dimples, that attentive way of holding her head slightly to the side when she listened and got ready to voice her own opinion.

Nick leaned forward and kissed her lightly on her mouth.

"Sorry, babe. We got hung up last night and it was too late to call. Then we got stuck on a fixed post all day . . ."

"Look, Nick, when you walk out that door, I literally don't know if you're ever coming back. With all the crazies out there . . ." Then she took a deep breath and he knew she had been planning to say this for a long time. "I don't know if you're alive or dead. It would help to know, so that I'd be ready for whatever plans I had to make."

He responded, reacting to her tone. "Hey, if I was dead, someone would have come to let you know. And you wouldn't have to make any plans. The *department* would handle it. All *you'd* have to do would be to attend."

Of course, he had gone way too far. He always did when he knew he was wrong. He immediately regretted the pain reflected on her face and caught the way she ground her teeth and blinked hard. She turned away and he reached out for her.

"Hey, babe, I'm sorry. I'm really sorry. I should have called. Okay, Kath?"

She waited for a moment. "Can we have a nice, family kind of dinner tonight? Peter's been all tensed up. For once can we at least try to fool him into thinking we're a normal, happy family?"

"Hey, I can put on an act as good as the next guy."

She turned the coldest stare in the world on him: her black eyes froze. Kathy was a small woman, and when she thrust her chin up she looked like an angry child, but there was nothing childish about her anger.

"You bastard," she said softly.

CHAPTER 3

One of the selling points when the development was being planned up in Spring Valley was that each of its homes was to be set upon a full acre. Along with the forty-five-minute commute to the city, good schools, nice people, that damn full acre seemed to appeal to all the cops, firemen, sanitation men, and every other type of New York City Civil Service employee looking to get out of Queens, the Bronx, and Brooklyn. Looking to get anywhere, as long as it wasn't Long Island. It was not as crowded as the island and seemed a bit more laidback: no crowded beaches or day trippers. Mostly year-round homes, with some summer residents and weekenders who would move in permanently after retirement. Block for block, Nick's neighborhood was probably populated by more guys on the job than anywhere within commuting distance.

As Nick raked the leaves and Peter bagged them, the dogs dove into each new pile, scattering Nick's work.

A loud voice yelled from the back door, leading to the kitchen. "What's this all about?" Frank O'Hara, carrying a cellophane garment bag over his shoulder, shook his head. "Petey, you and your dad rake the leaves, the dogs scatter them? And who said you can't teach old dogs new tricks?"

As Peter led the dogs into the house, he was stopped by his uncle. "Here, kid, take your father's suit inside."

It was an implicit dismissal.

Nick leaned on the rake and tensed. He really didn't need this shit just now.

"Did ya a favor," his uncle said, "picked up your suit at Clean 'n' Carry. Happened to be passing and figured I'd save you the trip."

Nick nodded without responding, continued to pull the leaves into a pile.

"Jesus, why don't you break down and get yourself a blower like everybody else? Good for leaves—good for snow. Gonna be a real tough winter, lotta snow coming."

He hadn't come to talk about the weather and both men knew it. Frank O'Hara, a deputy inspector in the New York City Police Department, was one of those barrel-chested, wide-shouldered guys you'd want on your side if things got rough. The funny thing was, Frank was one of the gentlest men Nick had ever known. In all the years Nick had lived with Frank and his family, when he was growing up, he'd never seen him do anything more physically threatening than raise his eyebrows and lower his voice in a certain way. That was all he had to do to impress his sons, and Nick.

There was only one time Nick had ever seen Frank hit anyone. The family had been sitting around the kitchen table over hot chocolate one night. His aunt, Mary, got up from time to time to replenish a cup, get more cookies. Frank was a great storyteller and he had everyone roaring over some baseball goof-up he'd witnessed at Yankee Stadium when he was a kid. Frank suddenly flung his arms wide to make a point and caught his wife on the side of her head, knocking her out cold before she even hit the floor.

It was hard to know what was worse for Frank: his absolute horror at what he had done to his wife, or the way the doctors at the emergency room looked at him and coldly asked him what happened.

If any sixty-year-old man could be said to have an innocent face, that would be Frank O'Hara. His soft voice, sweet smile, and sympathetic manner had fooled many a culprit into a confession he seemed to think he was entrusting to a priest.

Frank sat on top of the picnic table that would soon be stored away. Another game of suburbia: take certain items out, store them away again.

Nick dropped his rake and stood in front of his uncle. He used the technique Frank had taught him when he was a kid. Just keep looking into someone's eyes without any expression whatsoever and wait him out.

Frank knew what he was doing; he shook his head and stood up. "Okay. Okay, Nick. I wanted to talk to you for a minute. Just wanted a word with you, okay?"

"About what?"

"You know damn well about what. Look, the word is out about your grandfather's party tomorrow." Even though Frank was no taller than Nick, he always seemed to tower over his nephew. "I've been picking up things from all over. There are going to be some very heavy hitters there. From Philly, Miami, Atlantic City. The whole damn East Coast."

"To wish him a happy birthday. To honor him."

Frank wiped his mouth roughly. "Yeah, well, you and Peter and Kathy are going to honor him for his birthday. So, okay, give him the hug and the kiss and the present and get on your way, right? Nicky, there's gonna be a lot of surveillance goin' on. Local, state, and fed. Combined task forces, the works."

Nick spoke very carefully, trying, but not really succeeding, to contain his anger. "Jesus, Frank, gimme a break. This is my grandfather. He's an old man—"

"He's the youngest seventy-five-year-old man in the world, Nick. He's still operating, still running things. He's still in charge. All these guys are coming to look over your cousin Richie. It's gonna be like—well, wadda ya think? Richie is the heir . . ."

"Richie Ventura is my shit-faced cousin. Period. That's all I know about him. He has nothing to do with me. I don't know and don't care a damn about anything he is or isn't going to do with his life, *capice?*"

"Nick, you're a member of the New York City Police Department. You gotta know what this party is: It's practically a commission meeting, to make the big announcement, right from the old man's mouth, that Richie . . ."

"Gimme a break, Frank. I see my grandfather, what, three, four fucking times a year, holidays only. He is my grandfather. Anything else, I don't know about. Period."

Of course, Nick knew more than enough about "anything else." He chose not to acknowledge what he would not discuss.

Frank shoved his hands into the pockets of his jacket; he wished he still smoked. "Your grandfather is head of the Ventura Enterprises, which is responsible for—"

"Ventura Enterprises runs legitimate businesses. He's a businessman with solid legal investments who pays his taxes, gives employment to a helluva lotta people."

"Tell me something, kid. How the hell does a 'businessman,' starting from scratch, get his hands into so many pies? Trucking; commercial laundries; restaurants; convenience stores; cement and brick factories;

used car lots; car parts; construction; garment manu-
facturing; food distributors. Not to mention chunks of
stock in hotels, clubs—"

Nick's blue eyes lightened to a nearly transparent
gray. "Ain't America great? Listen, Frank. I never discuss anything about his business with him; he never
asks me about my job. We love each other. We respect
each other. We have a purely family relationship. Period."

"Yeah. Family." Frank held up his hand. "Okay,
okay, Nicky. Have a good time. Just don't mug into too
many cameras; ya never know where the pictures will
end up. I don't want to spoil your visit."

"Thanks a lot, *Uncle* Frank."

Because his uncle looked worried, and because Nick
loved him, he said, "Hey, Frank. I don't give a damn
about any of these heavy hitters from Miami or
wherever. I have enough trouble having to be in the
same room with my cousin Richie. Okay?"

"Don't underestimate your cousin Richie. He's a very
dangerous man." He bit back whatever else he was
about to say, grinned, and said, "Hey, your suit's in the
house. Jesus, that thing still fits you?"

Nick sucked in his stomach and shrugged. "I haven't
gained an ounce in ten years." He reached over and
patted Frank's stomach.

"Hey, I just look big. Have a nice time, kid."

Nick watched as his uncle walked through the yard
in his surprisingly light step that's always unusual in a
large man. He hand-combed his thinning blondish gray
hair into place, and without looking back, waved at
Nick.

CHAPTER 4

Nicholas Ventura's large split-level house was one of six in the private enclave known as Westwoods. Each house was set on a minimum three-acre lot; by common agreement, plans for each house had been submitted to a committee of residents for approval before being built.

At the entrance to the estates, there was a small booth manned by two men in brown uniforms who checked a clipboard at every arrival; each car was further carefully scanned by three or four men with scowling faces before being waved on toward the birthday celebration. Additionally, just outside the enclave, official surveillance was openly maintained by groups of government types equipped with video cameras, walkie-talkies, and whatever other equipment they deemed necessary. There was no communication among the various segments who, in one way or another, watched over the procession of those attending the Ventura seventy-fifth birthday party.

Ventura's immediate neighbors were a psychiatrist to the east, and a Wall Street attorney to the west. His back lawn touched hedges with those of a pediatrician who had written several popular best-sellers about raising children. Directly facing the Ventura property was the Tudor-style residence of a retired nightclub performer, who spent most of his life now playing golf.

Ventura knew the names and locations and boundaries of every resident in his community-within-a-community, technically part of Westbury, Long Island. He also knew each neighbor's gross and net worth and the various sources of their income. He could name the individual members of each household—family and hired help—and could describe each according to age, sex, sexual preference, appearance, and personality. He knew when and whom they entertained. He knew immediately if there was a change in the regular cook, maid, baby-sitter, groundskeeper, pool maintenance crew. If anything unusual happened, day or night, in the vicinity of the Ventura home, it was immediately noted and reported to him.

It wasn't that Nicholas Ventura was nosy, or even paranoid. He was neither. He headed one of the most powerful crime families in the eastern United States, and it wasn't just his personal safety that concerned him but the sanctity of his vast and widespread enterprises.

Nearly two hundred guests had been invited to the celebration, and there had been no "regrets" except on the behalf of one man who died the day before the invitation arrived.

Each arriving car, having passed scrutiny, was directed to a red-vested attendant who accepted the key, held open the car doors, watched as the guests were waved toward the house by one of many neatly dressed, alert-looking young men wearing sunglasses and speaking into walkie-talkies. In their self-importance, the guides never smiled, although they didn't look as unpleasant or threatening as the guys at the booth.

As Nick, Kathy, and Peter stepped out of their six-

year-old, somewhat beat-up Volvo station wagon, one
of the Ventura men approached.

"Jesus, Nicky." Fat Sam Lorenzo—who weighed
about a hundred and twenty pounds but had once been
very fat—pointed at the wagon. "I was gonna direct ya
to the rear of the house. Thought you was a delivery-
man."

Nick accepted the crushing handshake and grasp of
his forearms good-naturedly, then pulled away when he
felt a cold strong hand on his neck. Someone obviously
had beeped cousin Richie about his arrival.

Richie Ventura was almost as tall as Nick. Not quite,
but almost. An inch under six feet to Nick's inch over.
He was slightly heavier, which could have been due to
the muscle he had developed over the years through
weight training. Or to the huge appetite with which he
struggled all his life. His hair, dark with a great deal of
gray, was swept back from his high forehead and held
in place by spray. The thickness at the crown might
have been a weave, but if so, a good one. Maybe,
maybe not. He turned from Nick to Kathy.

"Will ya look at this one? She looks like one a' the
kids she teaches." He caught her in a huge hug. He
was not only impressed with Kathy, he had always been
somewhat wary of her. She was a smart, educated lady.

Next, he turned to Peter. "Look at this kid—damn,"
he bellowed, grabbing Peter into his arms, then pushing him back. "They feed you some kinna growing
beans or what? You gonna be taller than your old man."

"At least taller than you," Nick said with a smile. The
cousins had never been nice toward each other. Ever.

Richie turned his full attention to Nick. He shook his
head with a pained expression. His oldest son, Sonny,
stood next to his father with the same expression on his
face: amused disdain. Together, they looked like the
same guy at age sixteen and forty.

"Hey, Pop, can't you get Nick a deal on a car? You see that station wagon they come in?"

Richie wrapped his arm around the kid's neck and told him to show some respect. He demonstrated by asking Nick how much he'd paid for the wagon new; when Nick said he'd bought it used, Richie gave up.

"Jeez, bet I pay more for a suit than you did for that wagon." He looked Nick over from head to toe, didn't have to say a word. He reached out and adjusted his tie and nodded approval. Of the tie. Not bad. He winked at Peter, smiled at Kathy, and told Sonny to escort them inside the house.

Despite the number of adults and children milling around the large entrance hall, the level of sound and activity was respectfully contained. Mothers hushed children, fathers grabbed at sweaty collars and glared at their well-controlled children, eager to join the festivities in the yard behind the house. All in good time; the procedure was orderly and on schedule. Members of the family and friends were escorted quickly into the library, where they could extend best wishes and beautifully wrapped gifts to Papa Ventura; he then dismissed them with a nod and a smile. Go enjoy. White envelopes were handed discreetly to one of Papa's aides.

Across the hall from the library, through a partially opened door, if anyone was indiscreet enough to look, could be seen a large, beautifully arranged dining room; a table set with magnificent linens, silver, china, crystal, under a glittering imported chandelier. There were some fifteen or so men seated around the table, each attended by his own people, whom they ignored as they spoke quietly to their table partners. They had been encouraged to eat until their host could join them. He had his hostly obligations. They were all well-behaved men; they drank very little wine, and ate sparingly, tasting every dish offered. But through all the courtesy and

mannerliness in the room, there was also a feeling of
tension, the electricity of a great massing of power.

Nick stood with his back against a wall, scanning the
crowded entrance hall, getting his bearings. He was approached by his great-aunt Ursula, Papa's older sister.
She was a childless widow who had attended to the
running of her brother's home from the time he lost
his wife, some thirty years ago. Nearing ninety, she was
still severely critical of window washers who left streaks;
the cleaning women who missed dust; the gardener
who failed to clear away clippings. Through the years,
there had been so many cooks in and out of the house
that it was finally decided she would be the main cook,
with help from a docile cousin from the old country
who lived in a small room at the far side of the house.
(That cousin, in turn, was assisted by kitchen maids
who actually did the work of peeling, slicing, chopping,
dicing, and stirring that neither would trouble about.)
Nicholas was an undemanding man with a moderate
appetite; anything pleased him, but he had learned how
much happiness Ursula drew from the heavy, earthy
foods she set before him.

She greeted Nick with a complaint. This was not *her*
party. Richie had insisted on bringing one of the best
chefs in Manhattan, along with his staff, to arrange the
dinner. Nick listened to the criticism of the menu, item
by item, and nodded sympathetically. When she
pointed toward the yellow-and-white-striped tents outside, she whispered, *There would have been hell to pay
if it had rained today.*

Of course, it hadn't rained.

The old woman glanced at Kathy and Peter as they
came alongside Nick. She had no idea who they were.
In fact, she had no idea who anyone was or what they
were all doing here. She'd have to find that stupid maid
and ask her what all this fuss was about.

Kathy grinned. "She still looks hale and hearty and angry."

Nick focused on his wife. She really was pretty: her shiny shoulder-length hair framed her face, yet moved almost with a life of its own. She turned toward him, stopped for a moment by the expression on his face.

"What?"

"Nothing. Just . . . you look great."

There was a slight hesitation, a fleeting suspicion. Nick wasn't very generous with compliments these days. She answered too quickly, which was one of the problems between them.

"You sound surprised."

He took a deep breath and caught sight of Tommy the Dog Bianco waving him toward the door to his grandfather's library. While no one called him that to his face, Tommy's loyalty was so doglike and unwavering that the name was part of his personality.

He nodded at Kathy and Peter, then leaned close to Nick. "He's been asking for you, Nick—the old man," he said reproachfully. "You and your lady and the kid. C'mon, he's waitin' to see you."

The room was lined with expensive, wood, floor-to-ceiling bookcases. The books represented decades of collection, and they were matched with a wall filled with classical records. Nicholas Ventura was a self-educated man whose culture had been painstakingly acquired.

The furniture embraced heavy English brocade and leather couches; shining warm tables and expensive brass lamps. The room accommodated two fairly large, collector's quality Persian carpets; the paintings over the fireplace were not mere decoration but fine art. While he had hired decorators for other parts of his house, this library had been furnished over a period of years by Nicholas Ventura, whose tastes and requirements were refined to a certain excellence.

Joe Menucci, fifty-two years old, stood guard over Papa Ventura as he had for nearly twenty-five years. He was not a physically imposing man, but it was known that he had achieved a black belt in karate and could be murderously swift if he needed to be. Everyone who knew him respected his physical achievements, but it was his reputation of being some kind of genius that gave him his nickname: Joe the Brain. It was said that Joe Menucci could recall every single word said in his presence. That he could listen to a boring televised political debate, turn off the set, and repeat every word spoken not only by the candidates but by the moderators. In real time. It would have been hard to find someone who'd seen Joe's talents in action, but no one was ever heard to question them.

The stories were based on a peculiar trick of nature. Joe had a very intelligent face. His eyes, large, shiny, and dark, seemed to reflect an alertness to everything around him from infancy on. The fact that he wasn't a particularly good student meant nothing. What could schoolteachers know of someone with such a blessed gift?

Joe Menucci was a good-looking man. His dark hair had receded only slightly; he kept his weight down with moderate exercise, and he had never been passionate about food. He was a meticulous dresser whose clothes were made by Papa Ventura's own tailor.

If he appeared to be an extremely quiet man, it was because he had nothing to say. It was believed that he spent his time and energy absorbing everything everyone else said. When someone spoke in Joe's presence, his dark eyes focused on the speaker's lips, the way a deaf person tries to catch words as they form. There was a listening quality to his entire body. He seemed to pull every word into the very center of himself. He was always present at any meeting Papa Ventura held. Many a man spent a night terror-stricken at the thought that some offhand remark, softly spoken, would be spieled back to Papa Ventura in the privacy of his library by Joe Menucci.

Joe Menucci did have a real gift for understanding, installing, repairing, and adjusting any electrical or electronic system, no matter how complex. He had spent the morning setting up a number of video games in the playroom that existed for grandchildren, nieces and nephews, godchildren—any child attending his home. The kids loved this room better than any food or sweets.

He had installed a complicated PC system for Papa Ventura, complete with a shelf filled with software: Windows on the Whole Friggin' World. System this and System that. Papa had shaken his head. No. He had no need for anything like that. Joe could keep the damn thing, which lurked in the corner of his office. If he needed information, he could watch over Joe's shoulder as diagrams and words and numbers and pictures appeared and disappeared on the screen in response to the touch of a finger on a key or the slide and tapping of the gadget Joe called a mouse. To Papa, it seemed like witchcraft, magic. He had other uses for his mind.

When Joe the Brain spotted Nick and his family, he immediately went to the side of his Don, rested one hand on the shoulder of a smiling guest, edged the man away *just* a little. He leaned forward, spoke to Ventura, gestured with his chin.

Joe whispered to Papa Ventura that someone had messed with the music system; would this be a good time for him to see to it? Papa nodded; his full attention was on his grandson.

The birthday host finished his conversation politely, and fixed his gaze on his grandson. As Nick ap-

proached, for the first time that day while receiving
guests in this room the old man stood up and came
forward, offering his embrace. He stared directly into
his grandson's blue eyes and nodded with a deep satisfaction.

There was a strong resemblance between the two,
not just in the eyes but in the firm chin, strong nose,
and wide lips.

Nicholas Ventura had grown from an emaciated im-
migrant boy starving for all things, to a somewhat heavyset self-satisfied man who conceded nothing to age.
His receding hairline emphasized an intelligent high
forehead, and his remaining hair was carefully styled
for maximum effect. He was immaculately groomed
and his suit displayed taste and quality. Even at his age,
his vanity was evident. He took pleasure in the sensation he created whenever he entered a room. He
moved as a movie star, preceded not only by those who
served him but by his own magnetic field of power.

"Papa," Nick told him, "you never change. How do
you do it?"

"I change, Nicholas, I change. Except about one
thing—I do not see you often enough."

He turned toward Kathy with an admiring expression. A courtly man, Nicholas Ventura was courteous
and soft-spoken in social situations. He listened intently
to whomever spoke with him as though the speaker was
fascinating and what was said of great importance. He
tried to put others at ease graciously, as the Pope with
a group of nervous nuns.

Peter, his great-grandson, was a nice boy, more Irish-
looking than Italian. He was tall for his age, and thin
and intelligent. He was not afraid to admit that he loved
to read; that he loved animals and nature. From the
time he was a very small child, he had discussed these
things with his great-grandfather, whenever they met.

The Don listened to him seriously and asked his advice about his two water spaniels: be careful of heart worms, Papa; make sure they get their shots, and take their pills.

The boy took a deep breath and carefully recited his memorized birthday wish for the old man: good health, long life, happiness, and pleasure in friends and family. Peter's Italian was in a Sicilian dialect.

Smiling at Peter, who was slightly flushed, Papa said, "You didn't learn it from this one. He never could get the accent right." He poked at Nick, beamed at Kathy. "Look at this boy with the Irish face and the Sicilian eyes who speaks like a born peasant from the hills."

"But Papa, what are Sicilian eyes? You have blue eyes. My dad has blue eyes."

Nicholas laughed. "The blue eyes probably came from some crazy Norseman who must have stopped on my people's island a thousand years ago. All they left behind were some blue eyes, and maybe some broken hearts."

Papa nodded at Kathy and Peter. He could make his intentions very clear with the slightest gesture. It was time for him to visit with his grandson in privacy.

"You look good, Nicholas. You could do with a new suit or two."

"Thanks, Papa. Richie already told me that."

His grandfather brushed away the comment. It was of no importance. There was something else he wanted to speak about. He turned his unnerving stare on Nick. It was as though he could see through a man's brain, picking up thoughts and intentions.

He spoke softly but it was clear he intended to be heard. "Nick, your wife is a very fine woman. A man must respect his wife in every way. Respect his home, his family. You keep your job out of your home, I am sure. Very much like the men out here. Business is business. But your wife, Kathy, she has a sadness, deep inside of her. She smiles a wonderful smile—a quiet smile, however. There is a sadness there, Nicholas. Are you having problems?"

Nick felt like a kid again. Caught. Found out. Just tell Papa. Don't lie, above all things: don't lie. Tell the truth so we can see how to work out the problems.

Finally, watching his grandfather sit on the couch and indicate an easy chair for him, Nick said, "Married people have problems, Papa. You know that."

"There is a *deep* sadness there." He hesitated, placed his fingertips together under his chin. "Is it the gambling?"

Nick shook his head decisively and watched as his grandfather relaxed. All things could be worked out.

"You know, Nicholas, when your grandmother was alive—may she rest in peace—nothing ever touched our home. I was a man, as you are, so there were women sometimes. But it had nothing to do with my wife, my children, my home. You understand what I'm saying? Your son, he is a wonderful, gifted boy. But he seems a little, what? tense, nervous, unhappy? That shows when there is trouble between mother and father."

"Papa, you should have been a psychologist. It's just the job. You know. The house. The kind of stuff I deal with every day. All cops have these problems. We'll work it out."

"Cops have divorce rates as high as doctors. Did you know that? Doctors have one of the highest divorce rates." He smiled, enjoying showing off.

Nicholas Ventura was a man people were anxious to please, for he had the power of life or death. While he spoke softly, his words carried great weight. Anyone who had ever underestimated him rarely had a chance to do so a second time.

He had lost two sons in an airplane crash and one son in Vietnam. His only daughter had died six months after Nick's father of the family weakness—a failing heart. One of his sons was disabled by this condition, which had been handed down through generations of Venturas. His father had died before his fortieth birthday. His own heart troubled him from time to time, but medication kept it under control. Several among his many brothers, nephews, and nieces suffered from the genetic condition that had claimed so many Venturas.

In his seventy-fifth year, he had lost none of the glamour of a truly powerful man. He had many intermediaries to protect him from minor annoyances, and he expected his life to run smoothly. He was in excellent health; accepted bifocals and a hearing aid when it became necessary. He'd had a hip replacement, but walked without a cane, limp, or shuffle. His tailor accommodated his extra weight artfully, as did his barber with his thinning hair. What he retained intact was his knifelike intelligence. He retained all that was important; stored away the information and details necessary for his survival and the survival of the empire he had built.

He studied Nick intently, as though looking for something. He nodded abruptly, gestured broadly. "Go. Enjoy my party. See some old friends, Nicholas."

Some of the people Nick had grown up with looked very much the same as when they were children, only bigger. Junior Caniello, now a large man but who still looked like a hulking boy whose mouth always seemed to be rimmed with crumbs, waved at Nick with a smile. He held up a plate laden with food and looked very happy. In spite of the thinning hair, expensive suit, aviator glasses, despite the fact that he was an attorney, he was still chubby, sloppy, nice-kid Junior Caniello.

Nick's eyes locked on Funzy Gennaro and he felt all the hatred that had never been resolved between them. For whatever reason, they had fought constantly as children, bloodied and bruised each other with punches and kicks at every opportunity. Funzy nodded at Nick. After all, they were grown-ups now. Funzy had a partnership in a woolen goods factory. He had three daughters and led a respectable life. But when their eyes met, for one split second, they were two boys in the schoolyard again, wary, eager, and ready.

He watched Kathy, a breath of fresh air among the women who huddled together outside the entrance to one of the tents. They kept checking on their kids and catching up on gossip. Richie's wife, Theresa, was still a pretty girl. She stood next to her three lifelong best girlfriends and they looked remarkably alike. Nick had known all four of these women when they were kids. Now they obviously shopped at the same dress shops, visited the same beauty salons. Each had married a neighborhood boy. They all lived within a cul-de-sac in Massapequa, Long Island, and they all knew very little about what their husbands did for a living.

Nick glanced around the room checking out the various groups of men in their twenties, thirties, and forties. They were wire-tight guys wearing fifteen-hundred-dollar suits, Egyptian cotton shirts, silk ties and socks, and two-hundred-dollar shoes. Despite all the care and money and expert grooming, they were all a little out of whack. Just a little off. There was something primitive just under the surface being held in check. These guys were not very high up on the evolutionary scale. At any minute, they might forget themselves and begin to eat with their hands.

Many of the younger guys wore dark glasses, indoors or out, so that no one could see where the hell they were looking. They glanced around constantly without seeming to move their heads. They rarely made eye contact with each other. To do so would be to lose the advantage by a split second. Even in a safe place like a celebration for Don Nicholas Ventura, it was important, maybe even vital, to see who was talking to whom, off in a corner, trying not to be seen; who was shaking hands just a little too long with someone not known to be a special friend or ally. Were things changing? Alliances being formed or destroyed? Nobody trusted anyone else completely; if you did, you were a fool. Their world was in a constant state of flux, slow, tentative—someone might be trying out something new— or in an explosion of open violence, for all to see and think about. Those who didn't pick up the correct lessons rarely survived.

Nick watched Richie work his way through the crowd to his side. He put his hand on Nick's arm, ran it up and down. Nick stepped back, spread his arms.

"Wanna check me out, Richie? No wires. I do have my gun. Required, you know that."

"Hey, c'mon, Nicky, why the fuck would I check you out?" He butted his chin at the guests. "Brings back old times, all the neighborhood people being together like this, to honor the old man, huh, Nick?"

Nick glanced across toward the private dining room. "Not all old neighborhood people, Richie. Some guests traveled a long way."

Richie's smile was tight. "That's what they made the airplane for, Nick, so old friends get together from far away."

Nick dropped it. "So where's your father? I haven't seen him since last Christmas."

Richie's face changed. He looked sad. "My old man's not so good, Nick. Ya know, the heart. He can't travel from Arizona, too much hassle. He feels like shit he can't be with Papa on this day." Then, he brightened.

"How's it with you, Nick, the heart? You got any problems? We're some family for that, huh?"

The only thing that surprised Nick was that his cousin hadn't pulled a face, shaken his head, and mentioned the fact that Nick's mother had died of the "family problem."

"I'm fine. You haven't got the problem either, Richie, right? Hard to have a heart condition with no heart."

Richie didn't answer. He seemed not to have heard. Nick glanced over his shoulder to where Richie was staring, and together they watched as Laura Santalvo walked into the entrance hall and through the crowd toward Papa Ventura's library.

She stared straight ahead and moved as though she was the only person present. A silence fell around her, a pathway cleared for her automatically. Laura seemed completely unaware of the sensation she created. It wasn't that she didn't realize the reaction around her; it just didn't matter to her. She headed toward her target without acknowledging anyone until she reached Tommy the Dog, who whisked before her into Papa's domain to escort others clear of the inner sanctum. He beamed as Laura leaned toward him, brushed his cheek with a kiss, and disappeared into the room with Papa Ventura.

CHAPTER 5

Nicholas Ventura and Laura embraced. She sat opposite him on the leather sofa, kicked off her shoes, and pulled her legs up under her. Laura Santalvo was family in every way but blood, and her presence seemed to lighten the very air around Nicholas whenever she was near him.

As she sipped her wine, watched him closely, spoke about her travels, he remembered vividly the first time they had spoken seriously together. Laura was thirteen years old when her father, Salvatore, had worked for Papa Ventura as a collector. One day, making a collection visit, Sal had been stonewalled. Two young punks who didn't understand the sacredness of the unwritten contract showed the older man the door. When he spoke reasonably to them, quietly, they broke both his knees with a baseball bat and then for good measure cracked his skull and dumped what they thought was his dead body in an empty lot. Where he was found by some neighborhood kids, only just breathing. The next day, the bullet-riddled bodies of the two punks were found in a parked car on a busy neighborhood street: message delivered and received by all who needed to learn from their mistakes.

What was left of Laura's father was a shell of a man, non-functioning, almost an infant. He needed constant care, and so his wife, who had three boys and a disobedient daughter to raise, sent Laura for a talk with Don Ventura. Who else could straighten out this girl?

He remembered the angry though frightened girl, biting hard on her lip; not letting the tears flood from her eyes. Her mother wanted her to drop out of school—to devote herself to the nursing care of her father, so her mother could get a job in the garment industry. Did Laura expect her brothers to nurse their father? She was the girl; it was her duty. He asked her what she wanted to do, impressed by the strength of her voice, the straightness of her back.

She wanted high school, and college or design school. She was smart, talented. She would *not* become an old woman caring and tending to a lost man's fading body. She would not.

Don Ventura listened closely; nodded; expressed some surprise at the girl's ambition; wondered where it came from. He told both the girl and her mother a solution would be found.

Someone's distant cousin came from Salerno to take care of Laura's father. Her mother was given a good paying union job. Her father was supplied with a small monthly "retirement" bonus. The sons were later set up in an auto repair shop of their own. And after high school Laura was sent to an eminent fashion studio in Milan, to learn the basics of fashion—design; sewing; the business of the industry. She was paid a small pittance as an apprentice, plus room and board.

When she was twenty, she was allowed to show some of her own basic dress designs at a renowned show held in Paris. She caught the eye—and interest—of an international group. She was invited to parties; was swept into an older, wiser, more experienced world than she had ever known.

Among her most ardent admirers was thirty-five-year-old Octavio of Florence—he said he was a prince, though he never really identified his pedigree. He was charmed by this passionate-eyed little girl who spoke excellent French and Italian. He loved showing her off in her exquisitely designed outfits. He lent her good jewelry, one piece at a time. Simplicity must be her style; nothing to detract from her natural, incredible beauty.

Almost before she realized it, he was planning their wedding at his huge castlelike stone estate overlooking the Mediterranean. She knew hardly any of the people attending. No one from her family could come: her father was too helpless; her mother too frightened; her brothers too busy. She sent photos home and to Papa Ventura, who sent her a check large enough to impress even royalty. Octavio promised to set her up in her own house of design—in a while. Of course, she had no need to continue her studies, he said; she knew enough. He wanted them to have the freedom to be able to fly off to his home in the Bahamas; to attend the Cannes Film Festival; to accept interesting invitations from his many friends, all of whom made a great fuss over Laura. She felt that they were watching her as though they expected her to perform some outrageous act for their amusement.

When they visited the large manor house of an aging dowager, high in the Austrian Alps, Laura sensed a certain excitement, a tension, not only from her husband but from the guests as well.

Their hostess, surrounded by her young lovers, male and female, had planned an event in which Laura was to serve as the centerpiece of everyone's desires. A sexual performance.

Seized with disbelief as much as fear, Laura removed herself emotionally from the event. She retreated deep into the pure, untouched center of her being. The body that they touched, penetrated, abused, raped, sodomized, and devoured was someone else's. She, Laura, was immune to all of their violations. No one realized that Laura had disappeared, that all they had to amuse themselves with was the empty body of an anonymous young girl.

When they returned to their home in Rome, Octavio seemed unaware of any change in his young wife. He never really looked into his wife's eyes; never realized the deep hatred and resolve that watched him through her ice gray unforgiving eyes. He saw only the slender, elegant, compliant girl. Who, in fact, was beginning to bore him as any overused toy tends to do.

There was a particular trip he was planning to the Greek Isles, where they would celebrate her birthday in May. She asked where they would be. Exactly. On what island. Near what town. She studied the map intently as he pointed out—if it amused her, why not?—precisely where they would be. How they would get there from the yacht. Along what roads to the villa for the festivities.

It was a quaint harbor. The peasants were dressed as though taking part in a musical comedy. Laura guessed that her husband and his friends had arranged the spectacle in her honor. The driver of the Mercedes that was to take Octavio and Laura to the villa was a tall, dark, pockmarked man who kept his face down as he loaded their luggage into the trunk of the car. He wore a driver's black outfit and thin leather gloves and shiny black boots. The ride was along a narrow road, and Octavio glanced at his watch again and again. He was the host; he had to be the first to arrive. He pulled open the small bar set into the back of the front seat;

opened a bottle of champagne, poured two glasses. The car lurched to a sudden stop: the champagne spilled all over them.

Octavio began to curse the driver, who had stopped because there was a small van blocking the way. The driver got out of the car—to speak to the driver of the van, it would seem. Instead, he opened the rear door on Laura's side, motioned her to get out alongside him, to stand back. She heard, rather than saw, the three shots fired quickly into Octavio's head: one behind each ear, one into his forehead.

The driver stepped back, took Laura gently by the arm, and led her away from the car. He reached in, removed the car phone, and handed it to her.

"Wait until we are gone, then phone for the police." He told her the number. He put his hand out and she gave him the diamond ring, bracelet, and watch she was wearing. He reached back into the car, removed her husband's wallet, then opened the trunk and went to the jewel case she pointed out.

He tipped his hat to Laura, gently touched her shoulder, and whispered to her, "Do not look at him. There's no need for you to see."

She nodded; watched him get into the van, which took off up the mountain. She called the police, and by the time they arrived she had vomited and turned a sickly pale green. They didn't question her too closely. She trembled and so could only whisper, "The driver, the driver." She had no idea what had become of him. No, she had seen no other car—not that she remembered. Someone had pulled her bracelet and ring from her—she knew nothing about anything else they might have taken. Please, she felt ill.

The investigation went nowhere. These terrible things happened all too frequently everywhere in the world.

Two weeks later, Laura made a *second* phone call to
Nicholas Ventura. She had returned to Milan. She was
preparing to open her own studio.

She was a very wealthy widow, at twenty-one years
of age.

Papa Ventura watched her now, appreciatively. At
thirty-seven she wore her black hair cropped very short
and it framed her face to perfection. Contrasted with
the boyish haircut, her face, with its high cheekbones,
appeared exotic. She had large gray eyes with thick
black lashes; a straight, aristocratic, modified Roman
nose; full lips that glistened with what seemed to be
natural color—a deep wine-flesh tone. No other
makeup. Her black dress skimmed her body, subtly
suggesting her hip bones, narrow waist; the only orna-
mentation was a gold cat-pin he had given her years
ago. She wore it to please him.

Her eyes went to his most recent acquisitions: two
Chinese temple tiles, mounted and displayed in a spe-
cially lighted case. She reached up, lightly touched one
warrior, commented on the fact that his mount was a
dragon.

"And, I would guess—it is highly illegal? One of
China's treasures smuggled out of its proper home?"

Papa Ventura smiled and shrugged. "A work of art
has a proper home wherever it is treasured and loved.
These warriors are between two and three hundred
years old—they will surely outlive me."

Laura turned, surveyed him carefully. "You will outlive us all, Papa. I cannot imagine a world without you."

"Not for a long time." Then, like a child, he stood
up eagerly, eyes glittering. "So, you've kept me waiting
long enough. What is my gift to be?"

"You mean besides myself? All right." She dug into
the small black leather bag that hung from her shoul-

der. "Hold out your hand. No, don't look at it yet."

She closed his hand over what was obviously a coin, then let his fingers open.

"I don't have the provenance but I trust my source. It was struck in Rome. Pure gold. Museum quality. Caesar Augustus."

"Yes," he said quietly. "Yes." He studied it for a moment, then slipped it into his trouser pocket. "Thank you, my Laura. Now, go. Treat the party to your presence."

"Oh? Are there other people out there? I hadn't noticed!"

"Laura, you are still a bad girl. Maybe I should have put you over my knees and spanked you, long ago."

She kissed his cheek lightly, then whispered, "Maybe I would have liked it!"

CHAPTER 6

Nick and Richie watched as Laura worked her way through the crowd. She had stayed so long with Papa. Other people wanted to wish him well on his special day. Laura—inconsiderate as usual.

"She's some girl, huh?"

Nick replied, "I think the word is 'woman.' "

"Yeah, whatever. Uh-oh. Here comes trouble, if I know what trouble is." He sounded pleasantly hopeful as they watched Peter and Sonny coming toward them, followed by Kathy.

"Hey, Nick, we got us a problem here," Sonny sounded smug, sarcastic. Just like his father.

Peter shook his head. No problem; no big deal.

Kathy looked tense.

"So, whatsa problem?"

Sonny told his father, "See, I asked Petey to come on home with us after the party and stay over and I'd take him down to the San Gennaro with me tomorrow. I can't believe he's never been." He turned, the condescending male. "But Kathy says, she says *no*, but *I* think . . ."

Richie, glancing at Nick, then at Kathy, pulled his son by the arm, happy to watch. "*I* think you better butt out of something between a man and his wife, ya know?"

Kathy said sensibly, "Nick, tomorrow is a school day."

Richie grinned. "What kinda Italian we got here, never been to San Gennaro? Nicky, c'mon, how many times you take the kid to St. Patrick's Parade? Peter, ya gonna love it—great food, entertainment . . ."

"How would he get home?"

"Kathy, no problem. I'd have Artie Music—you know Artie, guy who drives for me—I'd have him take the kid home tomorrow night. Early, okay? Hell, this is a smart kid. So what if he misses a day of school? Bet you got a perfect record, right, Peter?"

Nick said, "He'd have a good time, Kathy."

Her face tightened. "Nick, I don't feel it's safe for him in New York City."

Richie let out a roar. "Jeez, not safe! Kathy, there's no crime in Little Italy, don't you know that? Safest place in the city—maybe in the country. Jesus, little girls, old ladies, anybody can be on the streets down there, day or night—it's protected. I swear to you. Hey, Sonny will be with him. And we got people there."

"I didn't realize you never went to the fair, Peter. Hell, Kathy, he'd love it—it's fun, the whole festival."

Peter, looking more worried than usual, assured him. "Dad, it isn't important, honest."

In her toughest voice Kathy said, "Nick, could I speak to you for a moment?"

Jesus Christ, Kathy, he thought, don't do this to me. Not here in front of these two cretins. Haven't you got any common sense? This had nothing to do with the San Gennaro. This had to do with a lot of other things.

"It *is* important, Kathy. This is part of his heritage. He's entitled."

She bit her lip. "Fine. Great. Look, I've done my

family duty. I've paid my respects. Now I'm out of here. Sonny, please get the station wagon out front for me." She turned away, then back to Nick and signaled him closer to her. "You can get home any damn way you can. Or not."

Sonny and Peter went off together to get the wagon. Nick watched as Kathy said her smiling good-byes through the crowd, without once looking back at him.

Richie shook his head sympathetically. "Nicky, Nicky. I tole ya and tole ya. You shoulda married one of your own kind."

He plucked Richie's pinkie-ringed hand off his arm. "I did, Richie. *I did.*"

CHAPTER 7

They hadn't noticed Laura until she spoke. "Richie," she said softly, "I think Papa wants to see you. *Now.*"

Richie moved quickly; now meant now. Laura took Nick's arm and pulled him. "C'mon, Nick. Let's get outta here. Papa didn't ask for Richie, but I assumed that sooner or later—"

She winked; Laura the brat, playing a trick. They moved through the crowd, who watched but pretended not to. It had gotten dark out, and the autumn air had a touch of winter cold just beneath the surface. Laura led him to a limo; a uniformed guy tipped his hat and held the door open.

They settled into the lush back seat; she leaned forward and asked the driver if he knew where Romano's was, in Long Island City. He nodded and slid the glass window closed, giving them privacy.

Nick leaned back. Very nice. "This yours?"

Laura shrugged and laughed. "Too big for me. But I get a good price for the rental—car and driver—when I don't feel like driving.

"So, Nick. How've you been? Haven't seen you in what, five years? Papa's last big birthday party." She reached out and poked him. "Hey, pal, we gotta stop meeting like this."

Years seemed to fall away; the tall, slender, sophisticated lady disappeared. His most vivid memory of her was as a child: stubborn, determined, unyielding. Laura would do things *her* way. Against all odds.

Laura chewed her index finger for a moment. "That thing with your wife, Kathy? Is it serious?"

Nick stiffened. Christ, a brief disagreement and everyone in the world makes it into big trouble. His grandfather with his radar; his rotten cousin, hoping for the worst. And now Laura.

"What are you talking about?"

She shrugged. Frowned. "So it *is* serious. Married people don't glare at each other that way over something minor."

Nick felt defensive, protective of Kathy and himself, his family. He felt a need to explain it away, even if he wasn't convinced himself.

"Look, I have a family—wife, son, house in the suburbs. The works. I think it's called commitment—"

"You make it sound like a sentence. No plea bargaining, Nick?"

"What the hell are you up to, Laura?"

She ran her index finger over her bottom lip. "You play around, Nick?"

"Jesus Christ."

"You Mr. Faithful or what?"

"Well, if I do and when I do, I make the moves."

Her laugh wasn't mean or smug. It was the sound of pure joy that he remembered from when she was a small girl observing the absurdities of the boys and men around her. Something in them she found funny, and nobody else could figure out why. She touched his cheek, leaned over, and kissed him lightly the way you'd kiss a child who was exasperated by teasing.

"Relax, Nick. I'm sorry. I'm just kidding. Hey, we're here. What do you say to an egg cream? Last place around for the real thing."

It *was* the real thing: a luncheonette out of a history book. The floor was made of small darkened white tiles; the ceiling of pressed tin. The counter was long, made of gray marble. The leatherette stools were locked in the same place as fifty years ago. The Coca-Cola clock was genuine; probably fetch more than a couple hundred in some antique store. The glass display cases, filled with heavy Danish pastry and cellophane-wrapped cupcakes, were sparkling.

The small man behind the counter, busy digging scoops of ice cream into a long banana-split glass, greeted Laura with a smile. Toast popped up, sandwiches were made then, finally, the old man held his finger up toward Laura.

"The real thing, right, Laura?"

He jerked his chin toward Nick, who nodded, and he presented them with two genuine, old-fashioned, only-in-New York egg creams. They picked up the drinks and Laura headed for the last table in the row, smaller than the rest, in a dark corner.

"When I was in high school," she told Nick, "I worked part-time across the street. In the old Wendy Pocketbook Company. I helped with the bookkeeping. This was my supper. The old man used to put an egg in. Said I was too thin."

Nick, his back to the wall, facing the length of the luncheonette, scanned the place quickly. It's something a cop does. Most people don't even notice. Laura was not most people.

"Any bad guys in the vicinity?"

"I'm not sure yet. You're the only bad guy I can see right now."

"Bad guy? Not *moi*, Nick. Independent guy, yes."

She always seemed to be on the verge of putting him down. Something about her was smug and irritating. Just like when she was a child: who the hell does Laura think she is?

"Hey, how independent can you be? You married money. You've been left pretty well provided for, right?"

She smiled, but her eyes were cold. "Whatever it takes, Nick. I learned that very early." She shrugged in imitation of a neighborhood wise guy. "Hey, ya gotta do what ya gotta do, right?" Then she stopped clowning. "Don't think I didn't earn every penny I ever got."

The playfulness between them was gone. He'd been spiteful, really, for no reason. She picked up her egg cream and gulped it down. No straws or sips for Laura. She wiped the back of her hand across her mouth, then took the napkin he offered.

"That's a nice-looking boy, your Peter. Looks like his mother. What eyes. How come you only have one kid, Nick?"

"How come you never had a kid, Laura?"

She pulled back against the leatherette seat and stared at him, then looked away.

"I would have had a child with my second husband. You heard about him, right? Emilio Sartucci, the skier."

Nick remembered. It had been a tragedy. He started to speak, but she cut him off.

"Two years after Octavio was killed, I married Emilio. He was an Olympic medalist, a national treasure in Italy—like a matador in Spain. Everywhere we went, crowds gathered, just to see him, touch him. We were married six months—to the day—when we went with some friends of his to Switzerland. The macho gang; Italian heroes. They were told the skiing conditions were dangerous; wait a few days. But it was a challenge, you see."

Nick reached for her hand and she pulled it away. "Laura, I'm sorry. I—"

"Oh, it was a long time ago, Nick. I told him it wasn't worth risking his life to impress friends ignorant enough to challenge death so stupidly. So three of them died—an avalanche. One boy survived with brain damage. Only Emilio's body was dug out." She paused. "My God, the funeral was incredible. Every celebrity, actor, athlete, movie star, politician, every wanna-be and almost was attended the funeral. A cardinal officiated. The press said I was 'beautiful and devastated.' " She shrugged. "What I was was angry. I hate stupidity."

Her expression now was placid, calm.

"Did you love him?"

"What difference does that make? We were good lovers."

"No one special in your life now?"

Laura closed her eyes, shook her head, and laughed. "Special? God, you sound like a high school boy. Lovers—yes. Who I choose, when I choose, for however long I choose. God, look at you—are you shocked?"

He didn't know what he was. The tone between them had grown edgy, antagonistic. He didn't know why he felt so angry, so judgmental toward her.

"So you're a pretty rich lady now?"

Laura nibbled on her pinky and grinned.

"Fly all over the world?"

He wanted to smack her or kiss her—either one, or both. She changed instantly as they got up to leave, as though she had pushed a button. Became a young girl, smiling, flirting with the counterman as they were leaving.

Maury wiped his red wet hands on his dirty white apron; offered his cheek for her kiss. "Any time, Laura, you come to me for the best egg cream in the world, right?"

"I come to see *you*, Maury. The egg cream comes in second."

"Ah, she makes me feel like a young boy, this one."

Nick knew exactly what the older man meant. He felt awkward, graceless, somewhat stupid.

She gave him a lift to the subway; he'd head for the precinct and get a car for the trip home. She put her face forward for a light kiss. Without a thought, Nick jerked her face to meet his lips. The kiss surprised them both.

It was nearly 1:30 A.M. by the time Nick reached home. Kathy had parked the station wagon right in the middle of the driveway, so he had to park in front of the house. She'd left a night-light on, more to discourage prowlers than to help him find his way in the dark. The house felt empty. He remembered that Peter wasn't home but looked into his bedroom anyway. The sleepy old dog, Woof, head resting on the pillow, grunted softly without really waking up. The other dogs were flopped out around the house. They all knew his step; no one had to go out.

Nick shared his glass of milk with the oldest of the family cats, a gray part-Siamese with pea green eyes. She sipped carefully, then washed herself and disappeared. No one really knew where she slept. She was the mysterious one of the group.

Kathy wasn't good at faking sleep. She breathed too regularly. He touched her foot lightly, shook it gently, and she didn't respond. Nick took a hot shower, then looked in the mirror when he brushed his teeth. He wondered what Laura saw when she looked at him.

He remembered the first time he knew he loved Laura Santalvo. He was eight; at his father's funeral. She and Richie listened when he told them he and his mother were moving in with his O'Hara uncle. Sure, he'd see them. He'd come back and visit.

Richie, heavyset with a wise-guy face even at nine, put his arm around Laura's shoulder and gave a squeeze.

"Don't worry about Laura, Nicky. I'll take good care of her."

Laura stepped down on Richie's foot, so hard he doubled over in pain and shock.

"Like hell you will."

Then, she took Nick's face in both her hands and kissed him full on the lips. She was eight years old, but the kiss was a helluva lot older. Nick didn't get kissed like that again for a very long time.

He turned out the light and started for Peter's room for an automatic last check, then remembered. He felt his wife's body tighten slightly when he got into bed beside her. When he touched her shoulder anyway, then the back of her neck, she pulled further away.

Nick rolled over on his side. The hell with it.

CHAPTER 8

Peter watched with admiration as the muscular, sweating men carried the massive platform on which the statue of San Gennaro, patron saint of Naples, had been placed, amid flower arrangements and candles and an assortment of holy relics and items. They moved slowly through the crowd, not stopping, just slowing a bit, as people pushed forward to slip five- and ten- and even twenty-dollar bills into whatever crevice they could find. If a bill dropped underfoot, it was a given that it would not be pocketed, but picked up and placed with the saint.

Sonny had told him that San Gennaro had been a humble priest in Naples who doubted his ability to turn wine and bread into the blood and flesh of the Saviour during mass—until one day a miracle took place, and he never doubted again. Even though most of the people at the celebration weren't Neapolitans, many not even of Italian heritage, the event had become a New York tradition of which few in attendance knew the origin.

Everything involved in the festival was traditional. Every single booth lining the way of the procession had been contracted for months ago. No one could sell so much as a hot dog without paying for the right to do so. All the food, in all the booths—the meats and pastas, breads, cakes, cheeses, wines—came from designated suppliers. Each supplier paid a fee for exclusive rights. The San Gennaro generated a great deal of money; a small amount went to the charity for which it was conducted. A great deal went into other hands that had nothing to do with charity. But what the hell. The wine was good. The food was excellent and the air was filled with marvelous fragrances and the noise of happy people.

Tourists ate too much, walked around a little, then ate some more. Their kids were splattered with sauce, their mouths rimmed in red, and though their bellies ached they pleaded for the original, incredible, tangy lemon ices sold nowhere else in the United States.

Peter was slurping his second lemon ice cup and was ready for a third. His cousin took him by the arm and led him away from the crowd.

"Look, kid, I gotta meet a guy over in Chinatown for a coupla minutes."

"Chinatown? Where's that?"

Sonny jerked his chin. "Not far, a coupla blocks away. You wanna pick a spot, I'll be back here, ten, fifteen minutes tops, okay? Get yourself a cannoli, something, ya got money?"

"I've never been to Chinatown, Sonny. I'll go with you, okay?"

The older boy narrowed his eyes, then shrugged. "Yeah, okay. But listen up. I gotta meet a coupla chinks, we got a little business to take care of. Now, here's the thing, Petey boy. This is strictly between us, right? Can I trust you to keep quiet, this never happened? Like, we never left the Gennaro until we headed home, right?"

For a minute, Sonny thought his cousin was going to

hold up his hand in the Boy Scout pledge. He ruffled
his hair; he was a good kid, if a little dumb.

They hadn't gone more than four or five blocks. The
noise and music from the San Gennaro could still be
heard, but it was as though they had entered another
world. On all the stores and shops, signs and legends
were written in Chinese. Peter was amazed that anyone
could actually make sense of the beautiful symbols. It
was like an ancient world. There were restaurants one
next to the other; open food stalls; real estate offices;
travel agencies; bail bondsmen; pool halls; meeting
rooms. There were people of all ages, single and in
groups, moving along the sidewalks, spilling into the
gutter, stopping to look into a window, to handle merchandise. There were medicinal shops displaying
charms and dried vegetables, roots, animal parts. There
were modern bookstores and video shops.

Sonny suddenly brought him to a stop. Then he
jerked his chin toward a narrow alley.

"You stay right here, outside. I gotta see these kids
for a minute."

Sonny entered the alley, then came back out. He
looked tense, angry. "They want you to come with me.
Lousy chink bastards, they don't trust nobody. You
keep your mouth shut, ya don't see nothin', hear
nothin', *capice?*"

Peter started to ask a question, but his cousin
stopped him. "Hey, dummy up. We'll be two minutes,
then we are outta here. And it never happened, right?"

There were four rail-thin Chinese boys, in their
teens. Everything about them was tense. Peter glanced
at them, surprised by their hostility.

Sonny reached into his pocket and took out a few
bills. He put his hand out and the tallest of the Chinese
snapped his fingers. More. Much more.

Sonny smiled, a tight, unpleasant expression.

"Hey, you gimme what I'm buyin', I pay for the whole thing, right? No games, you little weasels, ya not gonna screw around with me. You know who I am?"

The shortest, but obviously the leader of the Chinese, moved closer. "Fuck you and fuck who you are. You try to stiff me like you done with other guys, you don't be around to talk about it to no one no more."

Sonny put his money back in his pocket. He reached inside his jacket for a moment. The boy who had spoken pushed his hand against Sonny's chest. In a single moment, guns appeared, and were fired at Sonny, who had instinctively pulled back. He was hit in the stomach.

Peter O'Hara, who hadn't moved, was hit in the center of his forehead.

He was dead before he hit the ground.

CHAPTER 9

At the end of the 8:00 to 4:00 p.m. tour Monday, Nick and Eddie planned to spend at least an hour catching up on the paperwork that had accumulated since they had been stuck on the surveillance assignment. They handled the papers mechanically and without interest. Four or five squad guys were checking out the roster, catching up with telephone messages or just shooting the breeze.

A uniformed patrolman, young guy with a shiny new look, stepped into the squad room as though he had no right to be there. Someone waved him in, and he asked for O'Hara.

Nick and Eddie looked at each other. Neither one of them knew the kid. "Yo, I'm O'Hara. Wadda ya got?"

"Detective O'Hara? You're wanted in the captain's office. Right away, he said."

Nick nodded to the young cop, who took off after a hungry look around the room.

Nick told Eddie not to worry. "Hey, if *I* did something, don't forget, we're partners, right? I'll include you in for your share, good or bad." Then an afterthought: "Wait for me, you're my ride home tonight."

Nick tapped on the captain's door, and it was opened

immediately. Captain Nelson touched him lightly on the shoulder, stepped back into his office with Nick, and closed the door behind him.

There stood Deputy Inspector Frank O'Hara. Just standing there, his face expressionless but his complexion noticeably pale. A flash went through Nick: Oh, Christ, he's gonna ask me something about the party. Who was there? What did I hear? Oh, shit.

As he took a step toward his uncle, Nick remembered the last time he had seen Frank look like that. Drained of all color, even his lips pale. Eyes glazed and narrowed. He took a deep breath.

Someone was dead. That much Nick knew.

"Frank, what?" And then, "Frank, *who?*"

His uncle said one word.

"Peter."

CHAPTER 10

The hours following the murder of his son became a videotape forever spooling through Nick's brain. Some of it would come back in startling clarity: a segment-by-segment recollection of faces, voices, sounds, gestures; of locations, smells, light and darkness. Of sensations: panic, terror, anger, madness, sorrow, helplessness. But mostly, it was a feeling of unreality—this all happened to someone else.

He remembered inconsequential things: Frank leaning forward and touching the uniformed driver to slow down; no need to speed through traffic lights.

The thought flashed through his head as they entered the hospital: Good, St. Clare's. That's the cop's choice; always insist they take you to St. Clare's, no matter what. He noted there were a lot of uniformed cops, milling around aimlessly. Glancing at him, then looking away quickly.

Then he was in a small consulting room, staring down at a doctor who seemed too young to shave.

Nick rubbed his hand roughly over his face as he listened to the words.

Head wound.

He knew about head wounds; they said *instant death*.

He understood that. What he couldn't understand was what the fuck any of this had to do with his son, Peter.

His cousin Richie burst into the room. He looked like a crazy man. He was yelling, pounding his chest, the walls. There was blood on his knuckles. His wife, Theresa, came alongside him and watched as two of Richie's men came, led him away. She looked over her shoulder at Nick, reached out, without touching him. "They're gonna give Richie something to quiet him down. Nick, God, Nick, I'm so sorry. Sonny . . . he's in surgery."

She turned and followed her husband.

Then he was in some patient's room; there was a bed over by the window. Frank roughly drew the curtain across the slide and ignored the woman's weak voice: who? what?

Frank spoke quietly. "The kids walked over to Chinatown, Nick. After the San Gennaro. They walked right into a shootout between two street gangs. Sonny took two in the gut. Peter . . . in the forehead."

There were so many questions, but he couldn't seem to form the right words. Instead, he said, "Take me to my son."

They walked down a corridor and Frank stepped back knowing there was no way to stop him, no point.

"He's in there, Nick. Want me to go in with you?"

Nick didn't answer. Frank waited outside.

When he opened the door, a nurse quietly left the room.

There on a long bed, covered from his waist down, his head resting on a small pillow, his arms resting alongside his body, was his son, Peter Nicholas O'Hara. Aged twelve, no longer going on thirteen.

His face was very smooth. The freckles on his cheeks and nose were very pale against his even paler skin. His lips were parted slightly and Nick could see a glint of teeth. Someone had combed his hair. It looked damp. They must have used water. But they got the part wrong. Nick reached up and tousled the heavy dark hair.

There was absolutely no expression on Peter's face: the way he looked when he was sleeping and between dreams. Waiting for something, but not anxious. But there was, of course, a difference. His face seemed made of finely carved stone.

In the center of his forehead, near the hairline, was a small, nearly black circle. Some splatter of powder burns. He hadn't been dead very long. There was no obvious swelling of the head yet.

That was a cop's observation, not a father's.

Christ, this is my son. Nick reached over and picked up one of Peter's hands, so cold. Couldn't they at least have given him a warm blanket? Even as he thought it, he knew it was irrational. He brought his son's hand to his mouth, trying to warm the fingers; the way he did when they were out in the snow, when he was a little kid, didn't want to go inside, lips turning blue, warm my hands, Daddy, blow on them.

He leaned over, tried to warm Peter's face, with his hands, with his lips. His mouth tasted nothing of his son: just cold cold cold.

Frank O'Hara wrapped a strong arm around his shoulders and Nick didn't have the strength to resist.

They sat alone in a small room somewhere. Waiting for Kathy. Suddenly, it occurred to Nick.

"Christ, Frank. She'll think it was me."

Frank shook his head. "Your aunt Mary went to her, with Father O'Rourke. I sent Eddie Manganaro up in a car. They'll be here soon."

And then, "Tell her it *was* me. Oh, God, let it be me and not the kid. Not our son."

Nick had seen people in shock. They reacted in a hundred different ways. He'd once seen a guy who had been tossed through the windshield of his car in a head on, get out, blood streaming down his face, eyes staring, and start complaining in a whining voice about being late for his goddamn dentist appointment.

Kathy, in shock, was very calm and steady. Her voice was clear and she spoke carefully as she pulled back, not allowing his embrace.

"Well, are you satisfied now? Has he experienced enough of his heritage to suit you?"

His aunt Mary shook her head; don't pay any attention. Later on, Kathy would swear she didn't remember saying that, would be horrified that she had. If she said such a thing, God knows she didn't mean it. But the words had come from the deepest part of her brain, and had pierced the deepest part of his.

When his grandfather arrived, Frank O'Hara left them alone together. The old man was straight as a board. He put both hands on Nick's shoulders, and spoke from experience.

"It is a terrible thing to lose a son. A child. The worst thing that can happen to a man." Papa knew.

Nick nodded and wondered, Was this it, then? Finally. *The worst thing*.

He didn't remember his grandfather leaving; hardly remembered his being there. There were so many people, in and out of the small room; guys from the precinct, friends from their town, asking, What could they do? How could they help?

Nick heard a nurse ask if a cop had been shot, there were so many uniformed cops. Someone told her it was worse. A cop's kid.

Finally he found the room where Richie had been

checked into for observation, and asked they be left
alone. Richie leaning sideways in the bed, half-dopey,
pulled himself up.

"Jesus Christ, Nicky, Jesus Christ."

Nick began a slow, methodical series of questions.
He had to know the sequence of events.

Speaking slowly, his words slurring from time to
time, Richie told him: the kid got tired of the fair;
Sonny mentioned that Chinatown was only a coupla
blocks away, so he took the kid to see it. Peter couldn't
believe the place; he was all over, looking at the windows, the people . . . Then there was a fight of some
kind: then, *pop, pop, pop,* four kids shooting at each
other. And then gone. That's all. Peter on the ground;
Sonny moving toward him, not knowing he'd been shot
himself.

Richie started to cry again and Nick waited him out.
Witnesses? Jeez, Richie didn't know—ask the cops.
There were a couple of dicks outside—did Nick know
them?

He found Frank, who directed him to two detectives
from the Seventh Precinct Detective Squad. One of
them was familiar; he ignored their condolences and
got down to questions.

Witnesses? Gang affiliations? Were the kids wearing
gang jackets, headbands? Weapons? Who was working
the neighborhood? Did they have a good Chinese
American investigator? Would they take him to the location—

It was Ed Manganaro who convinced Nick he had
other priorities right now. He promised Nick he would
keep right on top of the investigation. Everyone assured
him. But it really didn't seem to make any difference
at all.

CHAPTER 11

It was amazing how little Kathy needed him. She took over all the terrible details involved in the death. She selected the funeral director. She picked the coffin, telling the salesman she was not interested in the most expensive one. She knew all the bullshit involved in funerals and he'd better back off.

Nick stood by, nodded agreement for whatever she planned. She scarcely noticed. Peter was to be buried next to his O'Hara grandparents.

She arranged the funeral service. Peter was carried by six of his friends: young boys with strong shoulders and hurting eyes. The mass and service were simple.

Kathy chose just the right people to speak and she trusted them to say the right thing. Peter's best friend— a goofy-looking, fast-talking boy named Patrick Riley— someone Nick never would have asked, spoke last. Kathy knew what she was doing. Patrick spoke so beautifully, in a voice so moderated and careful, that Nick cried for the kid's strength in spite of his pain.

Nick could hardly get through the prayers; Kathy took his arm when he started to ramble and firmly brought him back on track.

After the funeral, everyone but his grandfather and

Theresa went to Frank's house for food and for talking. Nick heard laughing, the kids getting a little loud, nervous when they spotted Kathy. She approached them, touched a cheek, ruffled a carefully combed head of hair. She gave a quick squeeze, a hard hug. Not letting them feel alone, or that they weren't acting properly. She told them that any way they felt was okay.

Laura was there, dressed in dark gray. She hugged Kathy; hugged him. Or did he dream it?

Then they went home to their empty house. Mechanically, Nick fed the dogs; some kids showed up to walk them. Kathy had made arrangements for all the dogs, except old Woof, to be temporarily "fostered" with a couple of other families. The in-and-out cat was fine.

Nick cleaned up the backyard. He raked the leaves, then forgot to bag them. He started to fix a loose hinge on the garage door and fell off the ladder, then couldn't remember why he had been up there in the first place. He went to the supermarket and forgot what he had come to buy.

He listened to the sound of voices, rather than the words spoken to him. Father O'Rourke, a sweet-faced young man new to the parish, spoke and Kathy answered while he nodded. His partner, Eddie, came over, spent an hour or two talking about absolutely nothing. His uncle assured him everything was being done to assure a good investigation into the murder of his son. Nick felt enclosed in a glass capsule, isolated with the one fact he had come to fully comprehend.

His son, Peter, was dead.

Kathy invited Peter's friends over, encouraged them to select any tapes, recordings, books, posters they might want. His clothes were dispatched to the St. Vincent's Society. All that remained in Peter's room were some team pictures, a plaque he'd been awarded by the Humane Society for his volunteer work. The room was emptier than any space Nick had ever seen. Only old Woof, lying restlessly on Peter's bed, seemed familiar. Each time anyone came into the room, he pulled himself up hopefully, tail wagging, then slumped into a semi-sleep.

Kathy went about everything with a brisk competence. In the middle of the night, he woke with a jolt: that something-is-wrong feeling. There was a light in Peter's room.

Nick approached his son's room. There was Kathy, sitting on the edge of the bed, cradling the dog. Nick came to her side and reached for her, but she shook her head and he retreated.

CHAPTER 12

Nick went to see his grandfather. He took comfort in the old man's presence. Papa never said he could imagine how Nick felt. He *knew*.

They sat quietly in the glass-enclosed porch overlooking the autumn garden. It was a view the old man had found soothing many times in the past.

"It is not right—not ever—for a man to bury his son. Nicholas, it will never stop hurting. It will hurt in a different way, not so sharp. But it is so bad."

"Papa, I can't seem to concentrate on anything. Sometimes, God, for a minute, I can't remember what he looks like."

"I know. And then it comes back. Yes. I know. Nicholas, I wanted to tell you two things. I hope the first will make you feel . . . if not happy, maybe comforted. The second thing—well, let's get to the first. Do you remember last Easter, when Peter and I had a long private conversation?"

Nick had watched the two of them walking through the blossoming garden, Peter speaking earnestly as Papa inspected the flower beds, stopping, listening, nodding.

"He told me something I had never heard. About the greyhounds from the race tracks."

Nick was surprised. "Peter told you about that?"

"We've talked about many things, Peter and I. I didn't know—imagine all these years I've bet on the races in Florida and never knew how these beautiful animals were treated. How they were destroyed if they won too many times, which brought down the odds. Or if they lost . . . not considered worth feeding."

Nick remembered his son's passion and anger: how can they get away with this?

"I asked him how I could help. He told me he'd read about a group that helped people adopt these dogs. He said people were trying to get the government to help, but they needed money." The old man smiled. "He told me, 'Adopting is good, Papa, but I don't know if you could keep up with a greyhound.' So instead I helped them out, gave them a little money for their legal fund."

Nick remembered his son reading nature magazines while his friends were still casting around comics. He'd matched Peter's fifty-dollar donation with his own. The kid saved every penny he earned at odd jobs, and dutifully sent in round amounts to help people who were helping animals. Most adults didn't have the kind of conscience this kid had.

"I also sent word to certain people, in certain places, that they would be made to account for each and every animal in their races. I would hold them responsible for any mistreatment myself."

Nick was touched by the old man's sincerity. He hadn't known about any of this.

"Papa, that was a good thing to do. In the spirit of my son."

Casually, to break the moment, Papa said, "The IRS will make my accountants crazy checking the donation.

Five figures to protect the animals? From me? Who's going to believe that? Hell, that's what I pay CPAs for. Nicholas, come, let's walk in the garden. Get my sweater over there, it's a little chilly."

In the center of the square garden was a small pool, with a flow of water from a simple statue. Bright orange fish, quick, fat, inquisitive, darted to the surface, then raced each other around in circles. Surrounding the pool was a series of intricate brick patterns. There was a heavy wooden container in each of the four corners. Herbal gardens, Papa told him. And the benches: not only copies of the ancient benches, but made by the very same carpenter who made those in the gardens of the Cloisters. Sweet birdsong could be heard over the splashing waters.

Papa Ventura stopped, pointed to the brickwork, which Nick hadn't even noticed. "These are called brick carpets, Nicholas. See the intricate patterns, the end row like fringe? Each one different; each one unique. And in the containers, all of the herbs were planted exactly like the herbs in those tapestries—you know, the Unicorn Tapestries."

Nick listened carefully to his grandfather. He seemed to be setting a quiet scene for something. "Who did all this work, Papa? Did you design it?"

The old man laughed and took his arm, led him to a bench. "Oh, if only I could. I saw this kind of work in a design magazine. Found the architect, an artist. She's designed these around the world, so I had her come out here. I liked the way she looked and talked. She knew her stuff. Brought brick craftsmen who had worked with her before. See that one, over there, leading to the trellis? The brickmen told her, no, lady, no, this is an impossible design. Cannot be done. My lady smiled and put her hands on her hips and told them, 'Of course it can be done. And you're going to do it.'

When they finished, she whispered to me, she really wasn't sure they'd be able to get that pattern—she'd never tried it before."

The old man smiled, sat very still, drinking in the strange atmosphere of separation: from the house, from the world. It was as if they had left time behind.

Finally, he patted the bench. "Come, Nicholas, sit here beside me."

"And the second thing you want to tell me, Papa. That's why we came out here, right?"

His grandfather's tone of voice was very serious. "This that I tell you now, Nicholas, it will never be spoken of again. By either of us. Ask any questions, here and now. And then it will be finished."

Nick knew something terrible was coming; something he had to hear.

"There was no gang fight in Chinatown that day. The gangs are well controlled and supervised. There were four boys involved in the shooting. Two were brothers. One of the other two had insulted a girlfriend of the older brother. They were there to avenge the insult to the girl."

"Peter got killed because one of those boys insulted a girl?"

"Exactly."

"Who are these boys? What are their names?"

An amazing change took over his grandfather. He seemed to slip out of his old age. His voice was strong and firm; it commanded caution.

"You don't need to know. Those boys no longer exist."

"What?"

"You know what I mean. You know *exactly* what I mean. They killed my great-grandson and wounded another. Nicholas, not only were *we* hurt, the Chinese community was damaged. Those boys violated all the rules by which they lived. It was dealt with. The way we would deal with such a thing."

"You had them killed?"

A nerve jumped in the old man's jaw. "*I* had nothing to do with it." He waited a moment, then broke the intense silence. "I have some connections in the Chinese community. It was in their interest that they deal with it. From the moment those four boys confronted each other with guns, in the street, their lives were over.

"None of this will make you feel any better. I understand that. Peter is still dead. But I didn't want you to spend any time, any energy on all of this. The police will be continuing their investigation, but nothing will come of it. But you had to know. *It is over.*"

There was nothing he could say. What could he ask? What was left for him to do?

CHAPTER 13

When he returned home, he was surprised to see that Kathy had suitcases on their bed. She was filling them with her things from the closets and drawers.

"Kathy, what are you doing?"

"Packing."

"Hold it a minute. What the hell's going on?"

"I'm going up to Boston, Nick—to my sister's. I . . . I'm leaving you."

"Will you please, *please* stop for a minute. Babe, c'mon, stop."

She sat on the edge of the bed. He pulled up a chair and sat in front of her.

"Kathy, in all this time, since . . . Peter . . . we haven't talked, you and me. We . . ."

She studied him with a puzzled expression as though she didn't understand what he'd said.

"But that isn't something we do, Nick, is it? Talk. You and I, talk. Not for, God, how many years?"

"You know how I always felt about the job, that I didn't want to bring any part of it home with me."

"Nick, you *brought* it home with you every single day of your life. But you kept it to yourself. It was your real world, out there. Here, with me, with Peter . . . this was your catch-up time. But Nick, what about *us*—you and me? Besides our son, what have *we* had between us all these years?"

Years of silence, subterfuge. Years of late-night phone calls with excuses, some valid, some not. Mornings of uncertainty—not knowing when, or if, he'd make it home for supper. He thought of all the broken marriages; cops' wives not able or willing to hack it anymore. The guys on the job were never at a loss to talk with each other: there was always someone who wanted to go over a case with him, a conflict, testimony, evidence, an event.

But they were always puzzled, the cops. Confused. What the hell did these women want?

"Kathy, remember a year or two ago, you wanted us to go for family counseling? Let's do it now. We *need* each other now."

She lifted her chin in resolve. "What family do we have left, Nick? We had Peter. Now we don't. Period."

"I love you, Kathy. I've always loved you."

"I know, Nick. Really, I do. And I love you. But I can't live with you anymore. You've created your own life. I've tried to share mine with you, but . . . what the hell. It never really worked."

"That's not true. Kathy, the things I didn't want to talk about, the job—"

"Let me ask you something, Nick. Do you think the women cops go home and tell their husbands about 'the job'?"

Quickly, he answered, "Yeah, I think they probably do."

She spread her hands out and shrugged. "So?"

"But that's different . . ."

"No, it's not. Women share. Men don't. Don't you think I've wanted to be part of what you are, of what you care about? And when's the last time we socialized as a couple with anyone but other cops and their wives?"

"Hey, in any job, people get together with others who have the same interests."

"And the evening ends with all the guys hanging in one room and the wives in the other. The men tell their war stories while the women either drink a little too much or eat too much cake or talk about their kids and their fucking housecleaning methods. Except for those of us who work and are uncomfortable talking about our jobs to women who feel threatened by the fact that we have a life outside of the home."

"Kathy, any time I ever went anywhere with your friends, your 'colleagues,' it always works out the same way. They tell me stories about the crooked cops they know, or ask about the best way to get a cop to skip a violation. Or they tell me about brutality, and how the kids on the street are really society's problem, brutalized—blah blah blah."

"Well, there we have it. Your world—my world. There is no 'our world,' Nick. *Peter* was our world."

He stood up and walked around. Was shocked at the sight of his face in the mirror: haggard, wounded, his eyes swimming red.

"Kathy, this is the wrong time—the worst possible time for you to do this."

"Is there a good time for a hard thing? One time is like another, Nick. This is not spur of the moment, and you know it."

"Kathy, *I need you.*"

When she stood up, her very posture defined her determination. "You never needed me. And you don't now. You have 'the job,' you have 'the guys.' That's your true life. Get on with it. I have to get on with mine. There's too much empty space between us."

She continued packing, speaking quietly. "Nick, I will always love you. But I can't live a half life anymore. I can't live here, in this house. I can't live in this town where Peter grew up. I can't teach in that school." The school where Peter had gone.

He felt desperate. "Kathy, please don't go."

She pointed at the largest suitcase. "Would you bring this down for me? I think I just heard the cab. I'm taking a shuttle up to Boston."

"I'll take you to the airport. We could talk."

"I'm all talked out, Nick. Listen, will you take care of Woof? And Cat. But if you want someone else to . . ."

"That's fine."

"The other dogs, they're adjusting to new homes. I'll be at my sister's for a while. Until I get located. You have her number?"

He nodded. When the cab driver honked, he helped her to the car with the luggage.

He embraced his wife, but after a quick light kiss she pulled back, and without looking at him again, she ducked into the cab.

"Kathy," he said softly to the retreating cab, "Jesus Christ, Kathy, don't do this to me."

CHAPTER 14

Eddie didn't see or hear from Nick for more than two weeks. He didn't answer his phone; his car wasn't in the driveway. Ed figured Nick was up in Boston, trying to work things out with his wife.

As he drove past Nick's house at the beginning of the third week, Ed spotted the old yellow dog sitting slumped against a tree at the side of the house.

"Hey, Woof, you guys just got home, huh?"

The dog moved sluggishly, rubbed his face against Ed's leg. The front door opened a few inches and a ragged voice called the dog, who turned and trotted into the house.

"Hey, Nick. You're home." The door slammed shut. He peered through the windows into the living room through the slit left open between the drawn drapes. He went around to the back and tried to see into the kitchen. After about twenty minutes, no response came from inside the house; no answer to his phone calls. Eddie Manganaro put in a call to Inspector Frank O'Hara.

Frank pounded on the door with his heavy fist, then shoved his weight against the kitchen door, nearly breaking the frame. The first thing he did was to cough against the stale air. He kicked his way through the kitchen, knocking empty bottles, pizza boxes, hamburger wrappers, and chunks of food out of the way.

It was worse in the living room. The smell of spilled Scotch and spoiled food filled the air. Woof let out a soft greeting, came toward Frank, limping. One of his paws was bleeding from a cut and he had what seemed to be sauce of some kind around his mouth.

"Jesus jumping Christ A'mighty. Nick? Nick, where the fuck are you, goddamn it?"

He heard a sound from upstairs and walked carefully through the cluttered hallway, tripped over a fallen lamp. When he switched on the overhead light, he stared in disbelief at the mess. He had seen crack houses that looked like this.

The dog limped after him, followed him to Peter's room, which was bare, clean, untouched. Then he heard a low, hoarse voice coming from the bedroom.

Frank stopped in the doorway and froze. There were bundles of dirty clothes, linens, glasses, bottles all around. Nick was slumped on an upholstered chair, his feet on an upturned wastebasket.

Frank grabbed his nephew by the shoulders of his filthy shirt and shook him. Nick's eyes were two blank light blue discs.

"Nick, c'mon, Nicky, you with me or what? What the fuck have you been doing around here? What have you done to yourself?"

Nick pulled himself up. He looked around, very agitated. "Holy God, Frank. Where's the dog? Oh, God, he's okay, isn't he? I wouldn't hurt him for anything—he's Peter's dog."

"He's okay, Nick. He's okay."

Nick hunched over the dog and touched his bloody paw. "Oh, God, Woofer, what happened to you?"

Frank placed his hands on Nick's shoulders, kneaded

them tightly. "He's got a little cut, that's all. From the broken glass all over the place. He'll be okay. Which is more than I can say for you."

He left Nick, arms around the dog, who licked his face. He searched around the bathroom for some clean towels. He turned on the shower, regulated the water: lukewarm.

He lugged Nick to his feet, stripped off the shirt, dragged him into the bathroom, and shoved him into the shower. He held him firmly, face up, as he decreased the temperature of the water until it was as cold as it could get. Nick shook his head, raised his arms, tried to push Frank away, finally slumped into a sitting position, his head down. Frank slowly increased the water to warm.

"Don't come out until you lose the brewery smell. You got any clean clothes around this place?"

Frank dug around and found some clean underwear, a pair of fresh blue jeans, a blue T-shirt that wasn't too dirty. Just not very clean.

"Get into these things when you finish. I'll be in the kitchen."

He snapped his fingers toward the dog, who followed him gratefully. Frank found a piece of cloth in the kitchen, and he cleaned off the injured paw, opened a can of dog food, and placed it in the backyard for the dog. He turned and looked at the mess, not knowing where to begin.

He found one clean cup, and set it up with powdered coffee. When he opened the refrigerator, the whiff of spoiled food sickened him. He searched the cupboards and found an unopened box of graham crackers.

Nick slumped at the kitchen table, drank a little of the instant, munched a corner of a graham cracker.

Frank was a compulsively clean and orderly man. He needed to feel control over some portions of his world that could still be brought to order. There was no way he could stop himself until he had cleared and cleaned most of the debris around him. His nephew was another matter.

Insisting he wasn't tired, Nick went upstairs when his uncle told him to just get out of the way. Within five minutes, he fell into a deep but restless sleep.

By the time Ed Manganaro arrived with two big shopping bags of food that Frank had ordered, the washing machine was churning and the drier was humming. Eddie looked around, amazed. The inspector was a good housekeeper.

Ed loaded his car with garbage bags and left the silent house.

Later, Nick barely tasted the fresh orange juice his uncle placed in front of him. He rubbed his reddened eyes, then the back of his neck. He stared at the scrambled eggs and toast, then lurched to the sink to throw up. It took a while for Nick to hold anything down, but his uncle insisted.

"At least drink fluids, Nick. You're dehydrated. Keep drinking—juice, water, soda. Boy, you are some piece of work."

Nick grinned weakly and shrugged. "Hey, I'm Irish. I'm supposed to drink, right?"

"You're half Irish, kid, and the Irish you're half of never were drinkers, so don't blame it on the green blood in your veins."

Nick started to laugh, but then uncontrollably he started to sob. His body was taken over with deep wrenching pain, as he was overwhelmed by the memory of why he had been drinking.

Frank went to him, his arm around him, feeling the shaking, trembling, gulping, as Nick tried to stop himself.

Softly, protectively, Frank told him, "It's okay, kid. Let it out. You got a helluva lot to cry about. Let it go, son, let it go."

CHAPTER 15

Frank drove them out to his cottage at Montauk Point, at the eastern end of Long Island. It was cold and gray, the air thick and damp. Then they drove a few miles further east to the Point, parked within sight of the lighthouse. The area was a national park, deserted now, dank and desolate.

They walked along the rocky beach, watching the Atlantic's heavy gray waves rise, roll toward land, peak, revealing flashes of pure green before crashing into foam.

They camped on concrete benches around the cement tables outside the closed, bleak restaurant. Frank had brought a thermos of coffee and a bag of sandwiches. They hadn't been hungry at the house, but now they were surprised the food tasted so good.

"Jesus, I remember going deep-sea fishing with my father," Frank said. "Your dad, Danny, he was just a little kid but he loved every minute of it. Our father turned green after about twenty minutes of our hitting the ocean. I lasted about two minutes after seeing him heave."

"Did my dad get sick?"

"Hell, no. He spent his time yelling that he spotted

whales. He kept snapping away with his Brownie camera. No one else saw anything like a whale. But damn, there they were when the pictures were developed. He was so damn proud."

"I never liked fishing," Nick said quietly. "Took Peter once, up in the lake at Bear Mountain. I caught a good-sized fish and took one look at Peter's face. 'Daddy, it's dying, isn't it?' I put the damn thing back in the water."

They sat silent for a while. Frank hunched his large shoulders into the wind and breathed deeply.

"Shame life can't be like this—pure, elemental, fresh."

"Yeah."

"So, Nick." Frank hesitated a moment. "When you planning on going back to work? You've just about used up all your time—vacation, holidays, compassionate leave, overtime."

Nick didn't meet his uncle's eyes. "You been checking up on me?"

"Well, you know me. I'm a nosy sonofabitch and got nothin' better to do with my time. C'mon, Nick."

"I'm not going back. I don't know what the hell I'm gonna do, okay?"

"No. Not okay."

"Hey, Frank. I'm on my own. I don't feel like doing anything. So I'm not going to do anything. You know why Kathy left me? Because of the job."

"There were other reasons, Nick. There always are. Don't blame it all on the job."

"Gimme a break, Frank. Leave it alone."

"Nick, there are some things I have to tell you. I know it's a helluva time, but . . ."

Kathy's words flashed through his brain. "But there's no good time to tell a bad thing. What have you got to tell me that I don't already know? What could be worse than—"

"A lot of things. Let's take a walk, Nick."

Walking along the cold, rocky, deserted beach, avoiding rushes of foamy water creeping higher and higher along the shore, Frank told Nick what he had never known. How Nick's father, Danny O'Hara, died. And who was responsible for his murder.

"It was an *accident*, Frank. He fell."

"Have you ever wondered why your mother didn't stay in Brooklyn, near your Ventura relatives? Why she moved in with us, and never went back to the old neighborhood?"

"How the hell should I know? I was just a kid."

Nick picked up a stone, tossed it as far as he could, watched it disappear as it caught a wave. Then he asked a policeman's question.

"How many guys were working up there—you said, what, twelve, fifteen?"

"Eighteen. Twelve came to me and told me the same story. Exactly the same story. The welsher got roughed up and tossed over the side. The bastards grabbed your father, to keep him from phoning the police. Your uncle Vincent dialed a number, talked to the only person in the whole world with the authority to give the order. Your grandfather."

"Papa loved my father. He always did. He felt like he was a son."

"What the fuck was he gonna tell you? And remember, Nick, Vincent *was* a son."

"You had twelve witnesses come to you? Okay, why the hell didn't you make a case?" Even as he asked the question, he knew the answer. Who the hell would dare testify against the Ventura family?

"Nick, right after your father's funeral, Vincent was sent to Arizona. Heart condition? Yeah, right. It was to keep him out of sight. And the two thugs with him, Nick. Guess what happened to them?"

Nick didn't have to guess.

"An unfortunate car 'incident.' The damn Olds blew up just as they started away from a restaurant. Helluva thing, could happen to anybody, right?"

Nick wiped the cold salty water from his cheeks and eyes. His breath was shallow and painful in his chest. "Okay, Frank. Tell me this." It was the only challenge he could think of. "If what you say is true, that Vinny killed my father, that Papa told him to, if that was true, then why the hell did you let me go to see him when I was a kid? I saw him every goddamn holiday, his birthday, mine. If he killed my father, why would you ever let me go near him?"

They stopped walking, ignoring wet shoes, damp pants, freezing hands, and stinging faces.

"Nicky, Nicky, you were eight years old. In nine months, you lost both your father and your mother. What the fuck was I supposed to do, kill off your grandfather for you too? I guess I was wrong, but as much as I hated that bastard, I couldn't do that to *you*. The years went by so fast, you didn't see him that often when you were older. Then you were off to the army, you got married. Okay, I guess I was wrong. I should have told you when you were a kid. But you loved him so much. And . . . he did love you."

"Then why the hell are you telling me this now?"

"I haven't finished, Nick. You've gotta hear all of it."

"*All of it?* What the hell else have you got to tell me?"

Frank turned his face to the ocean, trying to draw strength; wishing he could wash away all reality.

He told Nick how and why Peter was really killed— caught in the middle of a petty, street-level drug deal that went wrong between Sonny Ventura and some maverick Chinese kids who were carrying on their own business.

"Peter wasn't caught in any crossfire. He was shot from a distance of no more than two or three feet. Point-blank."

Nick had known this; of course he had known this. He had looked at his dead son's face; had seen the bullet hole surrounded by powder burns. His policeman's brain had noted that it was a close contact wound. For which there was no reasonable explanation according to Sonny's story.

"You know where Sonny Ventura is right now, Nick? They got him out of the hospital before the kid was fully recovered, so you wouldn't talk to him. Flew him, by private plane, to a hospital in Tucson, Arizona. He'll move in with his grandfather, Vincent. Two of a kind, Nick. They deserve each other."

Frank watched his nephew run along the edge of the beach, unaware of the fact that at some point the water was over his ankles. He became a vague shadow, emerging now and then in the heavy mist that was turning into fog. He waited. Nick was gone for nearly an hour, but Frank knew he would come back.

Obviously, he had slipped at some point: one side of his clothing was soaking wet. They walked up the steep sandy hill, crossed the deserted paved area usually filled with tourists in the spring and summer months, stopped at the benches.

"Nick, you *have* to go back on the job."

Nick's face was so blank it wasn't even clear that he had heard his uncle's words, but he had.

"Why? What for? Why the fuck should I go back on the job?"

Frank's body stiffened and he said, through clenched teeth, *"To get revenge."*

They spent the rest of the weekend at Frank's cottage, and Nick listened as his uncle spelled out, in detail, his plan.

PART 2

THE PLAN

CHAPTER 16

At Nick's precinct, there was a department leg-end named Sam Speigel, nicknamed "Singin' Sam." At his mother's behest, he had trained to be a cantor. His pure and beautiful voice brought tears and a sense of wonder to all who heard him sing. But what he had wanted, all his life, was to be a policeman, which his family thought was strange: What nice Jewish boy would want such a job? Sam Speigel did.

His voice earned him a unique place in the police department. Sam Speigel sang at any and every frater-nal dinner, convention, picnic, memorial service—in churches and synagogues throughout the city. He sang at weddings and bar mitzvahs, at anniversaries, birth-days, and funerals. He was invited to all parties wherever policemen gathered, and could sing in any language required with a soul-piercing clarity.

Which is why everyone who knew him and thrilled to his gift was shocked beyond words when Sam Spei-gel was shot in the throat, by a madman who had just killed his wife and children, and before killing himself shot Sam. Everyone rushed to the hospital to give blood, comfort, assistance of every kind to his family. What no one could give him were new vocal cords.

Sam was a plodder and an optimist and a man who concentrated on whatever needed to be done in order to survive. About a year after his release from his stay at a rehab center, Sam Speigel showed up in the precinct house, where his lifting voice had been heard for years practicing new songs for some party or traditional celebration.

He was warmly greeted, hugged, thumped, surrounded by his former co-workers, and then he waved them back and demonstrated his new way of speaking. Holding a microphonelike device over an implanted box in his throat, breathing in strange gasping sounds, Sam spoke to them. No one could understand a single word. There was a series of gasps and burps and loud electronic feedbacks and Sam grew red in the face with his effort. He scrambled around, found a piece of paper and a pencil, and wrote: *"I'm getting better at this every day!"* Everyone nodded, patted him on the back, and got very busy.

Sam Speigel was not deterred. Through the years, he would show up unannounced to visit with his chums. Nick had watched their response to his breathless performance. No one actually *looked* at Sam. They looked past him, around him, through him, but no one caught his eye lest Sam try to start a one-on-one conversation.

Nick O'Hara thought about Sam Speigel for the first time in years after he returned to the job. The precinct had been well represented at his son's wake and funeral. Guys had come to talk with him; kept in touch by telephone. But that was during the mourning period. Now that he was back at work he sensed a sudden quieting whenever he entered the squad room. He was acutely aware that everyone was very careful to gear their conversation away from anything to do with their kids, since his was dead, or to their wives, since his had left him. It was better to avoid him rather than blurt out something about a kid that might be hurtful to Nick.

Eddie Manganaro told him to ease up. The guys all felt so terrible about his son, they just didn't know what the hell to do about it. They didn't want to keep bringing it up or say or do anything that would make Nick feel bad.

"I feel bad every day of my life, Eddie. Nothing they can say or do about their own kid can hurt me."

Eddie squeezed Nick's arm. "They're trying, partner. Just let it slide. They'll come around."

"Well, what the fuck, I'll try real hard to be patient. I don't want to put pressure on anybody."

But Nick knew how Sam Speigel must have felt. He had become, if not quite invisible, someone to look past.

In a way, it worked to Nick's advantage. It gave him the freedom he needed to get on with what he had to do.

None of the men he worked with, except Ed, knew that in the past Nick had had a gambling problem. Hell, everyone bet on a prize fight, a ball game, an election, played the lottery. No big deal.

Years ago, he had gotten himself into a seriously embarrassing situation. He'd been sent down to Atlantic City to pick up a witness in a domestic murder case. The guy had been hiding out for nearly two months, trying to decide whether or not he should turn in his brother for hacking off his live-in girlfriend's head. According to the A.C. cops, the witness was flat broke and wanted to go home. So, the hell with his brother, who he said was a no-good lowlife anyway. Apparently, the murdering brother had failed to come through with a much-needed couple hundred dollars.

Nick got into Atlantic City a few hours early. He just

wanted to look around, check it out. Within an hour, he had run up his travel expense and pocket money from two hundred dollars to five thousand. Within the second hour, he was totally wiped out. Not even a coin to call home. He had to walk the couple of miles to the station where his witness waited. Deeply embarrassed, Nick spoke quietly to the detective squad commander. He explained how some light-fingered pro picked him clean when he was standing around, taking in the action at Trump's place. The lieutenant studied him with a knowing look, a slight shake of his head, then smiled and asked Nick if he wanted to make a crime report.

"Hell, no. The guy was so good I didn't even get a quick look at him."

The squad commander hit the squad's petty cash box, plus threw in a twenty of his own so that Nick could get himself and his witness back to New York. Didn't even ask Nick to sign a tab: he had no doubt at all that Nick would pay him back as soon as he reached home.

The witness who gave up being his brother's keeper complained all the way to New York about the discomfort of the crowded bus—all those old people with their rolls of coins. He had expected, if not a limo, at least a decent car ride.

After paying the money back, Nick vowed never to get in that position again. It was very hard. On the job, you get a lot of tips from people in the know. On the night their son was born, Nick took one look at them, Madonna and child, and promised Kathy he'd never bet again. It was all she asked him for a gift. But it was the night of the NBA playoff, and Nick, in a grand final gesture, made the right bet: He won eight hundred dollars. Kathy wouldn't touch it, so he lost it within two days. After seeing the hurt and disgust and sorrow in his wife's face, Nick never again bet on anything.

For a recovering alcoholic, the first drink is the fatal one. For a recovering heroin addict, the first hit is nirvana, the next moment filled with a need so quickly elevated, so persistent, that the clean years disappear and the horror is back.

For Nick, his return to gambling was ludicrous. He was standing on the elevated IRT platform in Brooklyn on his way back from trying to interview a complainant who never showed. A completely wasted day with an in-basket filled with cases. He stood, absently watching as a construction crew systematically took apart an old four-story industrial building, according to the faded legend on the old brick facade, once the home of "Mina and Mimmi's Customade Corsets."

The crew chief motioned his men away, positioned himself on a rig that operated a large iron wrecking ball suspended by long steel cables. In a jerky motion, the ball swung closer and closer to the standing wall, then hit it with a resounding thud.

He wasn't aware of the guy standing next to him until a raspy voice announced, "He'll take it down in two more hits."

Nick shrugged. "Naw, that's good construction. Take at least four."

"For ten bucks?"

Nick dug out his ten to match the other guy's. "You're on."

It took four more solid slams for the wall to collapse. That was Nick's return to gambling.

It wasn't the winning. No one could ever understand that it had little to do with winning. It was the chance, the dare, the sudden drop in the stomach, the rise in adrenaline, the breath held at the moment of truth: the challenge; the *possibility*.

It was a lot of things, but whatever it was, Nick was hooked again.

CHAPTER 17

As far as his partner could tell, Nick had settled into his solitary life without any complaints. Unlike other guys, he didn't blame or accuse his wife. He just never mentioned her name. He came to seem more at ease with the other squad guys—or maybe they grew more at ease with him. On a few occasions, he offered Eddie a tip on a horse race—good odds on an unknown young filly. Eddie laid down twenty alongside Nick's fifty at the local deli, where the book was run by a twitchy winking-blinking waif of a man who kept everything in his head: no slips, no pieces of paper. No evidence. It was Ed's first and last loss; he wouldn't bet again.

"Ed, I got this tip right from the cousin of the trainer down at the Saratoga dog track. These things are fixed, trust me. You can recoup your twenty in less than the minute it takes these dogs to run the course."

Ed Manganaro shook his head. "I hate losing, Nick. Thanks anyway."

The whole squad had been keeping up with the O. J. trial out in L.A. They began making bets on every aspect of the case: what color suit would Cochran wear; what would Marsha do next? Nick won a hundred bucks when she changed her hairstyle. They bet on how many jurors would be replaced; when; who would hit Geraldo for a TV interview. No one would take a bet on the verdict.

"He'll walk," everyone agreed.

Nick reported on his first 4:00 P.M. to 1:00 A.M. tour the day the case went to the jury. He offered odds, ten to one on a guilty verdict; top bet ten dollars. Everyone got in on the action. O'Hara was nuts.

"Hey, Nick, you gotta be kidding. You got some loose money you need to get rid of, give it to me. I'm your partner."

Nick shrugged. "You want a piece of the action."

Ed shook his head. "No way. I'm your friend, right?"

When the jury asked for a readback of the testimony of the limo chauffeur, who the prosecution said was the one totally disinterested witness, Nick offered to up the odds: Twenty to one, but no one took him on.

After the verdict, Ed drove the squad Chevy to the Avenue B location of a triple homicide. He glanced a few times at Nick, who didn't seem the slightest bit disturbed by the thousand bucks he'd just lost.

"C'mon, quit it, will ya, Eddie? I lost more than that on a single card. Hell, I'll recoup on the next ball game."

They waited for the Homicide Squad to take over, prepared notes and spoke to witnesses. The usual drug dealers' war: a couple of punks crossed to the wrong side of the street, a corner owned by another crew. Hell, they had to be taught a lesson.

Detective Tom Leary caught the case for Homicide. "Tomorrow, there'll be four dead—payback. Jeez, I wish they'd all get together in Yankee Stadium and have it out once and for all."

Nick grinned at Leary, who hadn't yet spotted him.

"What odds would you give and what side: Latin Kings or Island Starboys?"

"Jesus, Nick O'Hara, I haven't seen you in years. You disappeared on me."

"Uh-uh. You moved uptown. They got you back here, huh?"

"Temporary. I'm fillin' in. So, who do you pick of these two fine sterling young representatives of our brave new society? The punks or the punks?"

Tom Leary had been one of Nick's closest gambling pals. Between them they'd won and lost thousands of dollars. Leary played regularly in a heavy-hitters' poker game on the Upper West Side every Tuesday night, if he wasn't stuck with dead bodies. He wore a Brooks Brothers blazer, dark gray slacks, white shirt, neatly patterned silk tie, and a really good gold watch. He had apparently been doing the right things.

"Ever want to get into a game, Nick, gimme a call. Take my card—home number's on the back."

Nick played heavy poker for nearly a month, winning and losing several thousand dollars. He lost more than he won. It wasn't a social game: it was strictly business. Money on the table; out of money, out of the game.

Nick placed bets on any and every sports event—soccer, basketball, football, baseball: series; title games; hockey; races, horse and dog; tennis matches; boxing; wrestling. Even when you knew for certain it was a fixed match, sometimes you bet the underdog just in case. Just maybe.

Between extra assignments and extra tours and court time, Nick and Ed had plenty of overtime coming to them. When Ed invited him to come to dinner, Nick shook his head. Had plans.

"You seein' somebody? You holding out on me, pal?"

Nick smiled mysteriously. Less said the better.

He went to Atlantic City, and in four hours at the

Tropicana he won ten thousand dollars at roulette; in thirty minutes he lost twenty-five thousand dollars. His losses at the Tuesday night poker game totaled nearly thirty thousand dollars. His joint savings account with Kathy was cut in half.

It was a rotten thing to do to Kathy. He didn't want her to know about it. He went to the bank; couldn't take out a second mortgage. She would learn of it.

Mr. Grazler, a bone-thin man with strands of oily black hair stretched across his bald skull, looked exactly the way he did when Nick had seen him on his TV ads. "Need some cash? Bank turned you down? Debts getting heavy? See me. I won't turn you down. Grant Grazler will be there for you."

Nick examined the document, which seemed to contain print that got smaller and smaller as he read it. Bottom line: sign here for a loan of fifty thousand dollars, payable in x number of installments. Default and you lose the house put up for security.

"But the house is worth a hundred fifty thousand easy on the market today," Nick said.

Grant Grazler shrugged elaborately. "So? Sell it."

What he intended to do was to put thirty thousand dollars in the joint account with Kathy. That's what he truly intended to do. But somehow, he took the money in cash, and in a four-day time-off—which used up all his remaining overtime—Nick flew out to Las Vegas.

He didn't play right away. He wandered around; looked things over. He passed through the tourist games, the penny ante stuff; watched the frantic penny pinchers stuffing quarters into the hungry machines, guarding the machines with their bodies while husbands or wives ran over to turn tens and twenties into cups of quarters. This machine was due to hit any time now; damned if some lucky slob would walk over, drop a quarter, and hit big bucks. Of course, every now and then, someone *did* hit. Sometimes it was the first quarter dropped on an available machine. Lights would flash, bells ring, people would scream and point at the dazed honeymoon couple or fortieth-anniversary celebrants who just hit a cool million. From then on, there wouldn't be an available jackpot machine for days at a time.

He played the roulette table, craps, twenty-one. He won; lost; won; lost. Won more than he lost. Was up thirty thousand in a day and a half. He was noticed. He seemed a steady, serious, knowledgeable gambler. As he bought some fifty-dollar chips, a houseman, neat in his ink blue tux, approached, smiling: offered to comp his room and food service, a gratuity for our serious players. You don't have to be bothered with this: You are our guest.

Nick learned the house held a heavy-money poker game; discreet, invitation only, limited to eight players. It was held in a fourth-floor suite; food, drinks, any refreshments were served as needed. Inquiries were made, and within a few hours Nick sat across the table from some very serious people: a woman, about forty, whose makeup had faded as she kept licking her lips; a heavyset, white-haired man who affected western clothing though his accent was pure New York; a familiar guy—actor, singer, what?—he recognized from somewhere; a bookkeeper type in a buttoned-up, double-breasted brown suit, whose expression seemed frozen into a look of puzzled interest.

He began slowly; that was okay. The stakes were a thousand to open, a thousand a raise. Nick folded a few times, then began to feel a rhythm within himself: an electricity, a certainty. The world was right here at this round table with these strangers, all holding rectangular cards, all betting that he could be beaten. But he could not be beaten. This is what he realized at a particular

moment when he asked for two cards, and knew, *knew*
before he even looked at them, what they were. Two
kings; to go with his other two kings.

There was an absolute knowledge at a precise moment of each game: Drop out. Go for it. Drop; raise.
Scoop it up. Win. Win. Win.

There was a feeling of power that Nick hadn't had
in a very long time. An infallible, perfect knowledge
that this was *his* night. He was a winner and nothing,
no one, could best him. He *knew* how many cards to
ask for; how much to bet, raise.

By the end of the evening's session, Nick had won
one hundred and fifty thousand dollars. Chairs were
pushed back, cigars lit or stomped out, men stood up,
stretched; the lone woman had quit hours ago, tossing
her cards on the table without a word, and leaving un-
noticed. Nick stared at the black chips that had been
shoved toward him. As he reached for them, a quiet
voice said to him: "What do you say, sport? Double or
nothing? Cut for it?"

It was the accountant in the brown double-breasted
suit, whose eyeglasses had slid to the tip of his nose.
He was the house player. There was a dead silence in
the room. Nick felt a pounding in his stomach, a twitch
at the corners of his mouth. He started to say something, but instead he pulled his hands back and nodded.

From somewhere a cellophane-wrapped package of
playing cards appeared. Everyone seemed to come
closer to the table, although no one actually moved.
They were frozen to the sight on the table. One of the
house employees ripped open the pack; handed it to
Nick to shuffle, then to the accountant.

"Pick first?" the small, ineffectual-looking man asked.
Nick shrugged. Why not?

He took a deep breath, moved his hand toward the
pack on the green felt-topped table, let the tips of his

fingers stop at a certain point. Yes. He felt it. Yes. It was there, still for him. It was okay.

He held his breath, then let it out slowly. There was nothing in the world to worry about. It was still with him.

There was an audible sigh around the table as Nick displayed his card.

The queen of diamonds.

Nick kept his face absolutely still.

His opponent nodded slightly. He picked the top card without hesitation, turned it over, and placed it on top of Nick's queen.

"King of Hearts tops Queen, I believe. As it always has, as it always will."

CHAPTER 18

Kathy sat at the round kitchen table, her back not touching the chair. She breathed through her mouth, in gasps, as though she'd been running. When he placed a cup of tea before her, she never even glanced at it. She kept her eyes on him: watched every move, every gesture; pierced him with the anger and hostility she was trying to control. Still looking at him, she reached for her shoulder bag on the floor beside her foot and slid the bankbook from the outside pocket. She opened it flatly, held it so that the stamped words could be clearly seen: ACCOUNT CLOSED.

As he started to say something, Kathy held her hand up at him. "No. Not a word. Not yet. I've been up all night, preparing myself for this. I'm not going to let anything go unsaid, Nick. There was seventy thousand dollars in our—*joint*—bank account. Twenty we saved together. The other fifty came from *my father*. You remember that, don't you?"

Her father had been an unfriendly, parsimonious man who owned and ran a third-rate furniture store in the shabby section of Boston where he and his wife raised their five children. When they finally went suburban, it was on a G.I. loan for a cracker-jack box of a three-bedroom, one-bathroom house. All the kids who were old enough worked after school and summers, kicked into the family pot. They were all good students, able to qualify for minimum scholarships but unable to pay both tuition and board. One brother joined the army and served four years to get a head start on college tuition. Two brothers took on local construction jobs and ran their own company. Kathy and her sister, Patsy, worked at anything and everything, day or evening hours, weekends, summers, holidays. They baby-sat and cleaned houses, and tutored. They dog-walked and flipped burgers. They painted apartments along with their brothers. They did whatever they could in order to earn money to pay tuition for a teaching degree.

Her father never offered a penny to any of his children. Resented them wanting more education. That bastard, Kathy said; when my mother died he got her the cheapest possible funeral. He *argued* with the undertakers, said not to pretty her up—what the hell, the woman was dead. And then, two years ago, her father had died of a heart attack, right at his shop, where he was still working at age seventy-three. Her oldest brother, having put himself through law school, was the executor, and he called them all together.

Her father's estate totaled three hundred fifty thousand dollars, and was to be split among the five of them. He had maintained ten bank accounts—never trust the banks, he said; never bank more than the government insures. Forget stocks and bonds. None of them could have been more surprised if their father had jumped up from the grave and danced a jig. Through all the years when he could have helped his children—through crises with their families, rent, education—he had pretended not to have a dime.

Kathy's legacy was to see Peter through college. No

matter what else; the house could fall down. If I die, she said, cremate me and scatter the ashes, but don't touch Peter's college fund.

Her voice had taken on an odd, droning quality; her speech had turned into a recitation, but then she stopped speaking and stood up. Her face was a mask: the face of a desperate child who had suddenly become an anguished woman and didn't know what to say or do next.

"But of course, Peter's dead. He doesn't need a college fund, right, Nick?"

"Kathy—"

"I was planning to buy a four-room condo, Nick. Just outside of Boston, near the school where I'll teach starting in September. I have the papers all ready. Just needed the down payment. That's why I came into town. I wasn't even going to take the full fifty thousand; just twenty-five, for now." She picked up the bankbook and held it in front of her, an accusation. "You had it transferred out to Las Vegas last week. All of it. Account closed." She stretched out her hand. "Give me my money, Nick."

"Kathy—"

She clenched her hands to keep control. She shuddered with the effort and lifted her chin. "At least, Christ, did you have a good time, Nick? Did you win, then lose, then win, then lose?" Her voice went very low. *"Did you have a fucking good time, Nick?"*

There was absolutely nothing he could say to her. Nothing. Not a word. He couldn't bear to look at her. Her pain was different from when Peter had died. There was an ultimate, consuming anger mixed with a naked agony.

She turned from him, dug a cigarette out of her pocketbook, lit it and blew smoke at him. "Look at this. I took up smoking again. Yesterday. How about that?

Two packs since yesterday." She went to the sink, ran the water, dousing the cigarette. She kept her hands under the water, then sloshed her face lightly; blotted with a paper towel.

"All right. Here's what we are going to do. You are going to sign over the deed to this house. I contributed as much as you. I figured half of the selling price would be my nest egg, but it's going to be all I have. Get the deed." She checked her wristwatch. "We'll go to the bank. Right now."

When he didn't answer, Kathy drew back her arm, made a fist, and hit Nick in the mouth. Then, with the other hand, she punched him in the stomach, sobbing, gasping, hitting him over and over again, until her knees buckled. She shrugged his hands off her as he kept her from hitting the floor.

"Kathy. Babe, look. I didn't sell the house. I didn't lose it. It's just that . . ."

"It's just that—what?"

Unable to look at her, he stared across the room, noticed the array of snapshots still held by magnets to the door of the refrigerator. Bright photos of the three of them together. Of Peter with his animals; of Kathy, pretending to be sultry; of Nick, sweating over the outdoor grill.

"There's a lien on it. For fifty thousand dollars. We can't sell it until I pay that off."

It was as though he spoke a different language; she didn't understand what he was saying. "The house is in my name, too. You sign it over to me, Nick. I want the deed . . ."

"Kathy, I'll work it out. I swear I will. I just need a little time. Kath, there are some very . . . heavy hitters I owe a lot of money to. I gotta work it out. I will, I swear, I'll get everything back for you."

Her hands were shaking so badly, things began to

fall to the floor—her handkerchief, cigarettes, matches, car keys. She held the car keys out toward him.

"How about the Volvo, Nick? Maybe your heavy hitters could sell it—let's see, it'd be worth about fifty dollars for junk."

She yanked the door open, then turned to face him one more time. It was the cold, hate-filled face of a total stranger: a Kathy he didn't realize could ever exist. "I hope they end up killing you, Nick. I hope they kill you. I really—*really* do."

She didn't hear him say softly, "Me too, babe. Me too."

CHAPTER 19

He handled it as though it were an assignment. He spent hours watching, hunched in the seat of the beat-up old Ford he'd gotten from some rent-a-wreck dump. He was aware of who entered and never exited, at least not through the front door of the restaurant. He checked around the alley, found the back door. On the night he hit, Nick parked his nondescript wreck on a street adjacent to the back alley.

He huddled in the doorway of the deserted, rat-laden alley. Not even the homeless hunkered down here. Maybe a dead-out junkie or two. He took a deep breath, pulled the collar of his black sweatshirt jacket up; put on his dark glasses; slicked his hair back. He could pass for a Dominican, at least as he made his entrance.

There were a couple of elderly people finishing their late meal. The food smelled spicy; the air was steamy. There were closing-up sounds coming from the kitchen. The bartender, a small man with dark, bloodshot eyes, glanced around, made eye contact with one of the waiters, who slipped into the kitchen and emerged a moment later. Nick saw it all. He leaned one haunch on a stool, facing into the restaurant; clear view of the front door. He calculated quickly: four, maybe five workers—the owners, two brothers, Juan and Victor, did the cooking and serving. The bartender was an uncle or a cousin.

"Whut you want?" the small dark man asked him.

Nick ignored him, noting he had been addressed in English. He shrugged; watched as the elderly people paid their bill and left. Dominicans. They were a very proud people; they owned Washington Heights. Before the war, the wide streets and well-built apartment buildings had been dominated by German Jewish refugees. The Heights had been something of an intellectual center. They were people who attended city colleges, lectures, symphonies, ballets, the theater. They sent their sons to war; they opened prosperous businesses, and when the war was over, they took in relatives who had survived the camps. Then, they moved out, moved on with the great American suburban migration. Dominicans had slowly settled in the now shabby buildings; brought in illegals, gun runners. And drugs. Main industries, drugs and money. Money because the Dominicans, smart, better educated than some of the others from down southway, were proficient at the complicated task of laundering. They handled millions of dollars a month with such skill that a twenty-two-year-old could retire back home and buy himself a village. Or a spot in the local graveyard.

They made Nick for a cop from the moment he walked in, but that was okay. No problem.

A tall, well-built man, a little heavy in the gut but broad-shouldered, solid chest, dark skin, Indian nose, tight lips, black eyes, came and stood before Nick. Neither pretended anything. Luis had dealt with cops before. Had paid the price of doing business; but he didn't know this guy at all.

Making sure no one was behind him, Nick said softly, "I need some money."

Luis shrugged. "Who don't?"

"I need some of *your* money."

"Hey, don't you guys talk to each other? What, are you new around here? Who you work with, what squad? Who's your boss?"

Nick casually, but quickly, took hold of the man's shoulder in a terrible grip. He dug the nose of his automatic into the man's belly and whispered, "Tell everyone to back off."

Luis started to speak in Spanish, but Nick jerked him hard with the gun. "English. I know some Spanish, but you be very careful, right?"

He backed them all into the kitchen and they lined up against the wall opposite the large dirty stove. There was a smell of rancid oil and fetid food everywhere. The men glanced at each other, but, as Nick knew they would, took their cues from Luis, the oldest of them.

"Okay, you tell me what you want. No problem."

"No problaymo, huh?" Nick shoved Luis toward the large freezer next to where the men stood. "Get in there. Now. Reach into the bin where you keep the pork."

Luis was more stunned than reluctant. "What you talking about?"

Nick slammed him across the face with his fist. "That young guy, what's his name, Jose, he's your son, right?" He gestured to the teenager whose eyes darted back and forth, from his father to Nick.

Nick shoved Luis toward the freezer and held Jose tight against his body; his gun rested on the kid's shoulder, pointed straight at his throat.

Luis did as he was told. His face went blank, unreadable. He entered the freezer, kept the door wide open; dug out a package, caught Nick's signal, dug out two more packages, and shrugged.

"I swear, that's all. That's it."

"Two more," Nick said.

It was obvious the cop knew what he knew. Luis shrugged; fuck, it was only money. He put the packets into a heavy brown bag and carefully handed it to Nick, as he was told to do.

Nick whirled around and ducked as one of the kitchen men came at him with a butcher knife. Propelled by his own momentum, the man slammed into the wall and slid down, stunned. The others moved in, but Nick moved too quickly, caught hold of the kid again.

"He's gonna come out back with me, got that? Then I'm outta here and you won't see me again. Until next time. You been giving table money to some dumbbells. I *know* how much you pull in every week. I know *exactly*."

The kid tried to resist, but his father gave him a warning sign: Go with the bastard. Just go.

Nick threw the kid into a pile of overflowing garbage cans, got into the car, turned the ignition, and took off toward the corner. He made a left turn onto 184th Street and was headed downtown when a large gray van cut him off. Ran him right onto the sidewalk. Someone pried open the passenger side door. Another man pulled his door open and grabbed Nick by the jacket so unexpectedly that he fell to his knees. Before he could look at his assailants, he was thrown into the back of the large gray van and it took him a moment to focus. All the equipment; the monitors; the reel-to-reel; the men with headphones. A police surveillance van.

He was almost right. He had been tossed into a surveillance van run by the Drug Enforcement Administration.

They were not happy with him at all. He had just disrupted a major drug money-laundering operation they had been tracking for nearly six months and were planning to close down within a week.

CHAPTER 20

The interrogation room in the federal building had been set up for intimidation: no windows, bright light, hard uncomfortable chairs. Only Nick was seated, dead center behind a narrow steel table as they stood around the room watching him. No one questioned him; he knew they were waiting for someone.

When their boss arrived, he walked directly to the table in front of Nick. Carefully he placed Nick's gold shield, his official notebook, his gun, methodically emptied, and his wallet on the table.

"So, Detective O'Hara, what were you doing uptown?"

Nick didn't answer. He studied the tall, thin man with a cop's interest. About forty-five; flat face with round beige eyes; heavy beige hair slicked back in the style models used in the expensive men's cologne ads. Well-dressed; good shoes; good build. He had the whitest face Nick had ever seen. His skin was smooth as a child's, as though he'd never had the need to shave. His lips were full and pink and pouty, again like a child's. But Agent Rodney Coleman was not a child, and Nick did not underestimate him.

Nick shrugged. "Picking up some money from some scumbags."

Agent Coleman pulled up a chair and leaned forward. "That much we know. That much we have on tape. Along with every word you said in that restaurant. What I want to know is this: How did you know about the money in the freezer?"

Coleman's eyes never seemed to blink. They were like round doll eyes. Nick wondered: If you laid him on his back, would they close?

Nick shrugged. "I thought everyone knew about that."

Agent Alexander Kantor, a young man with an old man's face, small eyes made tiny by thick horn-rimmed glasses, got into Nick's face. He smelled of some strong cologne, and Nick rubbed his nose. He was about five seven or eight, thin. His clothing seemed too large for his body type. His hair was pulled back into a scrawny ponytail. He was the agent who had watched as the others tackled Nick in the van. He was the only one present who had clearly identified himself.

"Only a very few select people had that information. Where did you get it from?"

"Don't I look like a very select person to you?"

Kantor pulled back, crossed his arms, and shook his head. "You look like gutter scum to me, O'Hara."

Good-guy Coleman, the calm one, put his hand on Kantor's arm. "Do you know how much money you walked away with, Detective O'Hara? Oh, that's right. You didn't get a chance to count it, did you? Sixty-five thousand dollars."

"Really? I thought it was a helluva lot more than that." He looked pointedly at Kantor.

"How did you know how many bags were in the freezer?"

Nick shrugged.

Coleman positioned himself on the edge of the steel table. "See, here's the thing, Nick. I may call you Nick? Here's the thing. We've been set up on this money-laundering thing for quite a while. Our information is very privileged and you just blew it wide open. No one, not the P.D. or their renegade bum cops who regularly collect from Luis and Victor, know the extent—or the real nature—of the business that goes on there. Internal Affairs got a few anonymous calls about the cop payoffs; the shakedowns, interfering with drug trade. But they never made a case. Drug trade, per se, is not what these people are all about."

"Really? And what—per se—are these people all about?"

Kantor picked up. "Who gave you the information on the money laundering? What else do you know about this setup? You been doing something undercover, what?"

After a while, their voices became a humming inside his head. He remained silent. They gave him a plastic cup of lukewarm coffee, which he drank straight down and nearly threw up. He offered them nothing; no excuses, no pleas, no could-we-talk-about-this? No appeal to his better nature—if he had one—could penetrate his weary resignation.

They watched him closely as Deputy Inspector Frank O'Hara entered the room. Nick stood up angrily.

"What's *he* doing here? This has nothing to do with him. *You got me. You got me.* C'mon, Frank, this has nothing to do with you."

Frank O'Hara seemed diminished; pulled into himself. His voice was hoarse, his color gray. He shook his head. "Jesus Christ, Nick. How the hell did this happen?"

Within hours, they knew everything there was to know about Nick O'Hara and his family. Sad about his kid, tough. And they knew how tough it was to maintain a marriage when you're a cop with endless hours and far-reaching involvements.

They knew about the gambling and his outstanding debt to some guys in Vegas. They didn't seem to know about the fifty thou lien on his house. Or decided not to mention it for the time being.

Agent Felix Rodriguiz, black penetrating eyes, kind face, reached out, squeezed his shoulder, leaned forward as though they were just two guys, in this together. The others were all busy elsewhere.

"See, Nick, we've talked about all the pressure you've been under. Hey, your uncle is a good advocate. If this was a P.D. matter, something could be worked out. But you really blundered into something out of your league. We've been working a Dominican-Colombian-Nassau drug money-laundering deal for a long time."

Nick looked at the earnest face; the guy was just doing his job. "Yeah? Which one are you—or does Hispanic cover it all? I never could get it straight."

Rodriguiz was an even-tempered man. He continued talking as though Nick hadn't said a word. "We even have a man inside. One of the kitchen workers. He was afraid he'd have to break cover when they came at you with the knife."

Curious, Nick asked, "Would he have?"

The agent smiled. "It would have been his call, one way or the other. But see, Nick, what you've done is, you tipped them off. You knew there was a large amount of money, how many bags were delivered. Their whole setup is blown. You're a cop—so the cops know, right? They are kaput and we've wasted six months of our time for nada. We risked the life of an agent for nada. We got to answer a lot of questions from people in Washington, D.C. You can understand our position. What have we got to offer? A narcotics dick from downtown who came uptown, just *happened* to hit the right place on the right night for what was the beginning of the largest stockpile of money being collected for shipment to the islands. The word is out; everyone is laying low." He shook his head. "And all we got is you."

"I'm not much, huh?"

"You're a helluva lot less than much, my friend."

Coleman didn't even have to exchange signals with Agent Rodriguiz, who left the room and was replaced by a couple of agents Nick hadn't seen before, along with Agent Kantor.

Nick stared at Coleman's smooth face; not a line or a blemish—it might have been made of porcelain.

Nick shrugged. "Hey, sometimes things just go wrong, right?"

Coleman reached behind him for a clipboard being offered by one of his men. He studied it for a moment.

"Well, we *do* have something else. Something that just *might* save my ass and the well-being of the rest of my squad. None of whom, by the way, would look forward to being exiled to the flat Midwest or cold regions of the Dakotas. These guys are all city boys— New York, Chicago, Philly."

He handed the clipboard to Nick, who rubbed his eyes, tried to catch the light. Kantor immediately put on a bright overhead light. Nick scanned the papers before him, then slammed the clipboard of the table. It made a loud ringing sound.

"Nick. Your grandpa Nicholas Ventura is a big-time operator. Everyone knows about him. Very honorable citizen. Pays his taxes; gives to charities; keeps his property well groomed. No loud parties. Runs a lot of un-ionized companies; pays fair wages. He can afford to. Hell, everything he owns was established on blood money. He's healthy, even in his old age—although who can picture Papa Ventura as an old man?" Coleman looked around at his agents. "You should see this guy. Strong, energetic. I hear he jogs two miles a day, rides his bike a coupla miles—hope I can do that when I'm his age. God bless him, no couch potato he."

Nick tried to blank out, but he heard every word the agent in charge said to him.

"Your grandfather's new alliance is with the China end of the worldwide drug trade, Nick. China White: purest, most potent, most valuable heroin beginning to flood our country. No way the China end can get infiltrated. It's been tried, trust me. Five or six Chinese undercovers wound up floating, without eyeballs or ears or testicles. And three of the top experts, men with sterling records, fifteen, twenty years unblemished, honored service, selfless men who never were tempted by all the offers they received all their lives—they all of them became instant millionaires through the good graces of the Chinese Triads. They're now retired in Taiwan or Hawaii; one guy is president of an import-export company in San Francisco, a semiretired man not worrying about his lousy retirement pay. The Chinese are smart enough not to murder top police officials. They don't want all the attention that would bring to them. They buy them instead; so the public anger goes toward the corrupted man instead of the corrupters." He raised his light eyebrows, an expression of admiration. "They are cool customers, Nick. That leaves us without a China infiltration. So, we have to go stateside—and you're our only option."

"That leaves you with *no* option."

"Oh, Nick. C'mon into my office. Want to show you our videotape. You look pretty good, and your voice is nice and clear." He leaned down and whispered, "We could send your ass away for twenty years. Of course, you wouldn't last a week inside. Word would get around fast, Nick. Narcotics dick. And if that didn't do the trick, we spread a rumor: that you ratted out your own grandfather."

Nick refused to make a statement of any kind. He asked for an attorney from the PBA. Instead, they sent in Frank O'Hara. He sat heavily in the small chair. His face was pained; he was suffering.

"I'm not gonna ask you why. You can't blame them for asking where you got the information. They've worked on this case a long time—now they're in big trouble."

"Street source. A junkie owed me big time. He's long gone. Don't ask me how an informant knows anything. Sometimes they just do. Sometimes they're wrong. This guy was right. What can I tell you?"

"Nick, if this was Internal Affairs, I could intervene. Let you resign; take what's available in your pension. You could start a new life. We all know how it's been for you, but these guys—they don't give a shit about you. If you take a deal with them, you turn in your gun and shield, and it all gets explained away: personal problems. You need a new perspective. Nick, you'd never be able to take a fall. You know it as well as I do. Their case is loused up; their careers are loused up—unless they can give their bosses something bigger: the big thing, Nick, the China White trade. You're just about their only hope for getting an inside line on the China connection. Even their longtime informants are deaf and dumb about this stuff."

Nick stood up and flexed his arms. "Can you see me working against my *grandfather?* Don't turn away, Frank."

Frank rolled his eyes up toward the ceiling; he stared at a small hole adjacent to the ceiling fixture. The tape recorder used previously had been taken away. Nick had spotted the bug at once.

Frank shrugged. "Look, kid, how about you give it some thought? A coupla hours, you go home, shower, get a few hours' sleep. Nicky, you've been goin' like a nut case. Shit, I shoulda looked at you more carefully . . . I didn't realize. . . ."

Nick slammed his fist against the metal wall. "Don't start on that guilt trip. I did what I did. You have nothing to do with it. Frank, I'm all grown up. Whatever happens happens." He rubbed his eyes, pulled a handkerchief from his pocket and wiped his face. "There is one thing, though, Frank. Christ, I hate to tell you this. About the house—"

Frank was genuinely shocked by the loan Nick had taken out. To do that to Kathy. After going through their bank account. To wipe her out like that.

"I can't cover that, Nick. Damn it, the gambling, I sort of understand how that gets a hold on you. But to do that to Kathy . . ." He walked out, shaking his head.

Within fifteen minutes, Frank was back. He shoved his hands into his jacket pockets and rocked back and forth on his heels. "They can take care of it for you. The fifty grand. From funds. Get the house back so you can give it to Kathy. Let her sell it. Hell, they'll take it from the money you took—confiscated from the Dominicans. Kid, I don't see any other way."

"Frank, will they let me walk outta here with you? Gimme a coupla hours to think things through? I got guys from Las Vegas waiting on me. I make a run for it, they turn me into chopmeat. Literally. What do they want, about my grandfather? I don't know anything about—"

Frank looped an arm around Nick's shoulders. "They'll tell you when they're ready. If you're ready . . ."

They gave him twenty-four hours to figure things

out. The rock or the hard place. Neither Frank nor Nick spoke on the way home.

Frank reached out, patted his arm. "Get some sleep. You look like hell."

Nick entered his kitchen, leaned against the door, and heard Frank's car drive off. He closed his eyes and took a deep breath.

What the fuck had he gotten himself into?

CHAPTER 21

When headlights lit up the driveway, Nick thought it was Frank returning. He heard the light tapping on the front door. Joe the Brain Menucci stood quietly waiting for Nick to let him in. His grandfather wanted to see him. Now.

"Look, I need a shower, gotta change my clothes, Joe. Go look at the TV for a while, or I'll put on some music for you. Won't take me more than fifteen, twenty minutes."

Joe Menucci shook his head. Not even one minute. He had been told. "Nicky. The man said right now."

When Nicholas Ventura was tense, the very air within his home changed. Best to stay out of the way, as Joe Menucci did when he left Nick standing in the doorway of the library. One or two of the outside men, who usually came into the kitchen for some coffee during the evening, stayed outside. Ventura watched as Nick entered the room; his eyes focused on his grandson's face, but he went right on speaking softly into the phone, in a very controlled tone. The conversation ended quickly and Ventura replaced the receiver. He stood up and seemed frozen inside his body. There was a slight twitching along his jawline. His breath hissed in and out.

When he backhanded Nick across the mouth, the blow wasn't very hard, just unexpected. Nick could not remember his grandfather ever striking him before.

"Stupid," the old man said. "Stupid."

It was one of the worst charges he could lay on Nick: stupidity.

"The gambling—you said no problem, eh? You come up short a hundred fifty thou and you don't call me, you don't tell me, I gotta hear about it long distance from some people don't like me, no more than I like them. And you go like a common street punk, hold up a goddamn spic restaurant and walk right into a trap. Christ, Nicholas, never, never did I think of you as stupid."

He walked to his desk, yanked open the top drawer and removed a folder; flipped it open, handed Nick a copy of his canceled bank account and his signed agreement for the fifty thousand loan on his house.

Nick stared at the documents. "How . . . ?"

His grandfather's lips drew back. "How, how, how? You don't know yet that I can find out anything I need to know? A man who wins a hundred fifty big doesn't walk away from the table out there. One cut, double or nothing. No way a gambler could resist, huh? One cut, double or nothin'—my God, Nick."

He picked up his glass and swallowed some mineral water, then looked Nick over. "You look like shit. You look like garbage. Tell me what the fuck have you got in your head?"

There was an energy coming from him that would be powerful in a man twenty years younger. He removed his fashionable wire-framed glasses and stared at his namesake.

Then, quietly, he asked, "What would you have done,

Nicholas, if you had won the money on the cut? Would you have walked away with the three hundred thousand?"

Nick turned away from his grandfather, who reached out with surprisingly strong hands and clamped his shoulders. There was a softening, now. The old man's face showed more than anger and disappointment. It showed concern.

"Probably not, Papa. Probably not."

"It's like the junkie's high and then it's gone and things are worse than ever. This is the kind of kick you need, the gambling? How long does it last, Nicholas, from race to race? Game to game? Cut to cut?"

He sat behind his desk, motioned Nick into a chair facing him.

"Nicholas, your grandmother and I, we had eight children. Two girls died before they were a year old. The two oldest, born in this country—your uncles Raymond and John—died in that Washington plane crash. They were delivering some money to certain people. They came in for a landing and the plane got caught in something called wind shear. Some people survived. My sons didn't." He looked squarely at Nick. "The money was never found. Maybe it was, but I never saw any of it."

"Papa, is that why you gave up flying? Didn't you used to go down to the Caribbean? Once or twice to Italy?"

Ventura didn't like being interrupted, but he shook his head. "I will never set foot on a plane again. Every coupla years, we drive down to Florida; once took a boat to the Bahamas. But no flying."

He picked up the story of his children. "And then your mother, my only daughter, died." He touched his chest. "Her heart. She was my treasure, Nicholas. You're not supposed to have favorites, but she was the

light of my life. My other two sons—Dominick and
Mario—they 'lost touch.' " His tone became venomous.
"They are *citizens*, Nicholas. Senior citizens now, but
still running companies I set up for them. Businesses
paying millions in taxes; giving employment to hundreds of people; money to charities. Huh—good citizens, living off of Papa's investments.

"I try to help everyone. I've paid for colleges for
many of your cousins. They are doctors and lawyers and
businessmen now. Even teachers. They've done well
with my help, whether they want to acknowledge it or
not. Only you, Nicholas, never accepted or asked anything from me. Even now. When you got *real* trouble,
you didn't come to me. Why? Are you ashamed of me?
My two businessmen sons are. They changed their
names, did you know that?" He shook his head wearily.

"I don't like to ask for help, Papa. I never have. I
got into this, I have to get out of it myself."

"Yes, you've done a helluva job getting out of it yourself. Nicholas, what do you think family is for?"

Nick looked up. "What about Vincent? You haven't
mentioned Richie's father."

His grandfather's eyes glared steadily, then he
blinked. "He has a bad heart. What killed your mother
stopped his life. He's been like an old man since his
early thirties." He raised his chin suspiciously. "Why
did you ask about Vinnie?"

"No reason. You just didn't mention him, that's all.
Like he was dead or something."

"No. Vincent is alive. Nicholas, I know what pain is
and what happens to a man when he loses a child. *I
know*. But you have to make a choice: to throw away
your own life, or get on with it. There's nothing you
can tell me about the pain. Never a day goes by when
I haven't had at least one single moment remembering
them. All of them: the tiny babies; my dead sons; my

daughter; your father. They are with me, as Peter is with me now. And with you. That will be forever, I know this. But is that what you chose for yourself? To become a bum? A degenerate gambler? A loser? Because if that is all you have learned about life, I have taught you nothing. The world is bigger than you and me." He waved his arm in a broad sweep. "There is a whole world out there, Nicholas, that you know nothing about. What the hell—in the end, we all die. Why not see a little more than what you've already experienced?"

Nick stood up and walked to the fireplace. "I don't have many choices at this point, Papa."

"I know. They're talking about putting you in prison. Do not look so surprised. I know what I need to know."

Nick had the feeling he'd had since childhood: his grandfather knew every thought, every deed, every circumstance of his life. Lying was not an option.

"Papa, they offered me a deal. I'm supposed to go to work for you and report to them. I'm to be their mole."

"What did your uncle Frank say to this?"

"He told me to be very careful. Papa, you're right, I should have come to you right away. I did a stupid thing. Okay, I'm turning to you now. I need money to get the hell outta here. You can send me somewhere, where no one will find me. Let me live somewhere, get my head together, decide what to do. I'll get the money I owe. Tell them that out in Vegas—"

"By robbing the spics, Nicholas?" Nicholas Ventura spoke at a slow, determined pace. "No. No running away. I've been thinking this through for a coupla hours."

Christ. The old man had all the inside information that had been restricted to a handful of feds. Frank had said Ventura had a pipeline anywhere he needed one.

"This could be a very useful situation. You tell them yes—"

"Papa, I'd go to prison before I . . ."

"You will keep quiet until I finish speaking," he snapped. "I will put you to work in my Queens real estate office. And you will come see me regularly. I will give you information, you will go to them with it." A slight smile pulled his thin lips; he was visualizing his future plans. "I will give you information they can act on. To my benefit and to the benefit of my colleagues— these chinks are hard to impress. We can use the DEA to eliminate certain competition. Christ, they're savages, these Chinese; they make the Colombians look like Boy Scouts."

"Papa, are you really going into the drug trade? I thought—"

"I deal in *money*. And *companies*. And *markets*." He slammed his fist on the desk. "How, where, from what source the money comes is not my concern. The end product, with which I deal, is green. I keep the economy going. I keep people working."

He sounded almost benevolent. The drugs were just an incidental way for him to distribute his good works.

"I will tell your cousin Richie that you work for me and he is in no way to interfere with you. He has his own work to do. And Nicholas, you will also bring *me* information from *them;* determine what they know or do not know about our operations. They gave you fifty grand, to get your house back. What did you think they'd want for their money?"

"I was going to give the money to Kathy. And . . . run."

"Give it to Kathy and stay."

Ventura dialed; he hated the buttons on the newer

phones. His fingers hit too many numbers at the same time. He waited throughout more than ten rings. It was 2:00 A.M.; Nick wondered who the old man was calling. Finally, he smiled and began to speak. Whoever it was must have come full awake at the sound of his voice.

"Marty, how are you? Listen, in a day or two my grandson, Nicholas, will stop by. You give him the keys to that nice little apartment in Forest Hills—by the tennis courts, yes." He listened; when he spoke again, his voice had tightened. "I know we have better apartments on Queens Boulevard. That is not what we are discussing. Good. Good. It's nice and clean, yes? Good. Anything he needs, you take care of for him, yes? Goodnight. Goodnight. Thank you, Marty."

He jotted a name and address on a slip of paper and handed it to Nick. "Marty Tortelli—at the agency, any time, whenever it's convenient. Go. Make your deal with the feds, Nicholas."

He spoke with the hard authoritarian voice of the patriarch, and Nick listened with respect as his future life was being worked out for him.

"Now for the rest of your problem, Nick, with the casino. I own a certain percentage of some casinos. We'll work it all out. Someday, you'll pay me what I take out of pocket. But there are conditions. You will not be permitted to enter any casino, not in Las Vegas, Atlantic City, any Indian reservation. No racetrack, no ball games of any kind. No card games. You're not even to buy a lottery ticket, *capisce?* I mean this very seriously, Nick. There will be no violation of these rules." He relaxed a little, thrust his hand out. "Your hand on this." His grip was strong; then he embraced his grandson.

"Nicholas, Nicholas. All will be well."

Nick held his grandfather in his arms; felt a remembered warmth and confidence fill him. But he pulled himself back abruptly, studied the sharp blue eyes. There were many Nicholas Venturas in this one body. Capable of many things.

As Joe Menucci drove him back to his house in Spring Valley, Nick felt a growing sense of numb unreality.

Then the bleakest, emptiest thought of all flooded through him. What the fuck did any of this matter?

CHAPTER 22

Nick spent a long day trying to avoid people. Everyone knew something was up; word got around very quickly. When Ed Manganaro waylaid him in the parking lot behind the precinct house, Nick was abrupt.

"I'm outta here, that's all you need to know, okay? I turned in my papers. They got my gun and shield. I never wanted to come back, remember?" He turned, his eyes even with Ed's, and asked quietly, "You got any questions?"

"Yeah, Nick. About a hundred. I been hearing some bad things, and—"

"And you're my partner—*were* my partner. You're not involved in any of it. You're clean, okay?"

"Jesus, Nick, that's not what I'm worried about."

"Eddie, don't worry about nothin', okay. Don't waste your time. I'm moving out of the house. I'm telling you just so you won't be stopping over. Kathy's gonna sell it."

Ed put his hand on Nick's shoulder. "Partner, let's you and me sit somewhere and talk. How about we drive up to the Valley together and—"

"How about you go fuck yourself and leave me the

hell alone?" He turned away from the stricken look, the confusion, the wound. "Eddie, grow up. Shit happens, okay?" He held his hand up. "Not another goddamn word, Ed. Not one."

He didn't look in the rearview mirror as he pulled out. He knew Eddie would be staring after him.

Sitting at their family kitchen table, he signed over the house to Kathy. He also signed the divorce papers. The lawyers studied everything carefully, but Kathy shook her head when her guy pointed out something in small print. She just wanted out of there. She left abruptly without saying one word to Nick.

"Mr. O'Hara, your wife wants you to know you can take all the time you need. To move out of the house. Also that she's taking the dog and the cat up to Boston with her. That's all right?"

"Whatever she wants. I'll be cleared out by the end of the week."

He wrote his Forest Hills address on a scrap of paper, just in case she needed him for anything.

It was a small apartment: tiny bedroom, twelve-by-twelve living room with one recessed wall containing a small gas stove, sink, and half-refrigerator. The furnishings were old but clean. The windows gleamed behind fresh, straight white curtains. The bathroom had been scrubbed. Whoever took care of the property had done a good job. In case his grandfather asked. The phone was installed and in working order, but Nick jumped when it rang unexpectedly.

"How ya doin'?"

"Home is where the heart is, right?"

Frank grunted. "Wanna have some supper? There's a great diner out on Queens Boulevard, not far from you."

It was a brand-new place, carefully designed to suggest the fifties. The menu was huge and the portions gigantic. Nick pushed the food around on his plate.

"How'd it go downtown this morning?"

"It went the way they wanted it to, okay?"

"Coleman isn't as bad as he seems, Nick." Frank picked up the large plastic menu and pointed. "Hey, they got some great desserts here. Did you see that revolving glass case by the entrance? Forget the seven layer and the cheesecake. Go for the Boston cream pie."

Nick studied his uncle. He was trying so hard. As if everything in his entire world hadn't changed. As if Nick was still the kid dazzled by Frank's charm and ability and success. As if Frank hadn't gotten him into something he wasn't at all sure about.

"Listen to me, Nick. I've waited for more than thirty years. When they took Danny out, I wanted to kill every last one—every shit in your grandfather's 'family,' starting with him. But the time wasn't right. Peter was killed indirectly because of your grandfather's involvement in the *babania* trade. That punk kid of Richie's dragged him into . . ."

Nick thought of his grandfather's large blue eyes, blurred by emotion when he talked about Peter. Even if he hadn't loved Nick's father, he surely loved Nick's son.

"Don't tell me the DEA and the P.D. and the ATF and any other goddamn enforcement group hasn't got informants. What's the matter, you guys don't share information? Why me?"

"Because you are who you are. You can get in real close." Frank studied the menu for a moment, then, "So, when you gonna start in the real estate business?"

Nick pushed his plate back and drank some tepid water.

"Monday. They're getting me a license. I'm gonna hang around the office. Get the feel of the properties.

I can't picture myself actually selling—" He slammed the glass down in exasperation. "Frank, this is getting very confusing. Papa is gonna feed information for me to pass along to Coleman. He wants *me* to get *him* any information about the DEA's actions. How the hell am I gonna get anything to give him?"

"You're going back to college, Nick."

Nick had attended John Jay College of Criminal Justice on and off for six years. He was just a few credits short of a degree.

"You're gonna take Constitutional Rights and Liberties. Professor Thomas Caruso. Know him?"

Nick thought for a moment. "Yeah. I took a couple of Police Science courses with him, years ago. But—"

Frank blotted his lips and signaled their waitress, an alarmingly alert, stocky, middle-aged woman who studied their plates and bit her lip. How come these two big guys left so much food? She jotted down their order for coffee and Boston cream pie. Within moments she delivered and set the coffee and dessert before them. She looked each man in the eye. "Enjoy," she commanded.

"It gets a little complicated, Nick, but you can work it out. Tom Caruso. He's DEA. *Deep* undercover. Only a few people know about him." Frank tasted the cream pie, and smiled. "He's your man."

"Spell it out, Frank."

"Taste that, Nick, is that good or what? Well, you'll bring whatever Papa Ventura gives you to Coleman. Nothing else. Remember, Ventura's got a leak in that squad and he'll be checking you out. Your grandfather will give you *real* information, but only stuff damaging to his enemies. As far as Coleman and his team are concerned—that's all they get. Now, Professor Caruso, you give him *all* the information you find: names, locations, meetings, company organizations, officers, deals, whatever. *Only to Caruso.* And he'll give you some tips to give your grandfather."

"But, if there's a mole in Coleman's squad, won't my grandfather wonder where I'm getting my stuff from? He'll know it wasn't from them."

Frank shrugged. "You got a lotta connections in the department, right? So, what does that make you, a triple agent?"

"It makes me a sitting duck."

"Not if you're careful. And I know you, Nick. You know how to play whatever game you gotta play."

"Right. I'm a natural-born gambler."

"No gamble, Nick. You're a team player. One other thing. You and me—we won't have any contact. Assume your phone is tapped and you're being followed. You reach me only through Caruso. Until this is over."

"And when will that be?"

"You gonna leave that big chunk of Boston cream? That waitress will trip us on the way out."

Nick leveled a cold stare at his uncle and deliberately plunged his fork into the cake, stuffed it into his mouth.

"Jeez, you're a selfish little bastard, aren't you?"

CHAPTER 23

Ventura Real Estate was housed in a storefront on Metropolitan Avenue, just beyond the fancy Forest Hills streets. The man there was Marty Tortelli, a mid-sixties, skinny guy who chewed on an unlit cigar that smelled terrible. No one would talk into a telephone after him: ashtray breath. He wore smudged glasses that needed cleaning and updating badly. He held everything he read at arm's length. He was out of the office more than in. He introduced Nick to Tessie Tortuga—"someone's aunt," Marty whispered.

Tessie was a slender woman, anywhere from mid-fifties to mid-seventies. With her dyed black hair and carefully applied makeup, impeccable grooming, attractive clothing, and high heels, Tessie had a sparkle. She trailed a whiff of light, pleasant perfume as she showed Nick around the office.

She set him up at a steel desk in the front window, so he could gaze over Metropolitan Avenue. Across the street were a collection of taxpayers: small shops at street level, small apartments upstairs. The neighborhood was clean and orderly. No troublemakers allowed. Nick took an armload of file folders, fanned them out on his desk. There were properties recently sold, recently rented, on the market. There were client lists—potentials to buy, sell, or rent. Tessie kept the files. Anything you needed to know was in Tessie's head, if not in her files. She scorned the computer—so call her old-fashioned.

Nick spent a week or so studying the files, concentrating on houses and apartments. There was another large section of information on industrial properties handled by Ventura Real Estate.

He was driven around Forest Hills, then Forest Hills Gardens, by Salvy Grosso, a hulking man who looked fatter than he actually was. His face was very broad and featured a solid block of black eyebrows straight across his forehead. He had the wheeze of a smoker, although he had never been one. He was a toucher—your arm, your shoulder, your sleeve. When he knew you better, he might loop an arm around you.

Salvy spoke in a soft, confidential voice, occasionally cupping his hand around his mouth, just in case someone, somewhere, was curious about what he was saying. He drove through the Gardens like a tour guide. He had grown up in Woodside, Queens, and he felt that gave him, somehow, an insider's view. He stopped in front of a large house, mostly hidden behind bushes, trees, random plantings. Home of the first woman vice-presidential candidate. Neighbors went crazy when she was running: all the Secret Service, P.D., and media. If just for that reason, everyone was glad she lost. After all, Forest Hills Gardens was not happy with intruders. He pointed, vaguely, at what he said had been the home of a Transit Authority commissioner, "before your time, Nick." And you couldn't see it from here, but some older dame, a movie character actress, raised her kids here. And that actor from *NYPD Blue*, who claimed he came from hard times, he lived right in the heart of the Gardens. Some hard times.

It was a very quaint, self-contained old English Tudor village with an inn and a square and its own stop on the Long Island Railroad line. Salvy pointed out where the serial killer, Son of Sam, had murdered women on two separate occasions.

"Imagine a bum like that?" Salvy seemed to take the violation personally. "Ya know, Nick, I figured the guy to be a cop, ya know?"

"Yeah, why?"

"Well, he hit his targets at all hours. I figured he must have worked different tours. He turns out to be just another post office nuthead. Do they get like that on their job, or does the P.O. attract them? What?"

They visited several of the newer high-rises on Queens Boulevard, a futuristic collection of glass and steel buildings that would fit right in with any newly reconstructed section of Manhattan: all the same, without character or distinctiveness.

"When I was a kid living in Woodside, I worked for a garbage collection company. We'd pick up from restaurants, and some real nice private homes around here. Most of this section was empty lots—some parking lots for car sales agencies. Ya see the Kennedy House over there? Christ, I remember when there used to be a big mansion, with beautiful lawns and gardens, and a three-car garage in back. Must have been more than an acre. I guess the old folks died and the next in line sold out. Probably got a fortune. The developers just leveled the house. Guy I worked for, he got some of the woodwork—doors, shutters, and stained glass. He had an in with the construction guys. Shame, though, huh?"

When Nick got back to the office, Tessie, with a big smile, jingled some keys at him, then, with a jerk of her head, indicated a dark blue Cadillac parked across the street.

"Company rented it for you, Nick. Can't have you representing us in an old station wagon."

He checked the papers. Long-term lease. On the company. As he walked out, a shiny black Jaguar blocked his way. The window slid down and there was Laura Santalvo.

"Nick. Come for a ride with me. I have something I want you to see."

She handled the Jag with great authority, as she did everything else. She cut across Queens Boulevard swiftly, pulled into the U-shaped driveway in front of one of the newer thirty-story co-ops Nick had seen earlier. She left the car where she had stopped. The doorman hurried to help her, bobbed his head up and down.

On the twelfth floor, Laura led him to a door at the far end of the hallway, which she opened.

"Never live next to an elevator. I don't care how quiet they are, you can still hear them. Or feel them."

She flipped on a series of switches that lit up a large entrance hall, a huge living room, connected to a good-sized dining room, with adjoining eat-in kitchen. She preceded him rapidly, opening a door to a dark bedroom: even with the lights the room was dim.

"Master bathroom," she pointed out. "There's another bedroom, a little smaller; can be a den or office or whatever. Has its own bathroom, plus there's a small lavatory next to a closet in the entrance hall. There's a well-stocked bar. TV built in; music system—" She stopped speaking and watched him closely.

"Very nice. Laura, you have a very nice place."

She started to laugh. It was the hearty, honest sound that brought back childhood. She flopped sideways onto a soft beige armchair, letting her long legs dangle.

Her head fell back and she pressed her hands over her mouth.

"I'm sorry, Nick. My God, didn't Tessie tell you?"

"Tell me what?"

Laura stood up, came close to him, ran her fingers lightly over his lips; puckered her lips and began to laugh again.

"Did you think I brought you up here to seduce you?"

"You wouldn't have to . . ."

"This is *yours*, Nicky. Papa put you on hold over by the tennis courts because I had a customer from France over for a couple of weeks. We put him up here. He moved out two days ago. I had a cleaning service give the place a good workout. It's all yours."

"Like hell. I couldn't afford . . ."

"Ventura Real Estate owns this place. We use it for various clients. Sometimes I have European models stay here. Sometimes there are business conventions. Papa puts people up here. He's got a couple other apartments just like it in the building." She walked to the floor-to-ceiling, apartment-wide windows and pushed a button that slid the drapes open.

"Not exactly the Manhattan skyline, but not bad. If you don't like the location, there are others, all up and down the boulevard. You didn't want a house, did you?"

Nick stood beside her and stared at the panoramic view: Forest Hills at night. Across the wide boulevard were thirty- and forty-story buildings.

"This is not exactly my style, Laura."

She glanced at her watch just as the security phone rang. "Speaking of style." She grabbed the phone. "Good, yes, send him up."

She looked Nick up and down and shook her head.

He was wearing a slightly shoddy sports jacket and
wrinkled dark gray slacks.

"You look like a cop, Nick. We have to fix you up."

The tailor—Papa's tailor—was a tiny man with a bald
head, except for a thick white fringe around the neck-
line. He had heavy white brows and a thick yellowish
mustache. He arrived with a suitcase of samples; mea-
suring tapes; pins; men's fashion magazines.

Nick motioned Laura into the modern, glistening
kitchen: it was all silky brushed steel counters and ap-
pliances.

"What the hell is this, Laura? I don't want . . ."

Laura leaned back and smiled. He had a good look
at her; he had been so busy trying to absorb his sur-
roundings that this was his first chance. She wore a
gray, almost black pants suit and a very white shirt and
shiny black flat shoes. There was a gold ornament on
her lapel in the shape of a small cat. Without realizing
it, he reached out and followed the curves of the cat
with his fingertip, then looked at her eyes.

Nick, with all his police training, wouldn't have been
able to describe Laura accurately. It would be like trying to describe a color or the sound of a wave or the
smell of rain. He could describe the oval shape of her
face; the smoky quality of her dark gray eyes; her
straight nose and wide mouth and thick black brows.
He could describe the short-cropped hair that clung to
her head, leaving her face clean and untouched. He
could estimate her height and weight. He could describe everything he knew to a police sketch artist, and
no one, not the best in the world, would be able to
capture the essence and quality of Laura. There was
something so hidden and concealed and mysterious.
Even when she laughed, for a split second letting her
guard down, she drew on strong inner resources. No
one could ever take Laura by surprise.

She explained that his grandfather sent the tailor. After all, Nick was going to represent one of Papa's businesses. And he wasn't going to be spending all his time in the small Queens office. He would eventually do . . . well, whatever Papa Ventura wanted him to do. She shrugged; none of this had anything to do with her.

The tailor fussed and sighed; stretched and measured; slapped Nick's arm down when he needed to be sure of sleeve length.

He showed material samples to Laura, ignoring Nick as someone who wouldn't know anything. He flipped through some pages of magazines; a Sunday *New York Times* supplement on men's clothing. Stopped; took a signal from Laura; marked a page.

"Ralph Lauren. Yes. I think so," Laura said. "This gets priority, right?"

He glared his annoyance. She didn't have to tell him anything. He reached out without apology, the privilege of a very old man. He pulled her toward the light. His bony fingers ran up and down the edge of her jacket, examined seams and buttonholes.

Grudgingly, he said, "Good work. Yes." As he packed his battered leather sample case, he muttered, "But you stay away from men's clothing, yes?"

Laura hugged him from behind, which he acknowledged with a shrug and a sigh. He left without another word to either of them.

Nick hadn't seen her since the funeral mass for Peter. In fact, it just occurred to him that she had been there. And had left a card in his son's name. He thanked her now, apologized for not having acknowledged . . .

"Kathy sent me a lovely thank-you note. I heard about you two. Should I say sorry or what?"

"Don't say anything."

"You got it." He followed her into the kitchen.

"Watch carefully. So one day *you* can make espresso for me."

Nick loved watching her face as he teased her. The little girl appeared, mock angry. "Hey, that's *woman's* work. There are some things in this world that are—"

"Nicky, Nicky. You're still such a *Bensonhurst* boy. You still think like a Bensonhurst boy. It's been a long time since I've been with anyone remotely like you."

Impulsively, he asked her, "Are you happy, Laura?"

There was a split second of sadness over her face: eyes blinking, lower lip sliding between her teeth. And then it was gone and the mocking Laura was back.

"Bensonhurst boy."

"Bensonhurst brat."

CHAPTER 24

Nick studied the manual that came with the Apple computer. User-friendly? Tessie had tried it and lost five hours of work by tapping one wrong button. Or not tapping one right button. She told him he could play with it anytime.

He had some small knowledge: Peter had shown Nick a few basics. He placed the stack of folders into two piles and two-finger-typed, just like doing a police report, watching the letters appear on the blue screen. He entered all the data on each property: location, ownership, registration, history, size of property, number of rooms, special features, price, taxes, possible negotiations, problems re: mortgage, cash only, whatever.

As he reached across the desk for another file, he suddenly felt a cold round object dig into his neck. He froze.

"What the hell do you think ya doin', cuz?"

He whirled around, smacked the pen from Richie's hand. Richie took a step back, held his hands, palms up.

"Easy, Nick. I just really wanna ask you." He ran his hand over his thick black, graying hair, lightly skimming it. He pointed at the folders, then at the computer. His lips were pulled back into a tight grin that resembled the expression of a dog's face just before an attack. "What the fuck do you think you're doin'?"

"I'm supposed to tell you what my job is? You wanna know, ask Papa."

Nick clicked off the computer; collected the folders, and slammed them into the old steel filing cases.

"Papa know you making a record of all the holdings here?"

"Richie, I told you. Ask Papa what you want to know. What I do has nothing to do with you."

Nick had been working right out in the open; it was during working hours. Richie decided to give him the benefit of the doubt. For now.

"Old Tessie's afraid of that damn thing."

"I don't think Tessie's afraid of anything in this world," Nick said. He looked his cousin over: cashmere coat; dark brown suit and tie; pale yellow shirt; gold tie clip. He shot his cuffs so Nick could see his gold links.

No matter what he wore, Richie still didn't have it. Something gave him away.

"Well, I see they got ya wearin' some decent clothes. Christ, what are you trying for, the Ivy League look?"

"Just trying to avoid the rich thug look."

Richie drew his breath in sharply, glanced over his shoulder, making sure none of his men were close enough to hear the insult.

He snapped his fingers. "Close up shop, Nick. Papa wants to see you."

Nick followed Richie's black Mercedes, not quite keeping up as it cut in and out of traffic and ran red lights. They were waiting for him as he pulled into Papa Ventura's driveway.

There were more than the usual number of cars parked around the house. There was a gleaming black limo off to one side. A small man dressed in a black uniform leaned beside it, smoking a cigarette.

Richie put his hand on Nick's shoulder and said softly, "Papa got some chink he wants you to meet."

It was difficult to determine the age of Dennis Chen. His face was smooth except for a collection of crinkles at his eyes when he smiled, which was often, but it was not sincere. He was a handsome, soft-spoken man, meticulously styled by a good British tailor. There was an intelligence about his expression. His eyes seemed to see things not readily apparent to others. While at first glance he seemed Chinese, his face was longer, narrower. He had the healthy color of a man who spent time outdoors; no yellow-pale undertones. His nose was narrow and straight; his lips thin over sparkling white teeth. There was a blend of ethnicities. He was not purely one thing or another. He could be intensely Chinese when he wanted to be, but there was something of the British effete about him. More than just his Oxford education; the way he spoke, the slightly superior pull at the corners of his mouth, suggested he considered many about him to be in some way inferior. Or unintentionally amusing.

He gave Nick a cursory examination, but did not treat him with the warm respect given to his grandfather.

His handshake was weak—in the Chinese way, not from lack of strength. Though he was tall and slender, it was obvious, from the way his clothes fit, that he had a muscular, well-defined body. He wore no jewelry, no sign of his tremendous wealth. You either knew or did not know about him.

The three men sat near the fireplace, watched the play of orange and yellow flames. No smoke entered the room. It was sucked straight up the chimney without a whiff of pollution getting into the den.

"Your grandfather assures me you will be able to find

me a very comfortable house in"—he glanced at Nicholas Ventura to make sure he had it right—"Forest Hills Gardens."

"No problem, Mr. Chen. Just jot down a list of requirements. I'm sure we'll come up with something suitable."

Mr. Chen explained that he was only stopping over in New York right now for twenty-four hours. He was on his way to London; then to Paris, then to Rome, then back to Hong Kong. Business. He would return to the United States within a few weeks. He was assured a house would be ready for him. No mention was made of price, arrangements, or length of time.

Mr. Chen and Papa Ventura discussed art: Both admired the richness of the works Nicholas Ventura had collected through the years. Chen reached into his large briefcase and withdrew a small package, unwrapped it, and arranged four small paintings on the desk. Seventeenth-century Chinese watercolors, figures from a fairy tale. The colors were electric, the patterns intricate, and each told a small moment in the life of the person portrayed, from a mighty warlord to a simple peasant. The orange fish about to be chopped by a fisherman seemed to be fresh from the sea.

They were like two professors getting ready for a seminar. They were so knowledgeable, so scholarly; it was hard to believe that either of them could be involved in any sort of criminal activity. These must be cultured, decent, educated men.

Mr. Chen glanced at his simple gold watch. It was time to leave. He and Nicholas Ventura exchanged words and nods.

Then Mr. Chen turned to Nick for his handshake, but his hand tightened on Nick's and his eyes exuded a powerful force.

"I am saddened by the death of your son, Nick. I

know what it is to lose a child. One of the boys involved in that stupid business of a girl was my son."

The man's eyes were cold and emotionless. He dropped Nick's hand, and without another word, Dennis then left.

Papa Ventura had several pages of notes for Nick. It was his first assignment as a double undercover agent.

"The ship is called the *Golden Dream*," the old man said. "Very sad, how people treat each other. They are bringing in all kinds of goods—Eastern furniture, fabric, artworks—but the major part of their cargo is human beings. These poor people, Nicholas, the exploitation is unbelievable. We used to bring in relatives, we doubled up with families and friends. We worked with and for each other. These people, they've undertaken huge debts for being smuggled into this country. They are jammed in the cargo area with the clothing on their backs. They and their families are in debt up to thirty thousand dollars. When they get to America—San Francisco or New York—they are forced into servitude in garment shops, restaurants, laundries. They are given a sleeping place in a basement filled with other people; fed a meager diet; earn a small amount, which is held back to pay off their debt. And their families back in China must pay, or they are tortured or killed. Old people, children."

"Jesus," Nick said softly.

"Some of the girls and women are turned into prostitutes. These are young, ignorant country people. They are terrified. There is no one to turn to when they are here."

"What else is on the ship?"

Nicholas Ventura smiled. "Heroin with a street value of about forty million dollars. China White." He hesitated, then smiled. "A rival of Mr. Chen. So we get two birds with one stone. Save some poor souls—stop a rival. It is good for us to impress the Chinese. They are hard people.

"Nick, in the last three years, I've placed nearly three thousand illegal Chinese in factories, plants, fishing boats, laundries; some in construction. Some bright ones I've sent to school. A few young women have done very well . . ."

"What will happen to the people on the *Golden Dream*?"

"That is government business. I will not get involved." As though needing to justify himself, to be recognized for the good things he had done with his life, he continued, "The people I have helped, Nicholas, they become union members, are paid wages they earn, have lives of their own. These things, they make me feel good."

He read Nick's skeptical expression and his voice went lower and tighter. "As we get old, Nicholas, we see life differently toward . . . the end. Try to balance the scale, maybe. The world is a wicked place, grandson."

"And there are a lot of wicked people in it."

He could not see into his grandfather's heart; where one part of him began and another part ended. He was about to engage in one of the largest drug cartels in the world and he insisted on talking about his good deeds.

"Papa. One of the boys killed, who was involved in Peter's death. Was he really Dennis Chen's son?"

His grandfather nodded.

"Christ, what kind of man is he? Papa?"

Nicholas Ventura stood ramrod-straight, raised his chin, and said insistently, *"He is an honorable man."*

CHAPTER 25

DEA Agent Rodney Coleman did not do well in cold weather. There seemed to be a thin translucent sheet of ice over his face, and a shudder ran down his back.

Battery Park had not been his choice for a meeting. The choppy waters crashed against the bulkhead and the Statue of Liberty's torch could barely be seen through the sleety fog. He took hold of Nick's arm, turned him away from the water.

"A good location. Anyone dumb enough to be following you would have been spotted by now and the meeting aborted."

Anyone following him would have frozen to death if he had to stand in one place long. Nick shrugged his arm free, hunched into his lined hunter's coat: Thinsulate-lined, lightweight but warm. He moved quickly along the cement pathway.

"Well, Nick, the information you gave us on the *Golden Dream*—good. Very good. It was intercepted three days ago, just inside San Francisco Harbor. The agency is very happy with this; a great deal of China White was confiscated." He stopped walking abruptly, squinted against the glassy ice particles that hit him smack in the face. "But, Nick, here's my problem. This really doesn't connect the Venturas with the Chen Triad. What we're doing here is helping Dennis Chen take care of his opposition without him having to lift a finger. So to speak."

"You asked me to pass along what I heard. I gave you what I heard."

Coleman turned up the collar of his black coat, adjusted his Burberry scarf, and pulled the incongruous knitted watchcap down almost to his eyebrows. It gave him a slightly retarded appearance.

"You know, Nick, the coalescence of the Triads, the mob, and the Colombians is a very strange coming together. You know about the Triads? They go back hundreds of years, and—"

Nick hunched his shoulders as he walked, then moved slightly so that he was no longer acting as a windshield for Coleman. "Skip your history lesson, okay, Coleman?"

Coleman shrugged good-naturedly and continued. "The young bloods in the Triads know how to live well. Quietly, privately. Never flaunt their wealth or their power. The younger ones are not happy about sitting down with a gathering of old Mafiosa who think a trip to Disneyland is a celebration. A collision of cultures, as well as of age. Your grandfather is to their liking, but some of his colleagues—" Coleman shook his head derisively. "If they don't parade around with glitzy girls on their arms, who's going to know what big shots they are? You know, it's these old-timers, they're the ones insisting on the sitdown that's going to happen. They have that thing about 'looking a guy in the eye'—as though eye contact will tell them all they need to know. Wait till they see the poker faces on those Triad honchos."

Nick kept walking.

"The young Chinese, they'd rather do it all with no human contact. Via fax, anonymous couriers, coded messages. Computer discs. But they're willing to come together this once, mostly because they respect your grandfather."

"A lot of people respect my grandfather." Nick was surprised by the pride and anger in his voice. Who the hell was this little shit anyway?

He could feel the agent hurrying to keep up with him. He saw the two DEA agents moving out of the park toward Broadway.

"We know your grandfather will never fly." Coleman was smug; he knew a lot of things. "And the other old guys, they'd be lost in a foreign land. Without their people around them."

Nick gestured toward the figures waiting for them. "Those are 'your people,' I assume?"

Coleman laughed. His breath was icy. "They are indeed my people."

He followed Nick into a dimly lit coffee shop across from the park. In the overheated room, Coleman's glasses steamed up; he wiped them with his handkerchief, then dabbed at his watery eyes. He carefully hung his coat on the hook next to the booth where they settled. When he pulled off the watchcap, there was a dark red band across his forehead. He seemed to have two sets of eyebrows.

Coleman's eyes hardened as though frozen. "You do know, Nick—I assume you do know—that we're going after the whole operation before it gets going. Under RICO." He watched Nick closely. "If anything's a racketeer-influenced and corrupt organization, this bunch of thugs is. You do know about RICO?"

Nick didn't answer. The waitress delivered two coffees and Nick tasted his carefully. It was steaming hot.

"Years ago, we used to get the mob guys through

income-tax fraud. Until their lawyers learned how to avoid that. RICO is our big ace in the hole these days— it lets us cast a large net over all these various organizations. That's how we got Gotti and that whole bunch. Sent them away forever on a long, bloody laundry list of charges."

Nick stared coldly, unimpressed.

Coleman didn't seem to notice. "You're going to be our fly on the wall. These guys are running *billions* of dollars' worth of activities. If we can pull this off, tie them all up into one large package, do you know how much money the government will confiscate, Nick?"

Nick said softly, "Billions of dollars, you said."

Coleman's voice was controlled but his words were excited. "It can be the biggest roundup of its kind in history. Get them all together, then charge them as individuals. We put you right smack in the middle, get it all on tape . . ."

He stopped speaking abruptly. He lifted the steaming cup of coffee to his mouth and drank it straight down without stopping. It must have been near boiling point, but Coleman didn't seem to notice.

"So," he said, easily changing the subject, "you've gone back to school. To what end?"

"Well, I understand you need a college degree to get on the feds. Or is that just the FBI?" Nick sipped his coffee: it was very hot. "Let's say my plans aren't firmed up yet."

"Planning a fresh start, are you, Nick? Well, of course, your future depends very much on how well you handle your current assignment."

"I'm doin' what I gotta do, okay? Look, Coleman, I can only bring you stuff I get. You want me to make up stuff, just say so. Maybe you really don't need me."

Coleman grimaced. "If I really didn't need you, you wouldn't be sitting here with me. You'd be upstate,

Nick. Count on it. So, nothing to tell me?"

"Just one thing. Wait until *I* call you. I didn't ask for this meeting, you did."

Coleman carefully put his scarf around his neck, slipped his coat on, then his leather gloves. He held his hat until he reached the street.

Special Agent Alexander Kantor hurried after his boss, pulling his very large, lined trenchcoat around himself. Agent Felix Rodriguiz walked beside Nick.

"Hey, O'Hara, do me a favor, okay? Next time, pick someplace a little warmer." He shuddered, rubbed his gloved hands together. "This cold weather is murder, ya know?"

"Maybe ya never should have left your island."

Rodriguiz grinned. "I never did. Born and raised on Long Island. The weather doesn't bother me so much, but my boss—he's a fuckin' icicle to begin with. He's gonna break chops for the rest of the night."

"We all got troubles. Looks like he's waving for you, Felix. You better hustle."

Quietly, Rodriguiz said, "Oh, fuck him." At the same time he waved and nodded and headed toward his boss.

CHAPTER 26

Nick studied the boxes of frozen dinners: Healthy Choice, Lean Cuisine; pizza; roast chicken and noodles from the kosher deli down the boulevard. Sounded good.

As he tossed the package into the microwave, the phone rang. He lifted the receiver from the kitchen wall phone as his fingers played with the timing circles on the micro.

"Hey, guess who's downstairs? In your driveway. You hungry?"

"How'd you know?"

"Bet you're deciding which frozen special to have, right?"

"What are you, a witch?"

"Always have been. Put on something comfortable and come on down. I'm waiting for you."

When he got downstairs, she smiled and pointed to her car phone. "Handy device, huh? You're having home-cooked tonight."

"Your home?"

Laura Santalvo's home was a twelve-room duplex in the prewar Beresford Building, across from Central Park and the Hayden Planetarium. There were only two apartments on each floor, serviced by the various elevators. Nick glanced around at the small foyer, watched as she opened the door into what seemed to be another world.

It could have been a large old house in the country— a very rich, large, old house, with Mexican blood red tile floors and wood paneling in the huge entrance hall. Laura flipped some switches and made a sharp, clicking sound.

Cats came running from every direction: some leaping down the carpeted staircase, some sliding across the shining floor from other rooms. Laura motioned him toward a closet that was slightly ajar. She tapped on the door and a huge red-tiger cat with golden eyes stretched toward her. When she bent to touch him, he waved a threatening paw and gave a slight hiss.

"Rocky has a problem expressing love," she told Nick. "Well, here they are, all eight of them."

They pushed against her, rubbed against her legs, buzzed, cried for attention or stood quietly observing, waiting for a turn.

Nick had never seen Laura so relaxed. Everything about her was spontaneous, unguarded, natural. And joyful. She was totally at ease. "Our housekeeper, Maria, was supposed to feed them before she left for her day off, but I think she must have forgotten. Or maybe she did and Su-Su cleaned up their dishes. Oh well, they can always eat."

He followed the parade into the kitchen, helped her to dish out the bowls of food. Two black and white tuxedos—mirror images of each other—ate from the same bowl. Some ate on the floor, some on the table, some on the counters. She named them rapidly, and each cat, responding in turn, looked up at her. Nick had never seen a cat respond to having its name called, and when he said as much she poked at him playfully, cupping her mouth.

"Be careful what you say. Some of these guys are very sensitive."

Upstairs, the hall was stark white to better set off the artwork and photographs Laura had placed on the walls. The doors to the various rooms were dark wood, with gleaming brass doorknobs. Laura held her hand up to Nick: wait a minute. She tapped lightly on one of the doors, poked her head inside the room.

"Am I disturbing you?" he heard her ask.

She entered the room and Nick looked at the black and white photographs. They all were of a Chinese child: some at age five or six; then a little older, nine or ten. As he studied them, the subject of the photographs herself, now about eighteen years old, followed Laura from her bedroom.

Laura's hand rested lightly on the shoulder of a small, beautiful young woman. "This is Su-Su. Sus, this is Nick."

Nick glanced at Laura's face, and saw there a concentrated pride. The girl came forward, offered a small hand, a surprisingly firm handclasp.

"Nick," she said quietly.

"Su-Su. I was just looking at photographs of you."

The girl nodded, glanced at Laura. "My proud mom."

For a split second, Nick froze. Laura's daughter?

The girl caught his expression and said seriously, "I am her 'chosen daughter.' "

Laura added nothing to the explanation. She turned to the girl. "You being picked up or do you want me to call Marko to drive you?"

"Nope. All arranged. Nice to have met you, Nick." Her eyes, black and expressive, missed nothing. She smiled slightly, a familiarly mocking smile. Then to

Laura, "In about two minutes, Margaret will be calling from the lobby."

She had no sooner spoken than the house phone rang. She picked it up, listened, smiled, spoke softly. "I'm on my way." Then to Laura, "Not to worry. I'll call you tomorrow." She gave Laura a quick hug. "Fingers crossed for me, right? At about ten-thirty, have a thought of me."

"At exactly ten-thirty." She watched the slender girl in the baggy jeans and large black sweater dash into her room, emerge with a bulky garment bag. Before Laura could ask, Su-Su told her, "Yes, I have a very nice outfit with me. I will impress the daylights out of everyone at Yale." With a wave, shooing cats out of the way, she disappeared down the stairs.

"Pretty girl," Nick said.

Laura didn't answer. She pointed to the first photograph: Su-Su at five. The shadowed face, tiny, head down, eyes peeking at the camera, had a hopeless sadness.

"That's when I first saw her. In Bangkok, Su-Su had just arrived at a factory that supplied some fabric for my designs. Her parents sold her to the factory owners for about forty dollars. The factory owners had plans for her. At about nine—this is Su-Su at nine—at about that age Su-Su was to be sold to a brothel specializing in young virgins. For the foreign trade. They'd probably get around a thousand dollars. As you can see, by nine, she was already becoming the beauty she is today, at eighteen." She turned to Nick, put a finger on his mouth. "Not now. Let's just say my meeting with Su-Su was the most incredibly lucky thing that has ever happened to me. C'mon, I'll show you the rest of my domain."

She showed him the downstairs rooms: a dining room off the eat-in kitchen; a huge living room; a large den, which she called the media room, and a book-lined library. Everything formal, traditional: good dark wood, expensive carpeting, a few good rugs. She led him to a balcony off the living room, swept the view with her arm.

"Central Park."

She enjoyed watching him, trying to read his thoughts. "These rooms are off-limits to the cats. Too many scratch and puddle places here. This is mostly for company."

"Where do you *live?*"

She led him up the wide staircase. Her workroom was a huge studio, where sketches were tacked onto a long narrow board. Her worktable was cluttered with equipment, pictures, pens, inks. The floor was a washable white tile.

The cat room next door looked like a playground. There were carpet-covered climbing poles up to the ceiling, with shelves for perching and oval and box-shaped hideaways. There was a long, spiraling tunnel with several entrances and exits. There were cat-sized hammocks, chairs scratched to shreds; sisal scratching boards, toys that rattled, stuffed mice, things that dangled.

She gestured to the next room. Her bedroom. He raised his eyebrows. Laura shrugged and grinned. "Later."

"Suppertime for humans." She shooed the cats from the kitchen table, tricked them into the hallway, and closed the doors.

"I don't think you're ready to have Binkey or Precious Anne eat from your plate just yet."

"Hey, first time for everything."

"Yes. There is."

It was his first time for a vegetarian meal, and Nick

wasn't sure whether or not he liked it. It was interest-ing.

"That's a start."

"What wine goes with tofu?"

"Apricot juice cut with club soda." She studied him with a slight smile at the corners of her mouth; her eyes were glinting. "You don't want to blunt the plea-sure. Of the food."

The cats escorted them upstairs again and wandered into their playroom; one or two ran into Laura's bed-room and disappeared. It was as warm a room as the others on the second floor were cold and spare. Rich thick carpeting, deep red; dark red paisley wallpaper; huge mahogany headboard; paisley quilts and pillows; a velvet chaise, with a heavy, hand-knitted quilt tossed at the foot. Nick inspected the room quietly, aware of the tension building.

Laura stood against the window wall. The drapes were parted and the lights of New York blinked; traffic lights sent slashes of red, green, and yellow along the wet pavement. Nick hadn't realized it had started rain-ing until he heard the pelting against the window.

She just stood there smiling. That maddening Laura smile—wise guy, brat, superior to everyone in the whole goddamn world. The hide-behind smile.

He took her by the arms; was surprised by how frag-ile she was, how light. One hand pushed through the thick, straight black hair, held her so that her face turned up. And still that smile.

"What's funny, kid?"

Laura grinned. "You. Me. This place. The cat behind you getting ready to leap."

He turned quickly and a striped gray cat froze on the bed behind him, then dashed underneath. Laura ap-proached him, and when he turned she wasn't smiling. There was so much depth in her slate eyes. She bit her lower lip, and ran the tip of her tongue over her lips, then over his.

"Is this a game of some kind?"

Laura's hands went inside his open jacket, fingers exploring. Her voice was low.

"Everything's a game."

She made a game of undressing: pulled clothes from him, undid zippers; pushed his hand away when he began helping her. This was to be her scene. For now.

The first time was tense. They both seemed guarded, as though afraid this was a performance being judged by the other.

Quietly, she leaned over him and brushed the hair off his forehead. "I'm sure it will get better," she told him in the maddening, teasing voice.

Nick flipped her over and peered down at her. He nipped her lips, held flesh between his teeth. "You're a crazy girl, you know that? You are crazy-nuts."

"Of course I am. Isn't that what you've always loved about me?"

He pulled the sheet from her and studied her body. It was far better than he'd imagined. She was slim but not skinny. Her breasts were small, beautifully shaped with dark pink nipples; her hip bones were sharp, sculptured, the skin taut; her thighs were long and smooth, the hair black and thick; he tasted her everywhere. Finally, he danced his fingers on her knees and smiled.

"Damn. I knew it. I remember. You always were slightly knock-kneed as a kid. Looka this, little Laura knock-knees."

"Big Nicky big mouth."

She wasn't perfect. Almost, but not quite.

The second time was a little frantic; each felt lost, as though the other was in control. They devoured each other, consumed each other. Became each other for a brief and shattering time. It almost seemed an act of desperation. For both of them.

Later, over hot chocolate, Laura seemed to know his thoughts. "There are so many ways, Nick. That last time was scary; the next time, it'll be sweet."

And it was.

PART 3

LIVING THE LIFE

CHAPTER 27

Professor Thomas Caruso was a heavyset man with thick graying hair and a deep shadow over his jaw even just after he shaved. He peered over the tops of his half-glasses, noted the night class was about three-quarters filled. The night students were older; most of them were cops. Originally, John Jay had been part of the Police Academy. Ninety-something percent of the students were cops, firemen, or correction officers. For more than thirty years now it was an independent college, part of the City University system. Most of the day students were kids, some cop wannabes. His day class was repeated at night, twice a week. A throwback to when the students were mostly guys working around-the-clock shifts, so that they could eventually get degrees. John Jay College of Criminal Justice had, through the years, sent graduates on to Ivy League master's programs and law schools; it now offered a doctorate degree. Caruso liked the night students better. They had been there, done that. Some were old enough to remember when the *Miranda* warnings were unheard of; search and seizure was carried out without a thought. His course, Constitutional Rights and Liberties, had been a hard sell years ago.

Today, no one argued at having to take it—just argued their chosen side of the cases he threw at them.

The previous week's assignment had been an open-book, at-home exam. Each student was to assume the role of a Supreme Court Justice and issue a decision on a given case, citing precedents or establishing new guidelines.

"I'm basically just going to collect your blue books and give you a new reading assignment for next time. Make a short night of it. Any objections?"

A polite smile or two. They jotted down the reading information; a couple of students, bleary-eyed narcotics men who must have pulled a thirty-six-hour shift, were relieved to be able to return to their precinct and catch a few hours of dead sleep before they were due in court in the morning.

Professor Caruso slid Nick O'Hara's booklet into his briefcase without comment. He had felt the small hard disk containing the data Nick had been collecting. He nodded to Nick, spoke to a few others, and left.

Caruso and his people, whoever the hell they were, could do whatever they needed to do with the records from the Ventura Real Estate agency. Nick was ready for an early night.

Laura called him less than thirty minutes after he returned to his apartment.

"Guess who's downstairs? Got anything to eat or what?"

Nick thought about the steaks and chops in the freezer. "Nothing you'd eat, but there's a great little Italian restaurant coupla blocks away. You can eat pasta and sun-dried tomatoes. I understand the tomatoes are never slaughtered; they die of old age."

They went to the restaurant, but immediately decided to take the food back to his apartment. They could heat it up in the micro, later.

It had been years—if ever—since Nick had experienced such a continuously remarkable sex life. Instead of being sated, their lust fed on lust until Nick felt his body was about to disintegrate. Instead, slowly, steadily, he was renewed to meet her every incredible, growing need.

It was like a game; they were two very competitive players. Neither would give an inch. Yet, time after time, why did he feel that Laura dominated and possessed him so totally?

"I'll tell you a secret, Nick. Do you know the tango?"

"The tango? Well, sure. But I don't dance it. Why?"

"Well. Sex is like the tango. The man, very macho, in charge, dominant, deciding in a series of split seconds what move he will make, assured she will follow his lead immediately. He is not the one setting the pace; determining exactly what will happen next. *She* is. Always. At all times. Do you understand why?"

"No, but you're gonna tell me."

She raised herself, elbow on the bed, her face in her hand.

"Because she *permits* him. She allows him—to make the moves, the timing, the pace. She seems to follow him, but without her total concentration, the dance would be a farce. Don't you see? It is the woman who rules the dance."

"Well, I'm about to guide you toward the micro and put you in a position to hit some buttons, so that in about twenty seconds we can eat. Even though I *know* I'm only doing this—making you get the food—because you're allowing me. See how fast I learn?"

She pulled his discarded shirt on, shrugged the sleeves, buttoned some buttons. "Okay. I'll pretend this was your idea. Now, as for you, Mr. Bensonhurst. You set that table for two or we'll have to eat standing up.

Oh, and slice the bread; we'll—I'll—put it in the oven for a quick toasting."

The food wasn't as good as it would have been at the restaurant. With some things, microwaving just doesn't make it. She seemed to play with her food. Refused a refill of wine. Something was bothering her.

"So? What? You got something you want to say?"

He expected a quick wisecrack, a suggestive tone; something provocative. Instead, looking just past him, she said, "I have to go out of the country sooner than I anticipated."

Nick put his fork down. "I didn't know you were going out of the country."

"I thought I'd mentioned it. Well, anyway. I have to check out plans for next fall's line . . ."

"Next fall? It's still winter. You still got spring . . ."

"We have to do things far in advance. I have to check with my suppliers, designers. For silk—Bangkok. And Hong Kong for—"

It wasn't the way she said it: casually. It wasn't in the words, exactly. But there was some subterranean warning. Back off, Nick.

"That's a long way—Bangkok, Hong Kong."

"By plane, the world is very small."

"Have you been to the Far East often?"

She held his gaze, met his narrowed, questioning eyes for a moment. "I've been everywhere. Often."

All the fun between them seemed to dissolve. For some reason, they were being very careful of each other. He helped her clear the table, waved away coffee and the cannolis they had bought for dessert. He had lost his appetite.

Carefully, he asked her, "How long will you be gone?"

"Depends."

"When are you leaving?"

In that moment he saw that she regarded him as a stranger, who had no right to question her about anything. She had told him that at the very beginning: No questions, no promises. Only fun. When the fun is gone, well, who knows?

"I take a night flight to Tokyo tomorrow. Then, next morning, on to Hong Kong. So. I'll call you in a day or two."

"Laura—"

She reached out and removed his hand from her shoulder as though he had just made a social error.

She said good-bye to him at the elevator; she didn't want him to see her to her car. That's what doormen are for, right?

He slammed the door behind him. Straightened up the debris of their dinner. Thought, fleetingly, of Woof: that old dog would love these scraps.

Scrubbing his head under a hot shower, Nick tried not to wonder why in all the world—at this time—Laura Santalvo was going to Tokyo and Bangkok and Hong Kong.

CHAPTER 28

Nick was puzzled by his clients. The young couple, Mr. and Mrs. Lee Dong Wen, were well dressed, neatly groomed; both spoke with an upper-class English accent. Their Mercedes was brand-new; they were obviously wealthy people in their late thirties, early forties.

They rejected larger, more expensive houses in the Gardens very quickly. Finally said they preferred a more working-class area in Forest Hills, and when he showed them the attached, six-room Tudor-style house, with an updated kitchen but fairly small rooms, a tiny plot of a yard, a garage underneath the house, they glanced at each other and nodded.

When he asked if they had children, explaining that the public school was just down the street, they merely shook their heads. When he told them there was a bus on the corner that would take them to the 71st–Continental Avenue Independent subway, then twenty-five minutes to Manhattan, they said nothing. Realizing they asked him no questions, Nick shut up. This was what they wanted, for whatever reason. Outside, they stopped on the small square patio, glanced up and down at the similar houses on both sides of the street.

It was a quiet area. Generally older people; some re-tirees could be seen reading newspapers in canvas chairs.

They purchased the house for two hundred and fifty thousand dollars—the asking price. They put up a check for half the amount, asked for the soonest possible closing, at which time they would pay the remainder. They asked how soon they could begin shipping in their furniture, rugs, couches, screens, chairs, beds, all from Hong Kong. Nick told them he'd move as quickly as possible.

He looked over the record of transactions concerning this attached house, built during the Depression for thirty-six hundred dollars, five hundred dollars down, with the builder lending that amount if necessary. In slow, then in escalating increments, it was now being sold for a quarter of a million dollars. It didn't make sense. The last turnover was two years ago. It was sold by Ventura to a Colombian family for one hundred eighty thousand; bought back by Ventura for eighty-five thousand. Now it was sold to this young couple who mentioned they were planning to use it as their American stopover, not as a permanent residence.

There were several similar deals in the property records—quick turnovers, cheap buybacks, ludicrously expensive resale. An awful lot of money was changing hands—in a thoroughly legal way. Going back a few years, he saw that many of these small "first-home" houses had been sold to names he recognized: kids from "families" in Brooklyn or Queens, turned over within two years or so. Then, about three or four years ago, the houses had been bought, for the most part, by Asians. Word of mouth, right?

He jotted some financial details in a blue testbook. Not a bad way to launder money, inflated real estate transactions.

Laura called him at 9:00 P.M. The first thing he asked, immediately feeling stupid: "What time is it in Hong Kong?"

"I'm in Tokyo. It's ten o'clock tomorrow morning."

Well, that was a great conversation opener. He felt tense, wished he still smoked. "Was it a good flight? Nice hotel? How the hell are you?"

There was a silence and then finally she spoke. "It was a good flight. The hotel is fine. I am fine. I leave for Hong Kong in an hour. Anything else you want to know?"

"How long will you be gone? When are you coming back?"

He wasn't surprised by her answer or the tension in her voice. "Nick, this is stupid. I won't call you again. I'll see you when I get back."

He sounded petulant, even to himself. "Hey, you do what you wanna do."

"Always." Then, as if realizing how abrupt she had sounded, she allowed a small laugh. "God, you are such a big baby, Mr. Bensonhurst."

Without another word, Laura hung up.

Sharp, dismissive, unconcerned. Laura had just worked her every unpleasant trait into one conversation with him. No bullshit; no forced light conversations. All business. He thought for a moment. She was right. That was probably why he felt so much anger toward her. He really hadn't wanted a recitation about her flight, her accommodations, what she did, who she saw.

Yet he wanted to know every minute of every day she spent away from him. He certainly had no right, no claim on her. But still he felt the way he felt.

It was normal, probably, for her to be so offhand and casual and unimpressed about the exotic flow of her life. For her, all the travel was normal.

But he felt upset and uneasy. In a way, he wished

she hadn't called. And then it hit him: He had no way of knowing where she was, where she stayed. No way of reaching her, should he need or even want to.

He'd just have to wait until she returned. As Laura wanted it.

CHAPTER 29

A half hour before landing at Kaituk Airport in Hong Kong, Laura held her cupped hands, filled with cold water, first to her forehead, then her cheeks, then along her chin and neck. She had slept for about three hours flying out of Tokyo. She blotted her face with astringent-soaked cotton; slid on just a few drops of moisturizer, then some colorless lip gloss. She ran her hands through her hair, fluffed it, smoothed it, settled it. She brushed her dress with a small clothing brush, checked that the wrinkles were to a minimum. She looped a pale lavender silk scarf around her neck, twisted it into a distinctive knot, slid it around until it pleased her. She dug into her travel satchel, zipping and unzipping until she found an amethyst ring. It was the only jewelry she wore.

Most of the other passengers in the first-class section of the Northwest Airlines 747 were gathering papers, closing up laptops, checking pockets. And then checking out Laura as she walked to the last row of first class. She was the only woman; all the international businessmen enjoyed the sight of a beautiful woman at the end of the long flight.

When the plane had taxied up to the departure tunnel, the businessmen started to collect in the aisles. A bright, perky Chinese stewardess, smiling, held her hand up.

"For just a moment, please." She leaned down toward Laura, spoke a few words, still held her hand up for the other passengers to wait.

They craned to watch Laura as she was escorted, not to the debarkation tunnel but down a hastily supplied flight of stairs leading from the pilot's quarters. Several bent down, peering through the small thick windows at the procession: a few uniformed men touched their hats in salutes, glanced quickly at her passport and entry documents, smiled, extended a hand to help her toward the Rolls-Royce that waited just steps away. Her luggage appeared immediately and was placed in the trunk of the car.

"Well, what do you think of that?" One businessman on his way to a convention of cotton dealers asked his seatmate.

"Somebody's mistress," he answered.

Who else could she be?

Laura leaned back, deep into the luxurious silk-soft leather, stretched her legs, closed her eyes for a moment. Soft music came from the speaker directly in front of her as the driver, speaking into a small microphone, asked, "Is all right, the music?"

Laura smiled. "Fine. Thank you, Arnold. You always remember my favorites."

She opened the door of the small bar, reached for a blue bottle of mineral water, amused that it had been imported from Wales. She plucked a few green grapes from a perfectly shaped bunch. She hadn't eaten anything on the plane, a trick she learned through bitter experience. The fruit tasted clean and pure. She cut a plump peach in half, then in quarters, and carefully nibbled. She glanced out the window, then spoke to the driver.

"Where are we going?"

Softly, he informed her, "To the school, Miss. Before we go to the Great House."

She thought for a moment, then asked, "Is *he* there? At the house?"

"Not yet, Miss. But he will be in time for dinner. So you can visit for a while with the boy."

Laura felt invigorated. She bit into the peach with a sudden appetite. She hadn't seen him in nearly six months. When he was a baby, the time between visits was devastating. He was three years old before he recognized his auntie immediately at each visit. That's what he called her: Auntie.

The British School for Boys was in the British section of Hong Kong, outside the traffic and hustle of the incredible city. From the school grounds Victoria Peak could be seen, surrounded by fog, overlooking the wonderland that was this world center for commerce.

She had taken the boy up the cable car to the peak one time, a few years ago. His father was furious; why did she think the Rolls was available? The driver met them, nervously, at the end of the cable lift and the boy's face shone with excitement. To see the city laid out beneath them as though it was a toy metropolis, all steel and glass and bronze and lights, with heliports on the tallest buildings; to look down upon the brightly lit signs naming international banks and companies, the flags of various countries flapping in the wind. It was awe-inspiring. She wasn't sorry she had taken the boy. It was probably the only time in his life he hadn't been overprotected.

At his school, the headmaster, a tall, slender, gray-haired man with a rigid right arm from a war wound, offered his left hand automatically.

"Just a moment, Ms. Santalvo. I just have to check with—"

Laura nodded. She understood. No one questioned the presence of security people assigned to certain students. They were an international group of boys, many of whom had moved around the world's schools at their fathers' reassignments. Some were princes, some heirs who would one day rule exotic Arabian countries. A movie star's two sons were enrolled, guarded by masters of street fighting. Their father was a legendary hand-to-hand battling champion up from the streets, who had caught the eye of a Chinese filmmaker; now he had become a star so valuable that stunt doubles were hired to do the dangerous stuff for him.

The two men who entered the headmaster's office knew Laura. When she smiled and greeted them, they both bowed their heads ceremoniously. They would bring the boy at once.

"I don't want to interrupt his class," she said, not really meaning it.

"No, no, not to worry. Anthony will be so glad to see you."

He had been escorted from the playing field. His knees, showing in the space between his gray shorts and high knee socks, were scabby. His face was red from exertion and he seemed annoyed.

"Headmaster, why—"

His guards hadn't told him; they left discreetly, as did the headmaster.

The boy spun around at the sound of her voice.

"Anthony. Stop growing so fast. You're only twelve. You've time to reach six feet when you're twenty."

He flung himself at her from across the room, and she felt the impact of that strong, solid, muscular body. He smelled of sweat and dirt and boy. He pulled back and studied her face.

"Auntie, Auntie. You are so beautiful!"

There was such passion and joy in the moment. She reached out and caressed his flushed cheek, then kissed his forehead, still inches below her. She studied him hungrily: the set of his brows, the straight nose, strong mouth, black eyes. She saw much of his father in him. She searched for something of herself.

CHAPTER 30

With a soft purring sound, the Rolls glided up the steep twisting road, at times perilously close to the edge of the deep mountain rising to Victoria Peak.

Some tour buses were descending: Laura saw faces trying to peer into the blackened windows of the car. In the heart of Hong Kong, a Rolls-Royce didn't attract much attention. On the long narrow road, rising in solitary mystery, it was an item of momentary curiosity to tourists still gasping at their sky-high view over the top of the Hong Kong fantasyland.

She remembered her first ride in a car like this one. He acquired a new Rolls every five or six years, and kept two vintage models, just for the pleasure of viewing them. He never drove the Rollses; his cars of choice for personal pleasure were, of course, his Maserati and a succession of Jaguars, a remembrance of his university days in England.

Laura had met him many years ago, when she was married to the prince. She saw him as a somewhat exotic man, remote, cool: more an observer than a participant. He was courted wherever he went and expected to be; rarely accepted invitations. He had been interested in purchasing a yacht, a very expensive model, and the salesman who ran within the prince's circle practically tricked him into attending a dinner at a private club in London. He had spotted Laura at once—an incredible young woman who no more fitted the setting than he did.

She seemed to observe the others as he did, physically present but only distantly involved in whatever conversation or story flitted around the table. She drank sparingly, as he did. She pulled back slightly when spoken to directly. She answered softly, marginally polite; giving no offense, but also no encouragement.

Dennis Chen had been totally enchanted with Laura Santalvo, from the moment he saw her through all the years he had been her lover.

After the death of her second, younger husband, Laura had expanded her design house—had thrown herself into the business, with great success. He had seen her, listening intently, nodding, earnestly discussing some bolt of material at a silk factory he owned in Hong Kong. He waited her out, and then, as she prepared to enter her hired taxi, he had gently taken her arm. When she faced him, pleasure overcame surprise. They later confided each had fully expected that they would one day be together.

Their lives were as separate as they wished. Their time with each other was just that. Each had a full personal life, with no further explanation. When she became pregnant, he had no intention—nor did she want him—to leave his wife and two daughters. He was with her when she gave birth to Anthony, in London, and the child had dual British-Chinese and American citizenship. Dennis Chen traveled on a British passport, since he had been born in Hong Kong. Such passports were at a premium as the Chinese takeover of Hong Kong grew nearer, moment by moment.

Physically, he was her male counterpart. His body was long and slender; his movements easy and graceful. His muscles were as clearly defined as an anatomical drawing: everything in proportion. His skin was fine and smooth, its color an even, light honey.

His father, Lee Phon Chen, had been a very successful entrepreneur who had escaped China under the rule of the Generalissimo and stayed in Hong Kong when the Reds took over. He dealt in diamonds; gold; then, bored, had ventured into other fields. Eventually, the Chen name was on a multiplicity of things—from fine bone china to bolts of silk; from ivory jewelry to gambling devices. His investments included worldwide holdings in both legitimate and not-quite-legal enterprises. It was not until he met the quiet, fair-haired Englishwoman whose father worked in the British Embassy that he found something he wanted but did not have. He had his requisite wife, a Chinese beauty of the old style, who had given him four daughters and three sons. His home life was regular, his merest need and desire met instantly. But with the English girl, there was adventure—and treachery. Her father had conspired to have him killed. Instead, after a series of quiet meetings, after considerable money had changed hands, the Englishman had been reassigned to a post in South Africa. The daughter, by then, had made her commitment to Chen. Dennis was their only child; she died giving birth to a second child when he was six years old.

Facially, the boy would be defined as Chinese, yet there was something of the European mother to him as well. Something just slightly off-kilter for a Chinese boy. His hair was not quite so coarse, had brown glints in the sunlight. His cheekbones were not quite so high as his father's, his face not quite so broad. His color was light, and his mother kept him out of the sunshine;

by the time of her death, his amah knew he was to be always protected so that his skin would never darken.

He was taller than his father, as his English mother had been. Nor did he have the stocky, blocky build of his father's other sons. He had lived with his mother in a beautiful house—a mistress house—and when she died, he was sent to school in England. He knew of his father's other children; they knew of him. His father's will confirmed that he had been the favorite. The Englishwoman's bastard, legitimized by his vast inheritance. He had trained for business both at university and at his father's side. By the time he was to take over, Dennis Chen was a brilliant businessman. The directors of all the various companies had been carefully chosen. His older brothers were given important positions, but all were subordinate to him. They generally did not mind. Dennis Chen was ultimately fair to all of them; generous with praise, bonuses, even employment for his half sisters' husbands. Actually, his older brothers were relieved that the awful responsibility had not been theirs.

All the businesses, legitimate and otherwise, ran smoothly. Dennis Chen's venture into the drug trade— by far the most lucrative—was the one business he shared with no one.

Now he lay naked on the silk-sheeted bed, his head propped on his hand as he watched her move unselfconsciously about the room. She peeled her clothing off as carelessly and naturally as a child, tossing it to the chaise lounge, the floor, a chair. She wore the exotic, exciting underwear he had had made for her exclusively: lavender and deep purple silk. It pleased him that beneath her usual black, next to her skin, she wore his favorite colors. Whether she wore them when they were apart, he did not know or care. They existed for each other only when they were together.

Finally, naked, she stood very still, at ease, and looked at him. When their eyes met in a secret coded communication, the world became absolutely still. He pulled himself into a sitting position, then stood up from the bed and approached her. She remained motionless.

He ran his slender fingers along the sides of her face, traced her shoulders, circled her breasts, then leaned forward and tasted her flesh. He pulled back and slowly, carefully examined her without touching. He moved his chin just a fraction, and in response Laura turned and he studied her from behind. He ran his hands over her, cupped her buttocks. His mouth tasted her neck, her earlobes. He pressed into her, wrapped his arms around her. He felt the thick growth of black pubic hair, his fingers lightly touching, then moving to the very edge of her inner body. He felt the moisture he had caused and slid a finger into her. He could feel the slight contraction, her acknowledgment of him. He pressed her shoulder and she turned toward him, her head back so that they communicated again with just their eyes. Hers were a slatey gray; they darkened when he made love to her and he wondered if his changed in any way. He had to slow himself down; play with her; encourage her, all without a word.

For years, periodically, they had made love in many places and in many ways. Each knew the other's body, and each tried to find some way of surprising the other: some new movement, expression, hesitation, interruption. Sometimes they were subtle, other times very primitive. She had surprised him at the beginning, even though he knew of her marriage into the depraved circle of her prince husband. There was never anything vulgar or blatant about their lovemaking. Laura seemed to refine whatever vulgarity, whatever crudeness she had learned, into something special. Even when they indulged wildly, noisily, Laura brought something entirely her own.

As did Dennis Chen. He had absorbed knowledge from the most expensive and best-trained whores his father could provide, and then made use of his knowledge with an assortment of women whose experiences only further enriched his understanding.

But every encounter with Laura was special for one reason. No matter what technique, game, scenario, no matter how routine or familiar, there was always a difference.

Because she was Laura.

Her skin had a darker cast than his: both her parents had been Sicilian, but her coloring was neither sallow nor Mediterranean. Her coppery tone shimmered in the soft lighting of the room. Her face glowed as though reflecting candlelight, though there were no candles. She shone from inside herself; her face, in passion, still seemed to him somehow controlled. As though no matter how much of herself she gave to him, there was still some essence of herself she withheld.

They moved to each other's rhythm as though engaged in a dance. He would try to keep slightly ahead of her, but she would catch up immediately and smile up at him. As she rolled from under him, mounted him, rubbed her mouth over his, forced her tongue between his lips, nipping him playfully and then more passionately, he kept his eyes on her; in response she opened her gray eyes, which darkened as they continued to stare into his. There was something both knowing and impenetrable to those eyes of hers; he suddenly became uncomfortable because he could not see into her, and when he slipped from under her he turned her on her back more roughly than he had intended. She registered some slight surprise, but he kissed her gently and began the deeper movement of his body—no longer watching her face, his own eyes locked now. He felt her slight but growing resistance, felt her hands on his head, the known touch, the special signal, and he traveled down her body and tasted the contractions, felt them on his tongue, quick, decisive, then he raised himself and plunged into her. They moved and exploded as one. Whose body was this responding—was her body his, was his body hers?

She tasted herself in his mouth, the taste completing the joining and sharing. She had tasted his flesh many times, and the commingling with her own juices was a rare gift. She had taken his semen in her mouth, and then carefully moistened his face, his lips, his mouth with his own essence. He had told her no woman had ever done that to him, and when he asked if she had done this to any other man, she had put her finger over her own lips. No questions, no answers.

She had known, of course, of his visit to Papa Ventura, and of his plans to rent a house in Queens for a short period of time. They had never been together in New York. It was a mutual decision made without explanation, but in accord.

He propped his head on his hand, elbow resting alongside her. His tongue flicked to the corners of his mouth and he spoke to her softly.

"How did the boy look? How did he seem to you?"

"Ugly as ever."

"And stupid, right? So stupid a boy, who ever would want to know him?"

It was a game they played. He had told her of his amah's superstition: If you praise a child too much, an evil spirit might overhear you and become jealous and steal the child for himself.

In a conspiratorial whisper, breathy into his ear, she said, "My God, he is magnificent. So much like you."

"I see *you* in him. It's interesting that you cannot."

She thought of the boy's face: the cheekbones, the shape of his mouth; the way he held his head at certain moments. Yes. She nodded; there was something of herself.

"When he's in school in London," Dennis said, "you can stay in the apartment whenever you visit. He can stay with you for holidays."

"When will he go to London?"

"When the fall term begins. This summer I want to take him sailing." He gestured broadly. It was a world large with possibility. He studied Laura carefully, caught a quick expression. She was withdrawing from him into some secret sad place of her own. He reached for her face, turned her chin up. "What?" When she pulled her face away, he insisted. "Tell me."

"Does he know who I am?"

Dennis Chen moved away abruptly. They had had this discussion before. He stood up, wrapped himself in a long, dark, red silk robe, knotted the belt around his narrow waist.

She did not repeat the question, but she didn't take her eyes from him.

Finally, in a cold voice, he said, "You are his auntie. He loves you very much. *That is it.*"

She had agreed to all of his terms at the very beginning. She had at first wanted to have an abortion but he had wanted her to have a child for him. And if it was a boy, the child would be part of his life. In return, she could visit with him, love him, be "related" to him in some unclear way.

Laura hadn't meant to bring this up again. She had made the deal; she would abide by it. But she hadn't known how much she would love the child. Realistically, she knew there was nothing she could do about the way things were. She also knew he could close her out completely.

She did nothing to hide her bitterness. She shrugged slightly, more angry at herself than at him.

When she finished showering, he wrapped her in a large, thick towel. "Laura—"

"What?"

Not wanting to say it, but saying it anyway, Dennis Chen asked her, "Is this . . . all of this . . . just for the boy? Or—"

Laura stiffened. She smacked his hand away and glared at him. Her voice was deadly. "Do you think for one single moment of thought that I would come here as some kind of whore, as part of some agreement, that I would barter my body for . . ."

He put his hands on either side of her face, smoothed the short clean strands back so her face was naked in its anger.

"Forgive me."

He should have known better. Laura did only what she wanted to do. Nothing could force her into the kind of giving, the kind of sharing, they had between them.

Not even the boy. He was sure of that.

He was practically sure of that.

CHAPTER 31

Nick was impressed by the extent of his grand-father's industrial holdings. Other families went into the controlling of nearly every vital activity the city needs to run efficiently, services the average citizen took for granted—private garbage pickup, laundry services—hotels and restaurants and hospitals could not function without the services of the union members. The families controlled the fish industry, the meat industry. Won million-dollar contracts for building city-owned projects—even if their bid wasn't necessarily the lowest. There are always unanticipated cost overruns, after all.

Nicholas Ventura, of course, extracted a certain percentage of all such enterprises as his family's rightful share. But personally, with his own assets—and through the assets of his organization—he also owned a network of large storage buildings; small factories; car repair shops; hard use places; yards where scrap iron was stored, automobiles were crushed. Ventura Enterprises held leases on a tremendous number of neighborhood mom-and-pop stores; family restaurants, Italian and Chinese, Japanese and Thai. In some areas of Queens and Brooklyn, every Korean fruit and vegetable store was rented through Ventura, the owner. Every butcher shop, fish market, soft ice cream and yogurt stand; every bowling alley. No space, of any kind, was rented without certain upfront understandings: where the produce would be purchased, how delivered, where and how sold. There was a checklist of more than a hundred rented stores, some large ones situated in malls, some small stores in residential neighborhoods that used various Ventura storehouses for their merchandise, whether imported or not. Strewn about the five boroughs of New York City, as well as towns and villages in Nassau and Suffolk County, Long Island, were a large number of Ventura Enterprises, not necessarily identifiable by the specific name. Wherever there was money to be made, Papa Ventura held a lease. And a cut.

Locations for the dispersal of the China White, the purest heroin ever imported into the country, were ready. The Far Eastern network of suppliers and dealers was firmly in place in the West Coast: San Francisco, Los Angeles, San Diego; into Las Vegas, Denver, Chicago. South to Atlanta, Miami, New Orleans. Atlantic City and now the New York area. The Chinese Triads that controlled the stuff could now view the Red China takeover of Hong Kong as little more than a nuisance. Taiwan served as a major player in the drug trade: as had the Generalissimo in the good old days of cooperation between the Triads and all their criminal activities and the ousted leader and his defeated army. The Triads were powerful enough to have worked successfully with the Japanese invaders during the war. To everyone's advantage. They would eventually make their deals with the Reds.

The changing ethnic population in areas of Queens gave rise to many shops selling imported Asian furnishings, carpets, pillows, artifacts, herbs, vegetables, concoctions for every need. These stores had come into being within the last three or four years, as Italians, Greeks, and Irish moved out and Pakistanis, Chinese, Koreans, and others too exotic to be easily identified moved in. Whatever their background, from wherever they came, these merchandisers understood the protocol and accepted it as the price of doing business.

Nick and his grandfather dined together in a popular Italian restaurant in Nassau County, known for its fresh fish and northern-style cooking. The maître d' was a smooth-smiling guy about Nick's age, introduced to him as Charlie Napolitano's son, Little Charlie. He brought Nick to meet the cook, a cousin, who had worked his way from his own small Canarsie restaurant to run the large, spotless, modern kitchen that he delighted in showing to Nick.

"Cookie" Nostriana told Nick, "You be sure you come back here before you leave, I give you a little something to take home with you."

The little something was enough food for a four-course dinner for six. Nick regretted he had no one to share the meal with. For the first time in a long while, the bright, snub-nosed face of redheaded Eddie Manganaro flashed in his brain. That was one guy with a hollow leg for good Italian food. But he couldn't reach back. Not to Eddie; not to anyone. He hadn't spoken to his uncle Frank in weeks. He was sticking to the rules laid out for him.

Papa Ventura told him only what he wanted Nick to know, and what seemed important to Papa was that Nick understand that the Ventura family would not deal directly with drugs. Others would handle the delivery, dispersal, and monies involved in the multi-billion-dollar business. Within the boundaries of his influence, the Venturas would collect vast sums of money, though not from the actual handling of the Chinese heroin. They would merely make available, for a price, locations: storehouses, retail stores, business locations, apartments, houses, junkyards—whatever they were asked. What the customer did or did not do was their own concern—as long as they paid Papa Ventura's people a sum of money for the privately run businesses in which they dealt. The fact that many Chinese businesses rented large executive office space in the forty-story buildings along Queens Boulevard, for what to all intents and purposes was legitimate activity, was all to the good. Many apparently stand-up businesses were financed by drug money, laundered and scrubbed, so sanitized and profitable that no one could possibly compete.

Factories that paid desperately small amounts of money to desperately poor illegal immigrants, whose Chinese families were in debt for years, turned over tremendous profits on cleansed drug money. Items could be made for pennies and sold for dollars. Profit was everywhere; only a small number of people involved in all of these organizations really knew the financial facts. And of this small number, only a very carefully selected few knew the whole story. If any of them was found to be untrustworthy, he disappeared without a chance to say good-bye.

How the other families handled the Chinese heroin business was their own concern. Nicholas Ventura never even saw a bag of white powder; nor did any of his employees. At least, not to his knowledge.

Just when his grandfather had begun expressing impatience at the lack of any useful information Nick was passing along to him, Caruso offered Nick a big one.

"This is really out of the lines, Nick," the professor had told him. "Someone's gonna be very unhappy about this. But, hey, what the hell. You have to give Papa some really hard stuff every now and then."

It was very hard stuff. Two of Papa Ventura's top men, one in the steelworkers' union, another supposedly involved in illegal bidding in the city's construction business, were about to be indicted by the grand jury for collusion, bribery, and falsification of official government documents. The government was building a RICO case against both men—and by extension against his grandfather. Facing really hard time, it was hoped that one of the two, or both, would be willing to deal away years for names.

Nick got a call from Caruso the day the sealed indictments were handed down. Both men were to be arrested within the next twenty-four hours. He went straight to his grandfather.

Nicholas Ventura looked over the top of his eyeglasses, holding the notes his grandson had given him. "Tomorrow morning? You are sure?"

"Yes. I'm sure."

His grandfather went to the phone; made several calls. He spoke quickly, authoritatively, with great certainty.

He then considered Nick thoughtfully. "This could be a step toward building their fucking RICO case against us. How does that work, Nicholas?"

Nick had a feeling his grandfather knew more about RICO than he let on. "Well, Papa, they pull someone in under RICO, it doesn't matter what they have against you, personally, or your company. If you're dealing with other organizations, in any way, that are involved in a number of crimes—extortion, murder, arms dealing, importing and exporting of drugs, stolen cars, shipping girls for prostitution, illegal immigration, stolen credit cars, price fixing—any number of things, they get you in their sweep."

Nicholas Ventura shook his head. "All these things— what have I got to do with arms dealing, young girls?"

"If you deal with anyone involved in any of the activities covered, you don't have to be involved in everything they do. Just one aspect and you're vulnerable. When they got the Cosa Nostra, they had miles of bugged conversations on tape; it was all over."

Ventura was furious. "And this is supposed to be a free country? A man can't have a conversation in his own home? Hey, how stupid were those guys, they got bugs in their own homes?"

"They did it all legally, Papa. They even got Gotti on the street in his walk-and-talk meetings with his people. It was his main guy who gave him up."

The old man's face was hard, his eyes narrowed and blazing. "Scum. Not like in the old days. The vows mean nothing now. Nothing at all. This never would have happened in the old days—we had *honor* then."

Nick had studied his grandfather's weary face. "That's probably why they figured on picking up those two guys I told you about. Play them along. Probably got enough on them to convince them to make a deal. They're planning to grab a lot of people in your different organizations and tie them together. Leading to you."

"Well, they'll have to find them first, right? Hell, that's what private planes are for. And small islands in the ocean. You pay enough to some of these pompous niggers who run these little countries, they think you're the great white god."

He stared at the paper for a moment. "Tell me this, Nicholas. Where did you get this information?"

"Papa, c'mon. You get your information, I get my information. We're like reporters. We don't reveal our sources."

Nick realized what was going on in the old man's mind. *Someone else* should have told him this, too; should have had access; should have warned him.

He had come to a decision. "You go home now, grandson. This is a very good thing you've done. Very good. I have some business to take care of now."

He embraced Nick, kissed his cheek, and regarded him carefully. Then nodded, as though his trust had been well placed. He would bring Nick in closer. No matter who objected.

Nick continued to relay information, prepared by his grandfather, to Coleman. Information he gathered himself, to Caruso. From Coleman's office he picked up information, mostly useless, but enough to show his grandfather that Nick was doing his job. Caruso intervened just this once, a gesture valuable in and of itself, but also in helping to secure Nick's standing.

Yet Nick would awaken in the middle of the night in a cold sweat in his cold bedroom. Christ, did he give Coleman information meant for Caruso? Then his grandfather's mole in the DEA would know what Nick was doing. He felt like a traveler without a compass: handing off messages, some phony, some real; some important, some not. One mistake could trip him up. There were times when he longed to sit down with someone, outside of all this, and try to keep his balance. But there was no one. He knew things were moving rapidly. He longed for the whole thing to be over. He longed to stop being three different people. At times he really didn't know who the hell he was anymore.

He was getting ready for bed when the soft buzz of the house phone jarred him.

"Yeah?"

It was Fred, the retired-cop building security guard with a tight New York voice. "Young guy here, Mr. O'Hara. Don't much like the looks of him. Says he gotta see ya. Name's Vinny Tucci." Then, loud enough to be heard throughout the main lobby, he added, "Looks like bad news to me."

Vinny Tucci was the twenty-five-year-old nephew of Salvy Grosso, who had watched out for the kid since his punk father Tooehy Tucci got clipped in a dumb street thing. His sister kept nagging him: give the kid a job. Vinny Tucci helped around the Queens real estate office. Ran errands, made deliveries, picked up and sent out mail. Listened to everything that was going on. Sometimes he went down to Manhattan to run some errands for Nick's cousin, Richie. The kid was a wanna-be with never-be written all over him. A street punk.

"Put him on the phone," Nick said.

The kid sounded smug. He'd just shown the security guy something or other.

"Hey, Nick. It's me. Vinny."

"What, Vinny? *What?*"

"Oh, yeah. Well, your cousin Richie said . . . listen, could I come up and see ya a minute, okay? Tell Dick Tracy here it's okay."

Vinny Tucci was slender and badly dressed in baggy jeans and an oversized baseball jacket. He had a nice face that was spoiled by a nervous tic. Every few minutes his thin lips would pull out into a stretched, meaningless smile. The tic had gotten him into some serious trouble, from the time he was a schoolboy. When he attended a wake, he remembered to keep a hand over his mouth.

Nick led him into the kitchen and blocked his view of the rest of the apartment.

Vinny looked around, his small eyes darting as he waited to be offered something. A drink. Coffee. Something.

"What, Vinny?"

Nick apparently had no class. Vinny delivered his message, his hand cupped around his mouth. "Richie says to meet him at this place. Out here in Queens. In Forest Hills Gardens." He dug into two or three pockets, then found a smudged piece of paper with an address written by Richie in the clear, legible handwriting of his early Catholic school days. It was about all of his education he had retained.

Nick held on to the paper. "Okay, what else did he tell you?"

"Oh. Yeah. He said, uh—uh"—Vinny bit his lip, closed his eyes, then snapped them open—"Yeah, and he says do you know anything about bugs? Ya know. Not the creepy-crawlies. The listening things, ya know? Like a place being bugged. Ya know. Like you guys use. In the cops. See, he wants you to meet him there and check out the place. Want I should take you there? I got a car right downstairs."

Nick took Vinny by the arm, somewhat surprised by the good muscle development. He remembered the kid worked out, wanted to be a lightweight contender. Right. Sure. He led Vinny to the door, opened it, and not too gently pushed him out into the hallway.

"Thanks, Vinny. You do nice work. I have my own wheels, but thanks anyway."

As he closed the door, he heard the raspy voice offering to take him there, anywhere. Hey, any time. He could help Nick any time at all, all you hadda do was ask, okay?

Nick heard the elevator arrive, the door slide open. He watched as Vinny, grinning, stared longingly back at Nick's door, then left via the elevator.

CHAPTER 32

Forest Hills Gardens was a private community, a thirty-minute subway ride from mid-Manhattan. Continental Avenue stretched from busy, commercial, high-rise Queens Boulevard past a collection of shops, restaurants, newspaper stands, a movie, fast-food places, a big old five and dime, under the old-fashioned bridge of the Forest Hills Long Island Railroad Station. Once through that arch, there was a vast red cobble-stoned expanse: a town square setting. An "old English" inn, with an internal bridge, led across the road from one side of the elegant building to the other. There was a perceptible quieting once on the streets of the Gardens, which had been built in the twenties and thir-ties as an alternative for very successful professional and business people who did not want to live in West-chester or anywhere on Long Island. Appearances aside, Forest Hills Gardens was actually in Queens, New York.

The only thing not perfect was the limited amount of land around each home. Some of the Tudor houses would have fit in on acres of bright green, well-tended lawns overlooking the mists of an English landscape. Plantings, shrubbery, flower beds, and trees concealed

or revealed however much each owner desired. There
were street lamps in lavish wrought-iron shapes: lan-
terns, glowing mild yellow, that seemed to have been
lit by an ancient lampman. There were park squares,
with mellowed wooden benches for nannies to rest
while their infant charges slept in this oasis of isolation.

The only incongruous intrusions were the many signs
placed along the curbs, outside and within the private
parks, warning everyone that these streets were private.
Presumably, all illegal cars would be towed away at
their owners' expense. When they reclaimed their vehicles, paid a stiff fine, they would still have to deal
with a large windshield-sized sticker pasted with stubborn glue: that'd show 'em.

Not very long ago, many homes still welcomed guests
with shiny-faced black jockey boys, their glowing lan-
terns lighting their lawns. Most of the statues had disappeared, though one or two of the grinning figures
were resettled inside the private backyard gardens.

Nick pulled up just as a large moving van drove away
from the stone and brick mansion. Lights were burning
from every window. The neighbors might wonder why
anyone would be moving furniture in until eleven at
night, but no neighbors, curious or otherwise, could be
spotted.

Richie opened the door at Nick's lightest tap, put an
arm around him; without taking a full breath, he yelled
at one of his men.

"Hey, ya fuckin' moron, I tole ya no smoking in this
house. What, I gotta be like a schoolteacher? I gotta
appoint monitors? Take the butt outside, then come
back in. No smoking. We all got that, huh? Fuckin'
dunsky bastards!"

The culprit, shamefaced, muttering apologies, left
the house quietly trying to brush smoke outside with
him.

Richie was wearing a pair of good gray slacks, a bright red silk shirt, and a black leather vest. As always, he was meticulous, down to his shiny black shoes. He escorted Nick into the large living room. It didn't seem possible that this was the same vacant house Nick had carefully checked out just a few days ago. He had received the Hong Kong Enterprises check renting the house for one year for Dennis Chen, through his corporation, which had sprawling offices on a high floor in a Queens Boulevard office building.

Nick glanced around. Everything looked as though it absolutely belonged where it was. The rooms were completely furnished, including drapes and rugs; books in the bookcases, wood stacked in the fireplace. Every room but the dining room had been totally empty when Nick sent cleaning service in.

"How the hell you get this done so fast?"

Richie was modest. "We got a coupla guys from the stagehands union. A set decorator checked the place out and they fixed it up like this. Nice, huh?"

All the furniture was rented through some company of Richie's. There was a mellow, comfortable, old-money feel to the place.

Nick stopped at the open door of a room obviously intended as an office. Joe the Brain Menucci looked up from behind a table filled with computer parts.

"How ya doin', Nicky?"

Nick nodded. Richie pulled him along by the arm and said in a low voice, "He's got music piped into every room in this house, too. Ya know, Nick, I never believed all them stories about Joe the Brain. I never heard him say nothin' too smart." He shrugged. "Like, I know he's good with electronics and all, but I don't know about that other stuff people say. Wadda ya think?"

Nick said quietly, "I wouldn't know, Richie. But I'd be careful. You know, just in case."

"In case? In case a what?"

Richie sounded worried; he motioned Nick toward the dining room. It had been thoroughly cleaned. Centered beneath a sparkling crystal chandelier in the enormous room was an eighteen-foot mahogany dining table surrounded by twelve chairs. Other matching side chairs were placed around the room near various small serving tables, lamp and telephone tables.

"So, the kid said you got a problem. What's up?"

Richie looked over his shoulder, motioned Nick closer. He didn't want anyone to overhear their conversation.

"Well, I had the place checked out, ya know, for bugs. This room especially, because all this stuff was here for a while. This guy, the expert, come with a good recommendation, ya know? Like, he brings in all kindsa electronic equipment, sweep stuff and all. The guy finds this one device." Richie dug in his pocket and brought out a small square recording device. "It was wedged under one of the chairs. Near the head of the table."

Nick studied the device; it looked like a Cold War relic. "Anything else?"

"No, but ya know how ya get a feelin'? Like something just ain't right? The guy who come here, Johnnie Cheech sent him. Cheech ain't the smartest, ya know, but he said the guy's okay. So I just wanted you to take a second look." He wrinkled his brow. "Damn feeling I got, is all."

Nick studied his cousin's face. "Why the hell didn't you ask Joe the Brain? He's the expert."

Richie glanced over his shoulder. "Hey, c'mon. Joey works directly for Papa. I wouldn't never ask him to do nothing for me. And ya know, the chinks, they're gonna check it out and they find something, how does that make me look? Not too fuckin' good, right?"

"Uh-huh. Who's had access to this place recently?"

"You." Richie shrugged that away. "And the cleanin' people you sent . . ."

"I didn't send them. Tessie called the regular company that cleans up places for the agency. I didn't even meet them."

"So, okay. The bug guy checked, no signs of breakin' and enterin'."

"So just the moving guys and your people been in and out tonight, right?"

"They're *all* my guys—my moving company, furniture company. I vouch for all of them. So I just wanted you to take a good look. Ya don't got no equipment?"

Nick didn't answer. He asked questions, got seemingly satisfactory answers. Yes, every chair had been turned over and examined carefully. The table had been checked, under and over. The walls had been scanned; the edging on the chair rail. Shelves where some china was set on display. But still, Richie had a *feeling*.

Nick also had a feeling. Something in the way his cousin watched him, narrowing his bright eyes, almost daring him.

He checked out the telephone on a small side table and one on a small desk under the window. He re-checked all the furniture; searched carefully for over an hour. Then he approached a heating vent set into one wall. Nick, using a flashlight and a penknife, pried the grate from the wall. As Richie hunched over him, he ran his hand inside and removed a device identical to the one Richie had earlier shown him.

Richie shook his head and began to curse. "That fuck, that dumb sonovabitch. Wait'll I get my hands on Cheech and his shit of a friend, the dirtbag."

Nick watched him carefully. There was something not quite straight in Richie's anger. Nick had seen him go ballistic over small matters, and a hidden device was no small matter. His eyes locked on Richie's, and for a split second they tried to read each other.

Finally, Richie put his hand on Nick's arm, squeezing. "Christ, Nicky, ya saved the day. Jesus, am I glad I had that damn feeling, ya know?"

Nick said quietly, "I got a feeling now, Richie."

"Yeah? Like what?"

"Like if Cheech's guy overlooked one device, maybe he overlooked another. They don't all look like that, ya know."

"Naw, I think . . ." His cousin stopped abruptly and nodded. "Yeah, okay, ya wanna search some more, go ahead, be my guest."

It took Nick about fifteen minutes to examine the small leather-top desk in one corner carefully; each drawer was checked, and then finally, meticulously, he touched each item on the surface of the desk. The small tooled-leather letter holder had some heavy cream-colored stationery; next to it, a gold-colored stamp holder. A cup of sharpened pencils; a cup of pens.

Nick's hand covered the porcelain cup that held the pens, then, carefully, his fingers moved and he held up an old-fashioned black Waterman fountain pen, laced with an intricate silver design. He examined it thoroughly, then turned to Richie.

"Say a few words to the listening public, cousin Richie."

Richie stared, mouth open, as Nick removed the cap, then hooked a fingernail under the silver plunger used to fill the pen. Dark blue ink squirted, then dribbled down Richie's bright red silk shirt.

"Oh, Jesus, Richie. I'm sorry. I made a mistake. It's

just an old pen. In fact, it's *my* old pen. Must have fallen out of my pocket." He slipped the pen into an inside jacket pocket and returned Richie's glare with a smile and a shrug. "Hey, shit happens, right?"

Richie took a deep breath, and wordlessly the cousins acknowledged their wary dance. Richie had tested Nick to see if he would find, and reveal, the planted bug. Nick showed Richie he was wise to the test. Check. Checkmate.

Finally, softly, Richie said, "You playin' with me, Nick?" The slight smile pulled his lips back into a grimace.

"Richie, even when we were little kids, I didn't play with you. You know why? Because you cheated. All the time, Richie, you cheated."

Richie Ventura snapped his fingers, slid his arms into the black leather coat held out to him, his eyes fastened on his cousin. Years fell away and they were the same two boys vying for their grandfather's approval, the most important thing in their young lives. They should have finished with this shit years ago. Why the hell did Nick turn up in his life now?

"You take *good care* of yourself, Nick, ya hear me?"

"I *always* take good care of myself, Richie."

CHAPTER 33

It was a little past three in the morning when Nick let himself back into the Tudor. As with all unoccupied houses carried on the Ventura books, lights were programmed to come on and turn off to give potential housebreakers the idea that people were living there. He had no trouble with the burglar alarm; Nick had coded it himself.

He had parked his car several blocks away. It was dead quiet in Forest Hills Gardens. Nick went directly to the office, and with a small-beamed flashlight he studied the computer and then the music system Joe Menucci had installed earlier in the day. The listening devices were inconspicuous. Voice-activated, they looked like no more than another tuner button or selection device. He thought for a moment, then headed for the kitchen, another usual gathering place. He ran his fingertips around the edges of the table, chairs, light fixtures, frames on various pictures. There was a large spice rack placed on the wall near the table as a unit in a decorative arrangement. Next to it was a wreath made of twigs, clumps of dried flowers, and small fruits. Among the dehydrated grapes was a tiny recording device. Completely unobtrusive.

Nick traced the arrangement of music speakers throughout the house. At least one in every room. Then, just out of curiosity, he went to the basement. There was an expensively furnished playroom, a pool table, gym equipment in one corner. Most unusual of all was the small lap pool, fifteen feet long and eight feet wide, about five feet deep. It was connected to a motor that, when turned on, provided a swimmer with a strong current to work against. Someone had put a few outdoor-type chairs and a bundle of white towels alongside the pool.

Nick didn't worry about light showing. All the basement windows were shuttered. He poked and pried with his hand, then with a penknife. His arm entered the heating duct that led up to the dining room.

He felt around for a moment—and, as he withdrew his arm, his whole body froze in response to the cold circle of a gun barrel that pressed into the side of his neck. He held his breath as he heard the click of a hammer being drawn back, then turned in response to an angry voice.

"What the fuck ya doin' here, Nicky?" Playboy Pilotti asked.

CHAPTER 34

Pauly the Playboy Pilotti was nicknamed for his spectacular failure to stay married. When he was a kid, he was Pauly Pill, always the strongman of the neighborhood. He grew up demonstrating how he could lift heavy objects and straight-arm them over his head. He made a serious mistake when he was in his early teens, but it was a mistake that ensured him a lifetime job with Richie Ventura.

A kid named Ba-Ba-Boom—which was descriptive of how he liked to punch people out—socked Richie Ventura in the eye. As he readied his fist for the follow-up to the mouth, he was grabbed, hoisted aloft, cursed at, and then dropped from a height of nearly six feet. The fractured jaw wasn't the Pill's fault. The kid should have had sense enough to roll when he landed, like cats do to break a fall instead of a bone. When Richie kicked the fallen Ba-Ba-Boom, the bully got a broken arm and three busted ribs. Pauly Pill took the rap for the whole thing and spent nine months in a juvenile detention house. Which didn't bother his parents too much. They were small, nervous people, and between them they hadn't been able to manage his behavior since he was four years old and began breaking his little sister's toys and then his little sister's fingers.

Pauly spent years perfecting his powerful body. He entered contests and won trophies. To other bodybuilders, he was a thing of beauty. To the uneducated eye, he was vastly misshapen, carrying a small bullet head on a thick neck, set on massive bulging shoulders. His chest was huge, waist narrow, legs much too short for the top part of his body. He had to have his clothing custom-made. He had custom-tailored shirts made by the brother of the guy who made his suits. When dropped on the floor, Pauly's clothing looked like an outfit for a short, powerful ape.

He was a perfect man for Richie Ventura, who didn't really like to do his own dirty work. He was good with a bat, a cleaver, a gun. His hands could get a lock on a guy's neck that was a killer. Literally.

Wherever Richie went, Playboy Pilotti was either far ahead, for safety's sake, or slightly behind for backup. He worked long erratic hours, took vacations whenever Richie wanted a change of scenery. He went through three marriages before he decided he didn't really like having some woman asking when he was gonna come home. He had a nice apartment near Richie's house in Massapequa, Long Island, a good car with a cellular phone. He loved to eat at all of Richie's favorite restaurants, where no one would insult you with a menu. He also had a part ownership in a health and fitness club, and at times worked out for hours to the admiring gaze of club members. It all depended on Richie—his hours, his whereabouts, his activity.

He did a lot of different things for Richie. One of the main things was he kept his mouth shut. Whatever he knew, or thought he knew, was buried deep inside his closed mouth. Richie Ventura trusted him almost completely. After all, you have to trust someone in your

life—and this guy had taken a rap for Richie when they
were just kids. That kind of loyalty cannot be faked.

Nick turned and raised one hand toward Playboy's
gun, palm out in a pacifying gesture. He knew—Christ,
he hoped—Pauly wouldn't shoot him without Richie's
okay.

Playboy stepped back, admiring Nick's cool.

"You doin' a little plantin' of your own, cop?"

The tough-guy smirk, the wide-legged stance, the
chin thrust forward, eyes narrowed, were standard for
someone in the Playboy's line of work. He was known
to have killed at least seven people, possibly as many
as ten, for various reasons and on various orders. In his
early days, he had occasionally strangled a guy to keep
others in line. When Richie pointed, his man acted. He
had been charged, but never convicted, of murder a
few times; but aside from the open-dormitory time of
his adolescence, the only slammer time he served—
eighteen months—was for a botched burglary that was
someone else's fault.

It was recorded for future reference that Paul the
Playboy Pilotti had nutted out in prison. He couldn't
handle confinement. He had slammed his head against
concrete walls, steel bars, cement floors. He claimed
he couldn't breathe or swallow; couldn't sleep; couldn't
eat. His time was spent mostly in the prison hospital
for various self-inflicted injuries; for hysteria; for bi-
zarre behavior.

Nick took a calculated risk. "Playboy, ya wanna call
my cousin, call him. But I think I better tell ya what
I'm gonna tell him." Nick gestured to the open grille
of the heating vent. "I don't know who the fuck you
guys got to check for bugs, but the guy was a real am-
ateur. I bet no one ever checked out this basement,
right? I asked Richie if every room in the house had
been checked and he said no. Just the dining room and

kitchen. Anybody with any sense would check the whole house. I figured I'd start at the bottom and work my way up. The guy he paid to check shoulda done all this."

"Yeah? That's your story?"

"Hey, you want to call Richie right now, three A.M., and tell him you found me here checking, go right ahead. But I don't think he'd appreciate getting waked up for this little news flash."

"You find anything?"

"I just started. But like Richie said to me, 'I had a feeling.' Hell with it. Maybe I was wrong. It's none of my business anyway."

"Yeah? Well, it's Richie who decides, not you. Why didn't you tell Richie about your *feelin'*?"

Nick shrugged. "The less my cousin and me have to say to each other the better. For both of us." He studied the hulking thug, then thoughtfully asked him, "What about you, Pauly? What are *you* doing here? What the fuck you up to?"

The Playboy seemed uneasy; like a back-alley bully, he covered by getting very angry. "What the fuck that got to do with you?"

As they left the house, it hit Nick that Pauly must have been up to no good. Nick said, "You want I should tell Richie, I will. Maybe better neither one of us should say anything about being here."

"Don't try to pull any o' your wise-ass shit on me, Nicky. I ain't forgot you used to be a cop. Once a cop—"

"Like once a housebreaker? There are some pretty nice things here. Who owns all the stuff, the pictures and the silverware and such?"

Playboy Pilotti kept walking. When he reached his car, he turned and the scowl seemed scarred on his face.

"You and me, we better have no more business to-gether, you got that?"

Nick smiled. "Business? What business? I don't know what the fuck you're talking about. I guess Richie don't need you or me to tell him what to do. See you around, Playboy."

The man with the short legs seemed to disappear as he slumped into the driver's seat. Through the window, he looked to be about five feet tall, hat included.

Driving home, Nick thought about his grandfather. He was a man accustomed to dealing with colleagues face to face, either as friends or enemies. He found the Chinese unreadable. To him, everything about them was modulated: soft voices, quick, tight, meaningless smiles, slight head nods, controlled body movements. Obviously, he distrusted Chen and the men working with him. Joe Menucci was so good at what he did, it would take another electronics genius to discover all the hidden devices.

Richie clearly had no idea that Chen's house was very expertly bugged. Papa Ventura trusted no one com-pletely.

When he got back to his apartment, Nick punched the button on his answering machine.

"Guess who's coming home? I'll call you from JFK tomorrow night. Around eight. Go to school on the morning shift, okay?"

Even from across the world, she was calling the shots. What the hell, he'd take an office break, go to his class, come home and wait for her call. Just the way you want it, Laura, right?

CHAPTER 35

At the end of the class, Professor Caruso handed his students their graded midterm exams. There were a few groans, a few sighs of relief—or resignation—as the students went through the blue books to see why they got the mark that was printed in red ink inside the cover. Nick stared at the B−. He flipped the pages; didn't see many comments or checkmarks. He glanced at Caruso, who nodded slightly.

"I'll be in my office for the next hour or so. Anybody want to dispute the grade, see me then. Try to convince me; I'm a reasonable man."

Nick waited as the last of three students in line left the professor's study. He closed the door behind him and Caruso crossed the room and turned the lock.

"I'll change it to a B plus. I just wanted to get your attention."

Nick felt a little annoyed. His exam was certainly worth an A. He hadn't realized how important it was to him. He'd been doing some thinking about what would follow his current assignment.

Caruso told him that he was getting information from Chinese police and West Coast narcotics agents. Everyone was gearing up: a massive amount of China White was going to enter the United States very soon. By boat, by plane, in large shipments of consumer goods, commercial equipment, hidden in passenger carry-ons. Some would be picked up at LAX by a veritable army of sixteen-wheelers, which would cross the United States with stop-offs at various cities, unloaded at designated storage areas, and then distributed by various dealers into the communities. Some would be flown east to New York and Newark—large crates of merchandise consigned to warehouses throughout the area. Ships would be offloaded at major ports, designated as bulk items. Included with the valid material, unestimated kilos of China White.

He asked Nick if his grandfather seemed about to include him in the operation. Would he be in a position to gather crucial evidence?

"The information about the indictments, Tom, that really impressed him. He's also worried, I think, that his mole let him down."

"Good. That leak, by the way, has lead to a mountain of inside investigations. The two guys disappeared into thin air. No one, not their wives or kids or friends, seems to know where they are. There's even some talk going around that they've been . . . offed."

It was logical. It just hadn't occurred to Nick. "All I know is that my grandfather was pretty upset about the news. And very . . . happy with me."

"Good, that's what I did it for."

He told Caruso of the Forest Hills Gardens house rented for Dennis Chen, but they both thought it was too obvious a location for any real business to be occurring there.

"They're not gonna use a place we could stake out around the neighborhood, where it'd be easy to take videos of them arriving and leaving. That would be stupid. By the way, what the hell are you doing in my babies' day class instead of with the grown-ups to-night?"

Nick smiled. "I got other plans for tonight."

Caruso seemed hesitant. "Nick, there's one thing. I just want to sort of skim this past you, okay?"

Nick could feel the sudden, deepening tension. "What?"

"It's none of my business—except in a way, it *is* my business. About Laura Santalvo."

Nick sat up straight; his eyes narrowed and his voice went very low. "You're right, it isn't your business. Not in any way."

"But it might be, Nick. Laura might be connected. We know she's funded her own businesses, but she makes a lot of trips to the hot spots. We haven't been able to keep close tabs on her . . ."

"This conversation is over." Nick stood up abruptly. Then he turned, dropped his midterm exam on Caruso's desk. "This deserves an A."

Caruso shrugged. "You got it."

Laura called him early that evening.

"Hey, you. I'm at Kennedy. Wanna pick me up and buy me some supper? I'm starved."

"Yeah, I wanna pick you up. And buy you some supper."

Within forty-five minutes her luggage was secured in the trunk of his car, and she directed him to a small restaurant.

Laura stared so hard as he took a bite of rare hamburger that it seemed to turn to blood in his mouth. He swallowed, shook his head, sent the burger back, and ordered grilled swordfish. The waiter, a tall, thin, pale boy, glanced at Laura, nodded slightly in approval. Another barbarian turned?

"Please, no lectures, okay?"

Laura rested her chin on her hand. "I follow my own

beliefs. I never tell others what they should or should not do. If slaughtering animals after cruelly confining them doesn't bother you—"

He reached across the table and took her hand. "Hey. I missed you."

Her smile was the mocking, oh-sure grin that always got to him. She squeezed his hand.

"You are a hard case, Laura, you know that?"

"Is that what I am?"

"Among other things."

"What else I am is tired. Jet-lagged. My head is filled with too many words about textures and lines and flat hips and rounder bustlines and the excitement of clashing colors. Why don't we eat fast and get the hell out of here?"

She didn't want to go to his place. She wanted to go home.

As they drove along Grand Central Parkway, headed toward Manhattan, Laura leaned her head back, closed her eyes.

"You have a busy time?"

"I always do."

"How often do you take these trips? Christ, you hop around like a jumping jack."

Quietly, she said, "I take 'these trips' as often as necessary."

"What makes it necessary?"

Laura sat up straight. "You interrogating me?"

"I'm just making conversation. Relax, kiddo."

There was no further conversation, only tension. Nick reached out, put on a soft music station. When he glanced at her once or twice, her eyes were closed; her jaw was tensed.

Nick drove down the ramp into the garage beneath the Beresford. She directed him to her assigned space. He was surprised how light her luggage was.

"When you travel a great deal, you know how to pare it down," she told him. Her tone was conversational, neither friendly nor hostile.

The elevator opened at Laura's floor. As she inserted the key and pushed the door open, they both stopped short. There were lights on in the large square entrance hall.

"I didn't think Maria would be here." She mentioned the housekeeper. "I usually call her when I return. Su-Su should be at school."

Music came softly from the sitting room, which Laura used as a library. She looked at Nick, who dropped the luggage and motioned her back.

She followed closely behind him and they entered the mahogany paneled room. Stretched out in a deep cushy easy chair, feet on the square coffee table, latest copies of magazines strewn about, was his cousin.

It was a toss as to who was more surprised, Nick or Richie Ventura.

Laura pushed forward and in a steel-edged voice asked, "What the hell are you doing here, Richie? How did you get in?"

CHAPTER 36

Laura knocked his feet off the table with a sweep of her arm. Richie stood up.

"Hey, Laura. Relax. I just thought I'd save you a trip."

"I asked how you got in here."

Richie shrugged; smiled tightly at Nick. "Didn't you both notice the Playboy downstairs in the lobby?"

Laura didn't answer. She reached for the house phone, spoke loud enough so that Richie could hear her.

"Luis, this is Ms. Santalvo. Are you all right? Is there a gorilla-looking man there with you?" She listened, eyes riveted on Richie. "Luis, they will be leaving soon. You and I will talk. This won't happen again. No, no. Don't you worry. It'll be all right."

Then, to Richie: "You have fun scaring the hell out of a poor workingman? You, the big, labor-connected, concerned union man?"

As she spoke, Richie slid his arms into his jacket, snapped his fingers as though just remembering something. He dug into his trouser pocket and held up a key. Whatever reaction he expected, Laura remained stone-faced. When he reached out to give it to her, she didn't move.

"I want you to get the hell out of my home, right now."

Richie tossed the key on the coffee table. He shook his head; smiled his tense, leering grimace. "Nicky, you got a key to the place, too?"

Nick made a move toward him, but Laura intercepted by stomping on Richie's foot; as he bent over in surprise and pain, she smashed him with her clenched fist, right in the jaw. It wasn't the power of the blow, it was the unexpectedness.

Richie sprawled backwards, landing sideways on the couch. For a moment he seemed to fill with murderous rage. He took a deep breath, got control. Slowly he stood up, straightened his clothes.

"Jesus," he said, "you sucker-punched me, just like when we were kids."

"You were never a kid, Richie. Now get out."

"She ever do that to you, Nick, or don't you know all her little games yet?"

Laura said, "He's not worth it, Nick. Wait a minute, Richie. You said you came here to save me a trip. Fine."

She dug into her massive black leather handbag; unzipped a compartment, retrieved a small pink velvet ring box. She handed it to Richie.

Richie held the diamond ring between two fingers, letting the light send sparks across the room. He let out a sigh of delight, then showed it to Nick.

"For Theresa. Our twenty-fifth anniversary's coming up next month. We'll throw a big bash. Hey, you're both invited. C'mon, Laura. Friends, right?"

Laura said coldly, "You will send over, by special messenger—not your ape man—fifteen thousand dollars in cash. It's not that I'm trusting you with the ring, I just don't want to see you again. So get going, Richie."

"Fifteen thou, huh? Good price. Nick, ya know anything about diamonds? What'd this go for at Tiffany's, huh? About double that, right? The markup on this stuff—fuckin' incredible. But I guess your diamond-dealing friend—Mr. Chen, right?—gives you a special price." He slipped the box into his jacket pocket, patted it. "Theresa will be bustin' when she gets this. Hey, do I send the invitation to both of youse here, Nick's place, what?"

When no one answered him, Richie shrugged. They followed him to the door, stood watching him as he entered the small elevator.

Nick waited for her to say something, but Laura headed for the kitchen. Then, "I could use some strong coffee. How about you?"

Nick remained silent. Laura studied him, and her face became hard and her voice street tough. "You waiting for me to say something, or what? You have questions you want to ask? Go ahead."

Nick shook his head.

Laura jabbed her forefinger at him. "You fuckin' well better not. You want to know—what's with Laura and Richie? What's with the key? What's with the ring? What's what? But you're smart not to ask one single thing, Nick." She turned and slammed a coffee mug on the counter, dumped a large teaspoon of instant into it, grabbed the glass kettle just as it began to whistle, and poured. She banged the glass so hard it was a wonder the kettle didn't break.

"Why're you so mad at me?"

Laura took one sip of the hot coffee. "Because I can read your mind. You picturing Richie and me? You going to lie awake tonight and try to figure it out?"

Nick shook his head. "No. I can't see you with Richie."

"And if I was with him—*ever*—it would have nothing to do with *you* or anyone else." She studied his face; noticed him sucking in on his cheeks, biting on his lips. "And if I was with anyone, at all, at *any* time at all, it is *my* business. Nothing to do with you. Just the time we have together, Nick, got that?"

"No, I haven't got that, Laura. Is that how you do it, live in segments?"

She looked up at him steadily. "Deal with it. What you see is what you get. No more, no less. Jesus, where are the cats?"

She ran from the kitchen, up the stairs, and flung open the door to her bedroom. Cats came rushing from the room, yelling, crying, furious at having been confined.

"That goddamn Richie. Okay, pals, it's okay. I'm here now. You guys hungry, huh?"

She carried the gigantic white cat, a deaf oddity with seven toes on each of its front feet, past him. The cat stared yellow-eyed at Nick, then swiped at him.

"Angel, don't do that. He's not the man who locked you up." She put the cat on a counter and searched for the can opener. In a calm, friendly voice, she asked, "You wanna help? I've got a lot of hungry critters on my hands."

All the toughness was gone, the anger, the refusal to be put on the defensive. All that was over; done with; file and forget.

Nick shook his head. "I don't think so, Laura."

They stared, neither giving an inch. Laura shrugged. "You know the way out."

Then she turned her attention to the cats. "Okay, babies, let's see what you'll have. Some tuna and chicken or that salmon stuff or . . ."

He closed the apartment door behind him silently, leaned on it for a moment. All the way down in the elevator, all the way back to Queens, for the life of him, Nick couldn't figure what the hell was going on.

CHAPTER 37

There was something noticeably different about his grandfather. Their last few dinners had been tense, and interrupted by cryptic phone calls. Twice they were canceled at the last minute. While Nick was not specifically excluded from various conversations, neither was he included. He did catch his grandfather glancing in his direction as he pressed an arm, hugged a visitor. He seemed to be reassuring them: Nick was okay.

At one point, Papa Ventura said, "Nicholas, it is better that you do not know too much of what is going on. Actually, very few top people know. You notice your cousin isn't included, even as often as you. We must keep information very tight." He clenched his fist against his heart. "There is a job of work to be done. Soon." He measured his grandson carefully, then nodded, apparently pleased by what he saw in the younger man's face.

Nick spent hours trying to figure where the meeting of the various factions of the families would be held. He prepared a list of twenty possible locations: in private homes; in warehouses; in a large business office at some company's headquarters on Queens Boulevard. It

was physically impossible to wire all the potential locations. He felt certain of only one thing: it would be
in Queens.

It would all begin with the RICO enforcement, and
they would call it down upon themselves by meeting to
discuss the arrival and distribution of nearly a billion
dollars' worth of China White.

Nick was convinced that no one—except his grandfather and probably one or two of his counterparts outside of New York, and the head of the China Triad,
along with his top associates—actually knew the time
and place of the forthcoming meeting.

It was raining as Nick finally left the office. He had
parked half a block down from the real estate office, in
front of an Italian bakery. As he unlocked the car door,
a bulky figure, carrying a bakery box, darted toward
him.

"Hey, Nick. Hey."

It was Salvy Grosso, clutching a white cake box to
his chest. "Can ya gimme a lift to the boulevard to the
Independent, Nick? My car's at the service station—I
gotta subway home."

He apologized for getting the car seat wet. Offered
Nick a fresh-made cannoli. There was something quick
and furtive about Salvy. He glanced over his shoulder,
swiveled his head left to right. His voice was a little
shaky.

"Hey, Nick, could ya do me a favor, huh?"

"Sure. You want the Continental Avenue station or
want me to go down the boulevard, what?"

"Well, there's a flower shop, ya know, right across
from the cemetery over on Metropolitan Avenue.
Could you take a run over there? I'll buy the wife some
flowers. It's her birthday and I forgot."

For some reason, Salvy asked Nick to park across the
wide street on the cemetery side where it was dark.

Instead of getting out of the car, he leaned back in his seat, took a deep breath.

"Hey, Nick, look. I gotta talk to ya. This is just you and me, okay?"

Nick regarded him coolly without answering.

"Jesus, Nick, this is so hard for me. Ya got no idea."

"What? *What?*"

"I don't know how to say it, so I'll just plain come out and say it, okay? Nick, you and me. We got something in common, ya know?"

Carefully, Nick said, "We sell real estate."

Salvy shook his head, hard. He waved his hand in front of his face, covered his eyes for a moment, then spoke very quickly. "I'm in the same line you are, Nick. Ya know. Ya give information, I do too. For about eight years, Nick. See, they got me, the narcs, on a dealer rap. I couldn't do no more time, Nick. I'm too old. Too tired. So I made a deal—I give 'em a few things. Here and there. Small stuff, you know."

"No. I don't know."

Nick could feel the man's desperation, smell the rancid odor of his wet clothing. And of his fear.

"Nicky, I'm in some trouble, ya know?"

Nick remained silent.

"Big trouble."

"Tell your priest. Why ya tellin' me?"

"C'mon, Nick. I know you're workin' for the feds. Nicky, I'm working for the local narcs. Eight years. I faced fifteen, Nicky. I never gave up nobody important. Just street stuff. But they been pushin' me now with all this, ya know, activity goin' on."

"What activity is that?"

Salvy dropped his head, rubbed his face roughly. He looked up at Nick, his squinty eyes blinking rapidly for focus.

Nick wondered if this guy was so good an actor. He

didn't know Salvy well enough to guess the source of his fear. Salvy's hands were shaking and he dropped the cake box and swallowed a huge sigh. He sounded like a drowning man.

"Nick, I can prove . . . wait, look." He dug into his inside pocket, removed a large leather wallet. He pulled a folded news clipping and pointed to a picture, which Nick did not look at.

"I think you better get the fuck out of my car, Salvy. If you're lucky, this won't go any further. I have to think about it."

Salvy Grosso reached out, grabbed Nick's arm, held it hard. "Nicky, I'm in big trouble." He glanced around, checking the windows. "I . . . I skimmed some cash. From some of the business deals. I . . . they're gonna find out soon. Nick, they'll kill me. Please. Nick, ask them to bring me in. To gimme witness protection. Like they're gonna do for you when this is over, right? Nick, please."

Nick pried the strong thick fingers from his arm, flung Salvy's arm away from him. "You're a dirtbag, aren't you, Salvy? Who the hell do you think you're tellin' this stuff to? Ya been stealin'? Sure, they'll find out. And you'll get what you got coming. What's the deal, comin' to me? Someone told you to do this?"

Salvy Grosso crossed himself frantically. "On my mother's grave, Nick, I'm not lyin'. I been giving local narcs things, ya know—all this time. Now they owe me. *They gotta get me out.*"

Nick reached across Grosso, unlocked the passenger door, and shoved the terrified man. The rain was slashing into the car. "Ya want the subway, Salvy, you can walk it."

Grosso handed Nick the clipping, unfolded it carefully. He reached up and flipped on the overhead light.

"Look at it, Nick. See? Those are the fed DEA guys . . . that's the boss, Coleman. . . ."

It was an old picture and hard to see, but Nick quickly scanned it and the short paragraph identifying the feds responsible for a big drug arrest. The picture was dated several years ago.

Grosso pointed a trembling finger at a figure to Coleman's right. "Him, see, there, him. Felix. A spic. Rodriguiz. Ya know who he is, Nick? Ya know?" Without stopping, he went on quickly, "That's Ventura's man in the DEA squad. He's the tip-off man. How do you think your grandfather knew about your troubles so quick, Nicky? Because of this guy. Lemme tell ya something . . ."

Nick crushed the picture and tossed it into Salvy's face.

"Wait, Nick. A couple weeks ago, the grand jury brought down indictments against two chief executives of your grandfather's companies. Rodriguiz musta tipped your grandfather; before the indictments were delivered, the two guys were somewhere in Europe, Nick. Check it out. Rodriguiz, anything he thinks the Venturas should know about, he gives the tip. He's your grandfather's man. Nick, please, tell them to get me out. Nicky, they'll kill me when they start checking the money—"

Nick reached over and shoved Grosso out so hard that he fell onto the sidewalk. Then he picked up the box of pastries and tossed it after him.

"You ever come near me again, I'll kill you myself, you little weasel."

From the rearview mirror, Nick got a fleeting glimpse of Salvy Grosso, still sitting on the wet pavement, reaching out his arms toward the departing car.

Nick drove into Manhattan, stopped at a public telephone. It was raining even harder than before. He punched in Caruso's number and spoke quickly.

"Don't understand the last part of the reading assignment. I'm in Manhattan."

"C'mon over and see me."

In less than half an hour, they sat across from each other in Caruso's office. Caruso shook his head.

"Grosso doesn't mean a thing to me. He said he was working locally. Did you check with your uncle Frank?"

"Just you."

Nick didn't identify himself when Frank picked up his home phone. "Mr. O'Hara, I'm with Robinson Associated Travel, and you've just won a free vacation—"

Frank slammed the phone down; within fifteen minutes, as expected, O'Hara called Nick at Tom Caruso's office. He listened, shook his head. "Never heard of the guy. Look, I'm gonna move around a little. Check things out. Get back to you."

Everyone who has ever worked as a cop suspects every telephone he uses to be bugged. Move around, leave cryptic messages, prearranged signals. For nearly an hour, Inspector Frank O'Hara's command post was a series of phone booths both inside and outside a large, suburban mall, filled with umbrella-carrying shoppers.

Finally Frank got back to him. "Called four main sources; guys who would know. One guy who knows everyone listed or not listed in the numbered file of informers. I got the best possible information, Nick. The guy was just a lowlife off the street when he went to work for your cousin. He was sent out to give you a song and dance, to see what you'd do. Listen, did anyone see you pick up Grosso?"

No one had. Nick was the last one out of the office. He'd been alone for about an hour and a half.

"Good. Good. That'll account for the time since he laid this on you." Frank's voice was low and serious. "It's that shit of a cousin of yours, Nick. Richie is playing his 'I'm gonna getcha' games. Grosso's not on any confidential agenda. His street record is for two-bit stuff—three-card monte and shit like that. He was a very bad pickpocket—got caught on the subway when he dropped the mark's wallet and hunched down collecting the money. A dummy. He's no informant."

Nick licked his lips. "Ya sure, Frank? Ya gotta be sure. The guy really was scared."

"Probably afraid he couldn't pull it off. Tomorrow, they'll all be laughin' and smackin' him on the back. Nick, get on the horn and call your cousin Richie. Anyone seen when Grosso left the office?"

"No. He left before me."

"Tell him it happened, like, ten minutes ago. Ya thought you should let him know."

Nick remembered Salvy's face; the trembling hands and dry lips. "Jesus, Frank . . ."

"Jesus, Nick. You know your crud of a cousin. He thinks he's laying another trap for you. Go on. Do the right thing. Hey, and keep in touch, okay?"

He waved good-bye to Caruso, who nodded. Frank would know, right?

Nick drove back to Queens and called Richie at his home in Massapequa. He repeated as much verbatim as he could remember, and with each word he felt surer of himself. Richie was playing again. He knew it. Richie didn't bluster and yell and curse. He just very quietly said, "Thanks for callin', Nick. Ya done the right thing. Ya done the right thing."

Nick stared at the phone, and for the second time since he'd last seen her he dialed Laura's number. He had no idea what he would say to her, what he wanted to say to her.

He just knew that he missed her. A lot.

CHAPTER 38

It was a quiet day at Ventura Real Estate. Nick checked records of industrial holdings: current rentals, pending rentals, bills collected and bills due. Tessie pounded at her typewriter, then announced she had an appointment down the street to get her hair done and to get some new look for her nails. For months, Tessie had been experimenting with long, clawlike fake nails, decorated with paste-on objects resembling—to Nick— broken glass. To those in the know, Tessie told him, they looked just like the real thing. The only problem was breakage: typing was tough with these fingers. Nick teased her: Wouldn't the computer be easier on her? She made a face.

Salvy Grosso hadn't shown up, but then he worked on his own irregular schedule. In the early afternoon, a young couple in their twenties introduced themselves as "Augie the Butcher's" son and prospective daughter-in-law. You know Augie, he's known the family for years. Nick sat with them, went through lists of houses—moderate, ya know, like cheap but it don't look cheap. There were some houses toward Metropolitan Avenue, unattached, one-family. Nice tree-lined streets. Unless they might be interested in an attached, more into the central part of the residential area of Forest Hills. He drove them around for a while. It was refreshing to see an honest reaction to such extraordinarily inflated prices. They seemed discouraged and somewhat bereft when they returned to the office.

Nick knew that some properties were kept at a good low price for "special people"—family-recommended, kids who needed a break on a first house. He cheered them up with the suggestion that he might—might—have something for them. Something he couldn't talk about right now. Nick winked.

"It might be exactly what you're looking for. In your price range. Good area . . . your father, he's Augie the Butcher over in Woodside?"

These two looked like the kind of nice kids who could use a favor. He would run it through the files; check it out. Nick had seen other young buyers fall into "wonderful deals." He told them to call him in a day or two.

As he watched the kids cross the street to their car, he felt a surge of pleasure. They walked arm-in-arm, the boy opened the door for the girl, kissed her, went around to the driver's side.

It'd been a long time since he'd seen something resembling innocence. Of course, he could be wrong.

He'd been thinking about Laura. Should he call again? When the phone rang, for a split second, he thought it was her. It was his grandfather.

"Nicholas, you come out to my house. I need to speak with you. You gonna leave now?"

All the way out to Westbury, Nick felt a cold inevitability deep inside his gut.

CHAPTER 39

Richie Ventura stood near his grandfather's fireplace, ignoring the nearly symmetrical flames that threw little heat into the room. He watched Nick refuse an offered drink, watched as his grandfather led him to the massive desk, picked up an envelope, and shook out the collection of Polaroids.

Nick took them one at a time as they were handed to him. The first photos were of Salvy Grosso, looking bewildered as he faced the camera. Then his face seemed to sink into itself, his eyes narrowing with fear, then terror, then horror, escalating with each photograph. The final photos showed Grosso's corpse. The wire cut deeply into his neck; surprisingly, there seemed to be little blood. The bullet hole in his forehead, small, blackened, seemed almost gratuitous. Further documenting the disposal of Salvy Grosso, there were additional snaps of his corpse being fitted into a plastic garbage bag, which was then stuffed into a trunk of a car. Obviously others were present, but only their shoetips showed in the photographs.

Nick could feel the blood drain from his face; his brain felt depleted. Finally, he looked into his grandfather's deep blue eyes, which had been watching him intently.

Papa Ventura then handed him about four or five more Polaroids. Vinny Tucci had met the same fate as his uncle.

Before Nick could say a word, his grandfather took the photographs from his hand, gestured with them to Richie, who carefully placed them in the flaming fireplace, one at a time.

Realizing he was speaking, but feeling remote from his own words, Nick asked, "Why Vinny? Why the kid?"

His grandfather shrugged. A gesture conveying, off-handedly, why not?

"Because we couldn't take a chance. Let me tell you, Nick. For a long time, we didn't trust Salvy. Sometimes you get a *feeling*. It wasn't just the money—you know he'd been skimming, right? It was that certain pieces of information had been getting into the wrong places. What he told you last night was the final proof."

"Papa, I didn't really think—I thought he was just . . ."

Nick shook his head, covered his eyes. His grandfather handed him a double shot of Scotch. "Drink this. I know what you thought." He glared at Richie, who shrugged. "No, your cousin wasn't testing you—no more of that crap, right, Richie? Nick, this doesn't happen very often anymore with us. Not like in the old days. But what was done last night, to both of them, was absolute necessity."

"Was that Richie's decision?"

His grandfather's face stiffened; his voice was hard and his tone was ice. "Anything like this is *my* decision. *You* got that?"

Nick nodded. He flashed for one split second: *Anything like this is my decision.*

"It's just that . . . I worked with the guy, Papa. I fig-ured him for the nervous type. Christ, could he have been *this* bad?"

As though answering a challenger, Nicholas Ventura said softly, "Obviously. Or else this would not have taken place." Then, seeing the distress on his grand-son's face, he placed a hand on his arm, then embraced him and pulled back.

"Nicky, Nicky. Let it go. You weren't responsible for this. Salvy was. Forget about it. He was nothin'. He was street scum, garbage. He could have loused up a multi-billion-dollar deal with his scared little rat mouth. And his nephew was no better—snoopin' around, get-tin' into things. Wouldn't have taken him long to make trouble himself. Now, no problem, okay?"

Nick shook his head slowly from side to side and shrugged. He glanced at Richie, who watched the flames consume the last of the photos. Richie turned and stared at Nick with a strange, small smile pulling at his lips. His eyes weren't smiling.

"Okay, Papa."

His grandfather suddenly changed. He let everything unpleasant leave him. He approached his desk, picked up a piece of paper, and handed it to Nick. "Hey, I got a phone call, you seen Augie the Butcher's kid today, right?"

Nick no longer wasted energy wondering how his grandfather got his information. "Nice kids."

His grandfather nodded. "Good, good. So, okay, you give 'em a call—you got that property on Ingram Street, right, the attached right in the middle of the block. What you do, you rent it to them for a while. Keep the payments low, let them get on their feet. Then, we give 'em a decent price. Augie's good for it, but let the kids take care of things for themselves for a while, okay?"

"Okay."

His grandfather led him to the hallway, stopped at the heavy, ornately carved mahogany door. He glanced around, then told Nick, "Within the week, Nick, The big one. I want you to know fully why I want this so much. I'm an old man—I need to rest, but I wanna know I done some good in this world. The money this whole thing can generate for me—without me so much as touchin' a gram of that shit—I can build companies, factories. I can leave some good behind me in ways that the straight-arrow suits only dream about. And won't have to make all kindsa deals with the government crooks. It's what *they* do, in Washington, all over. Everything, anything for personal gain. I'm gonna make a contribution." He nudged Nick with his elbow. "Something *special* will be set aside for Peter's dream, Nick. Animal shelters. The kid would be happy. It will make me happy."

His grandfather's face was benign; his blue eyes narrowed to match his easy smile. He had a self-satisfied expression. All his life's work would be accomplished and on balance. He would finish his life as a good and honorable man.

CHAPTER 40

Without planning it, Nick O'Hara drove from Westbury, Long Island, upstate to Spring Valley. He drove past the house Kathy had recently sold, without a glance. Headed a mile up the road to Frank O'Hara's home.

He saw Frank's Oldsmobile pulled up in the driveway; saw lights on inside the house. He parked in front of the house, strode to the front door, and pounded with his clenched fist. His aunt Mary, book in hand, opened the door, stunned. Before she could say one word, Frank shouldered her aside.

"It's okay, Mary. Go back inside."

He looked around, checking the street for prowling cars; finally grabbed Nick's arm and pulled him around to the back of the house. Half of the double garage had been equipped with Frank's woodworking equipment; pieces of furniture in various stages of repair or construction were strewn about. Frank didn't put on any lights and he moved Nick away from the window.

"What the hell are you doin' here, Nick?"

Nick's jaw tightened. He raised his chin, and, staring into Frank's eyes, realized for the first time in his life that he was slightly taller than his uncle. Slightly larger.

"You checked him out, right? Nobody knew him? It was all a game, a trick of my cousin's? You know what happened, don't you?"

Frank had been told about the double murder; the two bullet-riddled bodies found in a parked car in Brooklyn. Had been told the identities.

"Nick, I swear to Christ. No one acknowledged the poor bastard. Maybe he was some old-timer's snitch, some guy who played it close to the vest."

"Who'd you talk to, Frank? You knew Salvy Grosso had to be deep under. Fuck it, Frank, he was right *inside* the family, every day. How could no one have heard of him?"

Frank earnestly studied his nephew; his face softened. He shook his head. "Look. If it's any consolation, the guy was a dirtbag. Street scum. He'd sell his own mother and kids if it would do him some good. He was one of the lowest of the low, Nick . . ."

"How do you know, Frank, if you'd never heard of him?"

Frank shook his head. "No, Nicky. I only heard about him after his body was found. And Vinny Tucci? He was at the wrong place, wrong time, but he was considered a loose cannon. Sooner or later, he'd have ended up the way he did last night. One thing you gotta believe, Nick. If I'd a found out Salvy was a snitch, I'd have told you." When Nick turned his head away, an expression of disgust and anger pulling at his features, Frank said, "Listen to me. I tried, believe me or not. But I will tell you this. One way or another, he was a threat to your life, Nick. It was you or him, simple as that."

"Simple as that? Christ Almighty. Know something, Frank? All the things you've said about Salvy are the same things my grandfather said. And Vinny was nothing. Scum. A dirtbag of no value. He told me, forgeddabout it. Good guy and bad guy—you both said·the same thing."

"You took a stupid chance comin' up here, Nick."

"Right. I won't do it again. Good-bye, Frank."

Nick drove back to Forest Hills, his mind a total blank. He purposely sang along with the radio. He didn't want to think about anything. At all.

Back home, he made himself a cup of instant coffee, drank a little, poured the rest down the drain. He stared out the window without seeing what was before him. Salvy had been so totally discardable; not worth a second thought. Vinny? Nothing. Absolutely nothing. Nick could see, feel, smell Salvy's terror. The Polaroids were imprinted on his brain, the last conscious moments of the man's life; the second of his awful death.

God, he needed to talk to someone. He needed to be . . . heard. He dug in a desk drawer, found his telephone notebook. With an index finger, he punched out Kathy's number—hit a wrong button. Stopped. Thought about a long time ago. He would come home from some assignment, agitated, worried, concerned, disillusioned, filled with conflicting emotions. He had talked, sometimes for hours, and she would listen. The process would be renewing, cleansing. He had needed her presence, her cool, clean, uncomplicated certainty that he would be okay.

On the second try, she picked it up on the first ring. Her cheerful greeting changed; her voice' changed. "Nick? Well, this is a surprise."

"How are you, Kath? I've been thinking about you. I . . ."

"I'm about to go to bed, Nick. I've had a long day and I'm very tired. Outside of that, I'm fine, okay?"

He was unnerved by the desperation in his own voice. "Kath, I'm in trouble. Big trouble. I've got to talk to someone. I've got to talk to you."

She broke a long silence abruptly. "You were right the first time. You've got to talk to *someone*. Not me, Nick. You and I, we haven't talked, really talked in years. There is nothing I could possibly say to you, about anything."

"Kathy, I need you. Kathy." He stopped speaking. When she didn't answer, he said quietly, "I thought maybe, as old friends, I could discuss something with you. You could give me another perspective or . . ."

There was a new, quick impatience in her tone, her words revealing more of her early Bostonian clip than he'd heard in years. "Too late, Nick. We haven't been friends in years." She hesitated; then with obvious determination, she said, "Nick, whatever it is, I'm sure you'll work it out. You always do. With or without me. I . . . I wish you nothing but the best, Nick. I have nothing more to say to you, to discuss with you. I don't want to hear from you, Nick."

She hung up without another word. He held the receiver in his hand for a moment.

In the past, he could always turn to Frank. But the Frank O'Hara he had grown up idolizing, loving, and respecting was gone. In his place was a cold-blooded, ruthless man. No excuses; no apologies.

He punched out Laura's number, but disconnected before the first ring. He couldn't expect anything from her. He had no right.

Nick flopped on the sofa; played with the remote control, flipping from channel to channel. A cop show: big case, heavy investigation, solution within the given hour. Coupla guys got clipped, but hey, so what? They probably weren't worth anything. He wondered what their obits would read, their memorials.

There was no reason in the world why he had any right to reach out, to expect any kind of help, concern, understanding, but somehow he had known all along that eventually he would call Eddie Manganaro.

Within an hour, Eddie arrived at his apartment. Eddie's presence seemed the most natural thing in the world.

They studied each other carefully, looking first for the familiar, then confronting the differences that had grown between them.

Drinking nothing but coffee, Nick talked while Eddie listened. From the very beginning. Eddie nodded, interrupted a few times. He had wondered about the sudden, reckless gambling. Attributed it to the loss of both Peter and Kathy, Nick's escape. Had never realized what a huge debt Nick had been carrying. Or why.

"But Jesus, Nick, why did the robbery at the restaurant have to be so damn authentic? They got you on tape—Christ, didn't you know the DEA had it staked out?"

Nick nodded. He knew. He also knew that his grandfather had sources that would verify the reality, spot any fraud. Yes. He had put himself totally in the feds' hands. His uncle had told him he would be Nick's safeguard, should anything go wrong. But now, Nick wasn't even sure of that.

"Hey, if I louse up—make sure you compose a real funny memorial for me. Hell, name names, it'll make everyone go crazy."

Eddie reached out and tapped Nick's chin with his closed fist. "I'll write one in poetry. What rhymes with 'bastard'? I got it. How about 'outlasted'?"

Eddie's questions brought some light to dark places. "Yeah, too bad about Salvy and his nephew Vinny. But that was a done deal, right?"

"I guess, but . . ."

"Jesus, Nick, I'm sure you feel terrible about it. Wish

you weren't the guy involved with Salvy. But, buddy, you were. And it probably saved your life in the long run. The guy was runnin' scared; he probably would have ratted you out in some way or other. Think about it." Eddie studied his friend's wounded face. "Ah, Nicky boy, don't tell me you *really* thought there are still good guys and bad guys? *They* do what they gotta do. *We* do what we gotta do."

Finally, Nick came to it. "Here's what I gotta do, Ed. I'm pulling out. I'm dumping the whole thing. I won't go to their fucking meeting wearing a fucking bug, won't write up reports, won't testify, won't name names. I'm bailing out."

Eddie Manganaro, the Irish poster boy, shook his head slightly and whistled between his teeth. It was a habit that indicated to Nick deep thought; a search for a solution to a tough problem.

"Is there anyone, at all, in the whole thing who you trust? *Really trust?*"

"Tom Caruso. I'm planning to tell him about the fucking agent-mole, Felix Rodriguiz. Christ, wouldn't you think they'd have run a check on their own guys? Just a basic background check on the guy's assets? He doesn't drive a Ferrari, for crying out loud, but he must have his dirty cash stashed away somewhere. Why the hell didn't these guys check out their own?"

"Maybe they don't want to? Who the hell knows. But look, Nicky. You've gone all this way. If not you—who? If not now—when?"

"That from an old song? Or a Boy Scout oath? Sounds familiar."

"Put it in perspective, partner. You're all they got to round these people up for RICO, for openers. And, sooner or later, there's always your big rat rushin' in to make the deal. Look at Gotti—Teflon Don, my ass. I'm

sure your cousin Richie has his very own Sammy the
Bull."

Nick nodded. "Pauly the Playboy Pilotti would sell
his sacred barbells to keep from going to prison. He
knows where the bodies are buried, who put them
there, when and why."

Eddie grimaced. "Pauly the Playboy?"

"Funny. Remember the old days? When we were
kids, we'd hear about it—the vow of silence. We
wouldn't even snitch on each other, even if we had to
take a beating. Code of honor? No more. They've been
selling each other out for years now."

"There'll be a big rush on—wait too long and you
miss your opportunity. That's how it works. Nick,
you're not thinking of bailing out because of your
grandfather, are you? You two been getting close,
right?"

Nick shook his head. "He's an old man. What the
hell could they do to him?"

Eddie shook his head. That wasn't what he meant
and Nick knew it. He had told Eddie the whole story,
starting with his own father's death and what had really
led to Peter's murder. One way or another, it was all
at his grandfather's feet.

"I want to look him in the eye, Eddie. I want him
to know that I know the truth. I really want that minute
between us. Everything else between me and my
grandfather is bullshit. Life and death, that's the real
thing."

Eddie advised him to get in touch with Caruso as
soon as possible. Get Rodriguiz out of the picture.
Hang in; see the job through.

"If you bail now, Nick, don't count on anyone—not
your uncle, or anyone—to take care of you."

Nick nodded. They rode down in the elevator together, looked at each other and grinned. There was

that old reliability, that old trust and confidence. You watch my back, I'll watch yours. They'd been each other's safety.

"I just wish I could help you in some way. Up close, ya know."

"You've helped more than anyone could have, Ed. I mean that. That was your role in all of this, okay?"

Eddie had parked down the block and they walked along briskly in the light rain. What Nick didn't notice as it passed them by, heading for the driveway to his apartment building, was Laura Santalvo's car.

She had been thinking about Nick. She had listened to the brief messages he had left on her machine, and she felt a hunger and a loss and a regret at the sound of his voice. She figured she'd surprise him; just show up. She wanted to touch him, to see him.

She watched the two men walk along, stop at a car. Watched them talk, then, finally, reach out and hug each other—not in the automatic, meaningless way men had been doing in her world for years, but in a way that meant something. Strong, meaningful, trusting. She sensed something about Nick. She could barely make out his expression as she drove slowly past, but it seemed to her that Nick looked relieved of some heavy burden.

She was starting down Queens Boulevard toward Manhattan when it hit her. That bright red hair: the Irish poster kid with the Sicilian parents. His former partner.

Why would Nick, at this stage of his life, be seeing his ex-partner, the detective?

It could be for any number of reasons. Nick had left the department under a dark cloud. He had severed ties with all his old friends when he joined up with the family, made a new life for himself. Which shouldn't include an old cop buddy.

Laura pulled off the boulevard, drove around for a while, then got on Grand Central Parkway and headed out to the Westwoods, to that private enclave in Westbury, Long Island.

PART 4

ALL FALL DOWN

CHAPTER 41

Papa Ventura knew more about Laura Santalvo than anyone in her life had ever known. Yet there were certain things she kept hidden deep within herself, and that was the source of her strength. They sat across from each other in his library, she with her feet neatly crossed at the ankles the way she sat when she was a child and had confronted him at their very first meeting. He had been impressed by her courage, aware of her fear. She had thanked him properly when he had made arrangements with which her family could be happy. She had written him a beautiful, formal note, and along the sides were her drawings of lovely figures wearing beautiful clothing. He had saved it through all the years.

She took a sip from the lovely crystal glass of white wine, then put it on the small table beside her chair. He waited her out.

"Papa," she said finally, "I get so tired. I'm still jet-lagged, believe it or not, but I . . . just wanted to see you." She held her chin cupped in her hand, her eyes, smoky, intent on his. "I always feel better when I see you."

He nodded. "So. You are upset. Is it about the boy? Or about Chen?"

She shook her head quickly. "Oh, no, no. Anthony's fine. He's spectacular. And Dennis, we have our understandings. You know. It's probably stupid that I came to see you. And so late at night. I apologize."

"Old people don't need much sleep. Don't worry about it."

"It's just a stupid, simple thing."

"Nothing about you could ever be stupid or simple, Laura. Is it about Nicholas, my grandson?"

She was silent for a moment, carefully weighing her words. Making some decision. Aware that he realized, at this moment, how her mind was working.

"We had a stupid argument. Last week. When I came home. I haven't answered his calls. Because he expects an explanation from me."

"And you give explanations to no one." He paused. "Even when you might be in the wrong."

She stood, picked up the wineglass and drained it. She told him how they had come upon Richie Ventura in her apartment. How Richie tried to make Nick believe that they once had been lovers. She told him about the key.

"Did he have a key? To your place?" He caught the angry expression and smiled. "No. Of course not."

"He and his Playboy ape man strong-armed poor Luis to open the apartment door. Richie pulled a key of his own from his pocket, so that Nick would think—whatever he wanted Nick to think."

"Why didn't you tell Nick?" When she didn't reply, he said, "Because Nick should know better. He should trust you. Because he knows Richie and his mean games."

She came beside him on the couch, snuggled against

him, played with his long fingers as he squeezed her arm reassuringly.

"Maybe I expect too much."

"Well, from Nick's point of view . . ."

"I know, I know." She turned away from him, walked about the room, hugging her elbows. She moved with an animal grace, a determined step, wary, yet at the same time certain of who she was. Taking her time. As she had when she was just nineteen and had completed her second year in the design school in Milan.

When Nicholas Ventura, after tending to some business in Rome, had traveled north to Milan to visit Laura, he stayed four days. He was her lover, her first, and thus her teacher. He had known many women, and had become a good, considerate, knowledgeable lover. There was an unexpected rapport between them over the dinner table at his hotel. It was immediate, electric. It was mutual. He was cautious; she was a virgin. He did not want her to romanticize anything that would happen between them. He wanted her to realize this had no place in their future: just now, just for this moment in time. And, he saw, she seemed able to isolate events in her life. It was the way she too wanted things between them.

Those four days in Milan were the only time they had been together, but neither of them ever forgot one single moment. Between them were nearly forty years, yet together they were ageless. Two entities, dissolving and uniting; giving and taking; serious and frivolous. Lovers of the moment, without age, without definition beyond each other. For that time.

He taught her physically, but he also taught her from his own best instincts. "Never tell anyone where you learned what you know. That knowledge is yours. Throughout your life, you will learn—and teach—many things. They are yours, exclusively." He told her he would forever be a telephone call away, wherever in the world, or in whatever situation, she might find her-'self.

When she was ready, she told him, "I was going over tonight, to surprise Nick. I drove toward his apartment. I was planning to tell him about Richie and his stupid key and—"

"And?"

"And instead drove out to see you."

For the merest second, he caught her hesitation, but she regarded him steadily, leaned forward, and kissed him gently on the lips.

"I guess I can be stupid about things, like any-one else. I always feel better when I talk with you. I'm just . . . I've been so tired lately, Papa."

Abruptly, he asked her, "Tired of what, Laura?"

It was not a casual question. She could not just brush it off. There were too many years of knowledge be-tween them.

"Is there something *else* you wanted to tell me, Laura?"

She sat tensely at the edge of the chair, leaned for-ward toward him. Her eyes were bright, a darkening thunderstorm gray. "Maybe I'm just tired of my life. Maybe I want to settle down. Maybe I did a terrible thing, allowing my son to stay with his father. I think I might have wronged Su-Su, in a way. You know, Den-nis found her for me. As a substitute for my own child."

"Have you been a good mother to her?"

"I think so. I love her very much. But how would she feel to know that she was *shopped* for? Like getting a puppy to replace the one that died."

"That might have been the motive in the beginning. But the girl is a beautiful, successful, self-assured young woman. Last year, I saw her at Christmas time. She and my great-grandson Peter, they were talking so seriously. I think maybe you need a vacation. Some rest; not to have to work so hard for a while. You have no problem with the girl?"

Laura shook her head. "God, no. She was accepted at Harvard, Yale—everywhere she applied. That's very unusual, you know. She was very concerned. She asked them, each one, flat out, at her interview, 'If I were accepted, would it be because I am a double minority? A woman and Chinese?'"

Papa Ventura laughed. "Sounds like she's got a streak in her just like you, Laura. How did they respond?"

"The man at Yale said, 'With a four point zero average for all four years of high school, with all your outside activities, political involvement, I wouldn't turn you down if you were a white, pale-faced young man from a family who came over on the *Mayflower*.'"

Papa Ventura didn't understand any of this. "Life is so funny," he said. "Times change; standards change; values change. That's why trust and honor are so important."

"I always feel better when I come to see you, Papa. I was wrong about Nick. I will get together with him. Again, I'm sorry I came here so late."

He rose and they embraced; kissed gently, as a grandfather would a beloved granddaughter. She stepped back from him and they regarded each other for a moment. He was not going to get anything more from her.

She walked from the room in her gliding pace, and in a tough, tomboy way, she waved good-bye over her head without turning to face him.

She might have been surprised, or concerned, or puzzled, by the expression on his face.

CHAPTER 42

Thomas Caruso had served two years in Vietnam as a member of a military intelligence unit. It was supposed that his law degree with specialization in constitutional law would serve his country well. When he returned to America, he studied for vows in a strict, contemplative Catholic society. Before taking final vows, Tom Caruso realized that withdrawing from the world was not right for him. His Father Superior suggested he study for the active priesthood. But he soon realized that he did not want to be in the position of listening to the sins of others, relieving them of their individual guilts, freeing them from a sense of responsibility after being assured of their repentance. In effect, telling them that he had intervened, explained all to God, and had received an assurance that a few prayers and rosaries would secure their purification.

He had known for a long time that no one else could secure your purity, your peace of mind. Some men could forget; justify; excuse the most disturbingly inhumane deeds. Others could not. For a while, Tom Caruso put his life on hold.

While teaching some courses in criminal justice, he was approached by a recruiter for the DEA. He was offered a position as a deep, undercover supervising agent, who would work from time to time as the only contact with a vulnerable informant who must trust him implicitly. At the same time, he could teach whatever courses he wanted at the John Jay College of Criminal Justice.

Through the years Caruso had felt satisfaction in teaching, but he was always uneasy running agents. He felt a heavy responsibility for each individual he took under his care. Nick O'Hara was functioning as a triple agent. He had seen in Nick the building tension, the growing confusion, the constant worry. He could imagine Nick asking himself, late at night, Did I do the right thing? Did I give the right information to the wrong person? Am I blown? Am I about to sink?

He shot a few baskets in the gym at John Jay. Nick had sounded quietly tense but insistent. He knew now that the murder of this guy, Salvy Grosso, and of his nephew, had shaken Nick. He had described the Polaroids vividly, repeating, "I should have known how scared he was, Tom. I should have known what it meant."

He hadn't tried to tell Nick that the death of these two men wasn't his fault. Nick would have to sort that out for himself. He hadn't commented on the lack of value in those two lives. Tom had seen too much casual death and killing; he had no words to offer. Nick would have to live with whatever degree of responsibility he felt.

He had known Nick was holding something back. He was glad it hadn't taken him long to make this appointment. Nick was dressed in black sweats, too. They passed the ball back and forth, shot baskets, ran up and down the court. Finally, Nick wiped his face with his sleeve and signaled a time-out. As they sat on the bench on the isolated far side of the court, looking straight ahead, Nick said, "I have the informant at the DEA office. Felix Rodriguiz."

Tom Caruso didn't react. He had known it could be anyone. The fact that it was Rodney Coleman's number one didn't surprise him or distress him. It made sense. He nodded and Nick turned to face him.

"I gotta ask you this. Coleman—you trust him? Because he's gonna be running me for the rest of this operation."

Caruso thought for a moment, then nodded. "I know Coleman is a pretty cold fish. We served together in 'Nam. He saved my life once. Literally. Then, again, I saved his life the next day. We were the sole survivors of a mission that went very wrong. Yes. I trust him. I don't particularly *like* him, but I trust him."

"Get Rodriguiz out right away. I have a meeting with Coleman tomorrow afternoon. In some office in midtown. Some advertising agency. Rodriguiz should get picked up right away."

"As soon as you leave, I'll pass the word. I assume you have some proof?"

"You guys get the proof. Salvy Grosso, that dirtbag—all thanks to him for all the good it'll do him now. He gave Rodriguiz up. I imagine the DEA can prove it out . . . but nail him right away!"

"As soon as you leave, Nick. I swear. Do you know why Coleman wants to meet with you?"

"It's gonna happen. Very soon. In a matter of days. I don't know where. No one does—except my grandfather and whoever else has a right to know. At the last minute, people will be directed by phone—public phones—to . . . somewhere."

"So no bugs can be in place."

Nick nodded.

"So it'll be up to you, more or less. You okay with that, Nick?"

"I'm not okay with that. But I'm not okay with a lot of things." He studied the bland expression on Caruso's face. "But I'll do what I gotta do. I'll tell you this, Tom. I came close to bailing out. After Salvy and the kid. Jesus, I thought we were the good guys."

"We are. Relatively speaking." He snapped his fingers, just remembering. "Here's something that might cheer you up. You're getting an A for the term." He reached out and thumped Nick's shoulder.

"Oh, yeah. That cheers the living hell outta me, Teach."

He had dinner with his grandfather after a quick shower and change of clothes. It was a relaxing evening; the old man showed him some new plants and arrangements he was cultivating in his greenhouse, to be added to his medieval garden in the spring.

It wasn't until he was leaving that the old man embraced him, hard, and whispered in his ear. "Nicholas. Tomorrow night. You come here by six o'clock." Then he pulled back, looked steadily at the blue eyes reflecting his own. "This shows my trust in you, grandson. You will be part of it."

CHAPTER 43

Dennis Chen carried his briefcase under his arm. The younger of his two assistants, Dong Zhue Wang, carrying a laptop computer, was noticeably excited. He had never been to New York; he had never before flown on the Concorde. Yang Bun Lau, in his forties, was a more experienced traveler. He carried the tickets and documents for all of them, had supervised the handling of the luggage; he would deal with all the necessary bothersome details that would get them from one place to another as simply as possible.

Heathrow was well policed; luggage was carefully screened, passengers searched when it was appropriate. Signs prohibiting unattended luggage were familiar by now, impossible to overlook.

Both men stayed close to Dennis Chen as he headed toward the Executive Lounge, where a quieter, more peaceful atmosphere prevailed. Then there was a sudden commotion: a woman's voice calling loudly, shocking well-dressed travelers nearby. She was apparently screaming at her husband to hurry from the newsstand as their flight was now boarding—*they'd miss the plane*. The man, tucking magazines under his arm, candy in pockets, clutching tickets in his mouth, ran haphazardly through the crowd, leaving behind him a trail of angry people. He had knocked into a baby stroller and the young parents, furious but grateful their child hadn't been harmed, waved fists after him.

The faster he ran, the louder his wife's high-strung voice. He turned to look behind him—could he actually have hurt anyone?—when he crashed into Dennis Chen, who had no chance to brace himself before the impact. The briefcase flew from under his arm; he twisted, and a pain shot through his right leg. He landed on his right shoulder, his right wrist crunching beneath him. His face slammed into the floor, blood clouding his vision.

His companions stood immobilized for no more than a second. Their decision not to pursue the vulgar runner was predetermined: their responsibility was to Dennis Chen. Out of a crowd of concerned but helpful people, two more men came to his aid—his chauffeur, who always stayed at any airport until Mr. Chen's scheduled plane departed, with the boss on board; and another aide, not scheduled for this particular trip, who carefully glanced around and retrieved Mr. Chen's briefcase and handed it to Yang Bun Lau, senior to himself.

Don Zhue Wang gestured the crowd back with great, calm authority. He caught the eye of a uniformed employee of some airline or other, ordered that the airport ambulance be summoned immediately.

As he was carried off by stretcher to the ambulance, a tall, thin, middle-aged Englishman identified himself as a doctor and volunteered to escort Mr. Chen and his senior assistant to the hospital.

Dennis Chen's eyes gleamed with pain and he pulled his lips back tautly. He felt the doctor's fingers lightly touching, exploring the femur. He glanced over his shoulder at Yang Bun Lau.

Then he leaned close to Dennis Chen's ear and told him, "Your leg isn't broken, Mr. Chen."

Through clenched teeth, Chen answered, "Then do what you have to do."

The doctor slid his fingertips along the injured right wrist, which was indeed broken. The doctor adjusted his eyeglasses, which had a tendency to slip down his nose. He then reached into the standard black doctor's bag available in every emergency ambulance and removed a pair of long, sharp, narrow-bladed scissors.

He admired the fabric of Chen's beautifully tailored suit, regretted having to destroy such fine work. He cut carefully, exposing the injured leg. He then slipped his hand into his trouser pocket and removed a surgical hammer, searched out the damaged but not broken bone that stretched from the knee to the ankle.

"Take a very deep breath, Mr. Chen. This will hurt like blazes."

In the middle of the advisory, unexpectedly, which was exactly as he intended, the doctor brought the hammer down on the injured bone with tremendous force and strength. Yang Bun Lau turned his face away, unable to bear the terrible sight. The clean but jagged white bone was visible through the tear in the skin for just a moment, then was hidden by spurting, bright red blood.

"Give him a shot of something. Please, Doctor."

The doctor shook his head as he wiped the surgical instrument clean and placed it back in his trouser pocket.

"No need. He's passed out. Just let me get some of this sterile gauze; must press it to the wound, stop the hemorrhaging. A clean compound fracture."

He had let some blood run onto Chen's cut trouser leg. As he pressed against the wound, careful not to further displace the bone, he said, "His wrist is a simple break. His shoulder—I don't know. May be dislocated. We'll let the chaps at the hospital sort it out."

He cleaned Chen's forehead, which was bloody but no longer bleeding. "Might have mild concussion. Likely, that."

Chen was semiconscious as he was loaded onto a gurney and wheeled, quickly, to an emergency room for evaluation. Yang Bun Lau pressed his hand and felt a slight pressure in return.

He leaned down and spoke to Chen. "The leg, a compound fracture, requires surgery immediately. You will be fine. I will wait in your room. I will be with you all the time."

He was later established in a large airy room, in the private section of the hospital reserved for royals or foreign visitors of rank. He remembered nothing of his ambulance trip. He had a vague recollection of being introduced to an orthopedic surgeon, one of the world's best. "Did up HRH's leg when he injured it in a polo spill. Not to worry."

He raised his right hand to brush his forehead and felt a terrible ache from his shoulder back to the plaster-encased wrist.

The nurse approached, needle filled with morphine, voice starched, clipped, used to being obeyed. "Now, now, don't play with that hand. Lie there still; this will help you out a lot."

Chen shook his head: No. The nurse said, "C'mon, now, don't try to be the hero. No point to it."

When she saw the determination glaring from his eyes, from his set lips, she told him, "All right, then. But when you want it, you just press this little button for me. I'll leave it here by your left hand, all right? No heroes, right?"

When he told her in a dry, parched voice that he wanted his associate to come to him, she started to protest; again, his expression allowed for nothing short of compliance.

Yang Bun Lau assured him that everything was taken care of. A collection of all eyewitness reports, doctors' reports, X-rays and charts had been compiled, taken to the concerned people, faxed around the world after further local evaluation. And wasn't it fortunate, he told his employer, that Dr. Heddington, a heart specialist from London, had been at Heathrow awaiting his own flight. Not to worry; arrangements were made for the good doctor to take another flight, with a limo back to the airport.

The police had questioned and released the very distraught passenger who had plunged into him. He seemed to be a straight-arrow clerk who had been about to embark on a two-week vacation in Spain and now would have to make other plans. Chen would press no complaint. Things happen. All the time. The policeman's report had been added to all the other information.

Finally, medicated, alone, drifting, Chen floated somewhere between ocean and sky; and in the dark, as it encompassed him, he heard Laura's soft, concerned, warning voice.

CHAPTER 44

Madison Avenue was a deep canyon, held in place by tall, shining black structures with the ominous feeling of a space movie. Nick lit, smoked, and dinched a cigarette before entering the huge lobby of the building where he was to meet with Coleman.

There was a collection of upscale storefronts all around one side of the lobby, with openings both on the street and inside. Music came from somewhere. There was a fountain with a marble figure of a child, pouring water into an oval green pool. He looked toward the ceiling, a good three stories high: long balconies extended from various restaurants at the second level. People seated at white-clothed tables ignored each other as they glanced around. Or ignored the atmosphere as they pressed on with their business meetings.

Nick went to the main desk, situated in such a way that no one had access to any of the banks of elevators without passing through security. Four uniformed, smiling people—two men, two women—worked quickly and efficiently with both phones and computers. Yes, may I help you? You are here to see? Your name is? You are expected? Fine, go to the second elevator to your right. No? Fine, you may use the courtesy telephone at the end of the counter and you can clarify and they will get back to us.

Nick was expected, cleared, and sent on his way to the elevator, which shot quickly to the twenty-sixth floor. The door slid open and he was faced with a large white marble table, behind which sat four women who might have been wearing uniforms. They were dressed in simple, expensive little black suits; one adorned with a simple gold pin; two with bright neck scarves; one with nothing ornamental. One was a redhead, one a blonde; one had shiny black hair; the fourth, a black woman, had a neat, attractive, scalp-clinging hairdo. She caught his eye and smiled an automatic greeting. She cocked her head, as though they were old friends.

"Mr. O'Hara? Hi. I'm Dianne. Let me take you to Mr. Coleman's office. If I gave you directions, you'd get lost. I'm not good at directions," she added with a smile, and led the way.

She was small, tidy, assured. As she reached an office crossroads she faced one way, then the other, before turning. She grinned at him. "See? I would have sent you out into space."

"Never to be seen again, right?"

She studied him carefully, then said, "Oh, I'd have found *you*, Mr. O'Hara."

"I'd have depended on it, Dianne."

She stopped outside a small office, no more than a cubicle, with frosted glass on the window. She tapped twice, opened the door, and extended her hand. She winked good-bye and went back where she came from.

Rodney Coleman was standing at the window, surveying the city that stretched to the south. He squinted and made out the outlines of the World Trade Center buildings.

"Great view," he said, then turned and looked directly at Nick, waved a hand. "Not a particularly great office. Sit down, Nick. Sit down."

The round beige eyes watched him with interest, as though Nick was someone from whom he expected unusual behavior. He accepted Nick's silence.

"I *am* sorry about what happened to Salvy Grosso. And his nephew. He wasn't one of ours, by the way. Not that I'm blaming the P.D. Apparently, they had run him at one time. His name never turned up on any computer, or in any deep-pocket list." He shrugged. So there you had it. Not our fault. He turned toward the window and tapped the tips of his fingers together and said, "We *did* have some . . . but not very much, suspicion about Rodriguiz. I take full responsibility for that." He spun the chair around. "You won't see him again, I assure you."

"Thanks to Salvy Grosso."

Coleman shrugged. "I understand you will be with your grandfather tomorrow night. It is too bad we couldn't zero in on the location. We do have some bugs in place, by the way. Including in your grandfather's house." Nick's eyes must have betrayed his reaction. "What? You seem surprised."

"Not very much surprises me anymore."

"But I see you doubt me." He opened the deep side drawer of the inexpensive, modern white-topped desk and removed a tape recorder. "Want to hear some after-dinner conversation? Let's see—I hear he's got some new plants in his greenhouse."

"I didn't say I didn't believe you."

Coleman nodded. "That's right, you didn't. We have about twelve places wired. It's hard to stake out twelve places for surveillance work. Your grandfather has always been very smooth and careful. So, that leaves it all up to you."

The bright light eyes widened, showing white on top

and bottom. For the first time ever, Nick saw Coleman blink. His lids were delicate lavender-pink; his lashes the same color as his eyes and hair.

"I know you've been having some misgivings, Nick. Well, in your position, I would too. This probably isn't a good time to say this, but say it I must." He leaned back in his chair, his voice pleasant, conversational. "We have the video showing clearly, and with sound effects, your robbery of the bar up in Washington Heights. It would be good for about ten years, Nick, but you'd never last a month inside, you do realize that, right?"

"If I had decided to bail out, Coleman, it would have been long before now. And you wouldn't have had a chance to act on your videotape."

A delicate shudder hunched Coleman's shoulders. "Oh, is that a threat? No? Just a statement?"

"Any way you wanna take it. Look, let's get this over with, okay? What do you want?"

"Well, first let me tell you this. We have evidence on incoming merchandise. Christ, these guys are clever. They're shipping about one hundred fifty million dollars of China White within the next two days. But none of our action will occur until we have your evidence." He reached into his pocket, dropped a small brown envelope on the desk, pushed it toward Nick. "I assume you've arranged a hand-off to your professor—oh, don't look surprised. Tom and I go a long way back."

He stood up as Nick, without looking, put the envelope into his pocket. "Nick, I want to tell you. What you've done, are doing, are going to do, it's remarkable. I do know there are some deep personal reasons involved—" As he was about to recite Nick's history, something made him pause. He shrugged. "I will assume your motives are of the purest. Oh, and we are *eternally* grateful to you for helping us catch the rat in our midst."

Nick put his hand out, palm up. "The video?"

"Surely you didn't expect me to turn that over to you right now? At the proper time, Nick. Well, if you don't care to shake my hand, go with my good wishes. God speed."

Softly, Nick said, "Fuck you, Coleman."

CHAPTER 45

The logistics of the meeting could not have been more efficient had they been arranged by agents of Israeli intelligence. Papa Ventura had final approval and had made some suggestions to Dennis Chen. No one else, at all, knew where or when the meeting would take place. The safe house was in fact a safe house.

Each participant had been given a phone number, no two the same. They were to drive through a specified area of Queens, and, at exactly 9:00 P.M., stop at the nearest public phone booth and dial the number provided—the number of another public phone. After two unsuccessful tries, but only then, were they to try the second number given. The slip of paper was then to be destroyed: Burn it.

The caller didn't know to whom he was speaking or even where his call was directed. A few of the callers noticed that their area codes were not in Queens. There were two Bronx exchanges; some in Manhattan. And one somewhere in Jersey.

As directed, each next drove into the heart of the middle-income neighborhood of Forest Hills. At a particular designated location, the passenger left the car, whose driver would return at the same spot within one and a half hours for his pickup. Each individual, family man—from Philly, Atlantic City, Miami, travelers from Colombia, China, Thailand—was met by well-dressed, soft-spoken young Chinese men who provided escorts anywhere from two to four blocks from the drop point, through the quietly suburban community to Ingram Street.

Another escort would arrive, take the lead down the long, sloping driveway leading to the back of the row houses where the garages and back doors were located. Others being escorted from the next street would approach from the other driveway. There was nothing to attract any attention from the families in the houses backing on the house they entered. Some bedroom lights shone; some flicker of blue-white TV. There was nothing heard or seen of the arrivals; no limos pulling up, no loud noises or disturbances.

Once inside, they were led to a small, twenty-by-twenty-foot semifinished basement. The fiberboard walls had been whitewashed. The flooring was plastic tile. The one small window, overhead, at ground level, was covered with rough fabric. In the center of the room was what appeared to be a Ping-Pong table. Around it was a collection of folding chairs. They were here for security, not luxury.

As soon as Nicholas Ventura, accompanied by both Richie and Nick, ordered the driver of the blue Camaro to pull up in front of the attached house with the small cement patio, Nick realized where he was. Although the attached houses were physically the same, Nick realized they were at the house set aside for Augie the Butcher's kid. Which would be made available to him for a good price within a week or two. When it was no longer needed.

They were greeted at the door by Lee Dong Wen, to whom Nick had sold a similar house not three blocks away. To anyone watching, they were house guests who entered quietly, and whose car was driven off toward Yellowstone Boulevard.

In the basement, Richie looked around, clearly annoyed by the tight quarters, as everyone stood to welcome his grandfather. Only bosses were present, no second-in-commands except Don Ventura's grandsons. They were a mutually agreed exception. The Don was growing older and seemed somewhat breathless. He gestured them all to sit down, then stood himself.

"Before we begin, I have one very important request to make of each of you. And then one important piece of information to convey. The first request applies to every single one of us—including myself."

The request was put politely, but it wasn't arbitrary: Every man present would be searched. The two Colombians narrowed dark cold eyes, stared through the walls, ignoring the indignity of a search for guns or hidden recording devices. No family member, from anywhere, searched any other family member. There was to be no favoritism and no chances.

Nick watched as his grandfather was searched by Lee Dong Wen, who in turn was searched by Don Ventura. Missing, obviously, was Dennis Chen.

When everyone was cleared, Richie leaned over and said to his cousin, "Nice ring ya got there. I don't remember you ever wearing that before."

Without looking at his cousin, Nick removed the ring from his pinky. His son's class ring from junior high school graduation. Richie dropped it, apologized for his carelessness, examined it closely, then handed it back. Nick removed a familiar fountain pen from his breast pocket, uncapped it, plucked at the gold lever, then smiled as the squirt of ink just missed Richie's shirt.

Papa Ventura admonished them in a whispery voice. No time for stupid games. No food was offered; nothing to drink. Afterwards, whoever wanted entertainment would have the whole of New York City to welcome them.

When he had everyone's attention, Ventura reached into his leather folder and extracted some documents.

"Now for the information. Mr. Dennis Chen, our esteemed colleague, is not present. His place is taken, for this time, by Mr. Lee Dong Wen, who has Mr. Chen's complete power and authority in this matter."

Before he could continue, one of the Colombians, a large, heavyset, muscular man with a glistening bald head, thick eyebrows, and semidark eyeglasses, spoke in a very loud, suspicious tone. "Why not? Why is Chen not here?"

Ventura was not accustomed to that tone of voice directed at him. He stared the man down for a moment, in silence, then looked away from him. Deliberately, insultingly, not acknowledging his presence, he said, "Two nights ago, at Heathrow Airport in London, Mr. Chen was waiting for his flight to New York. As he waited, an anxious passenger, afraid he was going to miss his own flight, ran through the airport pushing people aside and knocked Mr. Chen down." As though sensing unasked questions, he held his hand up. "There were many witnesses to this accident. The passenger gave the police his business card." He displayed a faxed copy. "Dennis Chen was in great pain and was taken by ambulance to the Royal Hospital. X-rays showed a compound fracture of his right leg. It required immediate surgery, which was performed by an orthopedist who has attended many of the Queen's own family members. His card is also here. He had a broken wrist, a mild concussion, a cut on his forehead, a shoulder injury." Ventura shuffled through the various documents, then distributed them to the others at the table. "Mr. Lee has acted for Mr. Chen on other occasions."

Several of the Chinese nodded their affirmation.

"Nicholas," the gravel-voiced man from Philadelphia hesitated, then spoke slowly, "this has been—all of this stuff, the accident and the injuries and all—this has been, ya know, checked out?"

Ventura nodded. "By our own people. And by others. Yes. So, is everyone comfortable now? I regret that the accommodations are not so comfortable as meetings on this level should warrant, but we all appreciate the necessity, at this point, for absolute privacy."

Still standing, Nicholas Ventura surveyed the faces around the table. Then, in a clear, loud voice, beginning with the men to his right and continuing around the table, he named each participant by way of introduction. Some nodded self-consciously, some shrugged, seeming embarrassed or annoyed by the personal attention. The Triad members, one at a time, stood up, glanced around, nodded slightly, and sat down quietly. The Colombians stared at Ventura, then glared around the room. They were obviously angry at being named, even in this tightly secure meeting.

They settled down and waited expectantly as men from both ends of the table pulled out various papers, faxes, charts, and documents, and passed them around. Each offering was studied carefully. Notebooks came from breast pockets, as it had been made clear all copies were to be returned. Nick pulled out a large white envelope and began doodling: a large blue ink puddle marred the paper and soiled his hands. His cousin looked at him and grinned. Nick pulled a ballpoint from another pocket, raised his eyes at Richie, silently offered the pen for inspection.

"What'll that one do, stab me in the eye?"

Nick shrugged. He made doodles, stick figures, suns and moons, then absently clicked the pen, in and out. In and out. He chewed on one end for a moment, then resumed playing with it, rotating it between his fingers.

Before them all, on the rough Ping-Pong table, was the detailed itinerary of the China White distribution plan, by which the Italian-Colombian-Chinese triangle would launch one of the largest heroin disseminations in the history of the United States.

Abruptly, after they had been present for an hour and a half, or just under, all papers were collected and returned to Papa Ventura and Mr. Chen's deputy. Everyone here would be kept advised, specifically, of all matters pertaining to his sphere of operation. Hands were shaken all around; some present looked wary, evidently uneasy at the nationality of their new partners. Others were more outgoing, inviting anyone interested to a tour of the best restaurants in New York City.

Each man then exited as he had entered, discreetly escorted to the place where his car waited to pick him up. A few men, looking for a personally owned Mercedes or Cadillac, hesitated for a moment, then remembered: these were all rented, low-cost cars.

Nicholas Ventura and his two grandsons, shown to the front door on the first floor, shook hands cordially with their "host." Papa Ventura directed Nick behind the wheel of the empty Camaro, and gave him the keys. Richie sat in the passenger seat, Papa Ventura in the rear. Ventura instructed that they be driven to Metropolitan Avenue, in the vicinity of the cemetery.

Joe Menucci opened the door of the small car for Papa, leaned toward him, and spoke quietly, directly into his ear. With his right thumb, he jabbed toward the house from which they had just come. He looked at his watch, held up three fingers.

"Three minutes, that's all, Papa."

Papa Ventura took Joe's arm; shook his head; patted his shoulder. Whatever it was that Joe wanted to do,

Papa decided this was not the time. Menucci nodded; helped Papa out of the car.

The old man leaned into the open window of the Camaro and spoke in a firm but pleasant voice.

"Nick, you drive Richie out to Massapequa."

Instantly, Nick said, "I'm ten minutes away from my apartment, Papa. Why don't I—"

"Yeah, but your car isn't," Richie said. Shrugged; *hey, don't blame me.*

"Your car is at Richie's house. I had it driven there— just in case anyone might be following you. Do as I tell you and pick it up there." He raised his hand, anticipating Nick's protest.

That was all he said. He settled into the rear seat of his dark-windowed limo and Joe Menucci slammed the door, got into position, and drove off quickly.

"I'd offer to drive this piece of shit, Nicky, but what the hell. You're used to drivin' crap like this—I'm not."

Nick didn't answer. He pulled the car quickly into the line of traffic, nearly cutting off an oncoming car. He slammed his brakes and ignored the angry driver. Richie had flung his hands out; they hit the windshield, instead of his forehead.

In a quiet voice, Nick said, "For Christ's sakes, put your seat belt on. How'd I explain your cracked skull to Papa if you went through the windshield? Besides, it's illegal."

The other motorist, shaken by the near miss, was walking toward them, but Nick O'Hara just tooted his horn twice, waved, and headed toward Grand Central Parkway.

CHAPTER 46

Nick ignored Richie's running commentary on the various men present at the meeting. He joked about pissing off the guys whose job it was to drive around Queens for an hour and a half. Queens, for God's sake!

"Hey, did ya notice how some of the guys—'Philadelphia Pete' Pisarano—did ya see his face when he spotted you with Papa?" Nick didn't respond. "See, me, he knows me, right? But you—I don't know, Nick. Coupla guys raised eyebrows."

Staring straight ahead, Nick said, "I didn't notice anyone askin' Papa anything, did you?"

They got on Grand Central Parkway at the Forest Hills entrance. Traffic was fairly heavy in both directions. Nick reached for the radio, pushed a button for 1010 WINS—all the news, all the time.

"How 'bout we try for some music? Hell, I gotta lotta great CDs in my car. What's so interesting about the news, anyway?"

Nick turned the sound up. He sensed Richie studying him, but he watched traffic carefully, made sure he stayed in the proper lane, didn't hang to the right cutoff when he had to stay with the left lane.

Along with their retainers, more than a dozen men from the meeting were on their way to a little-publicized but very popular restaurant in Little Italy. The cook had been carefully selected, the menu scrutinized. Even the Chinese, in their quiet way, would be pleased. Who the hell could not like pasta?

"How come you didn't go out to eat?" Nick asked.

"How come you didn't?"

Childishly, Nick said, "I asked you first."

He had a hunch that Papa hadn't invited him, either. But Richie had to save face. "I tole Papa I ate before I came. You know my wife—whatta cook!"

After a long silence, Richie snapped the radio off. "Ya know, I been thinking, Nick. If someone, somehow, had bugged that meeting tonight, Christ, they'd have everybody. Under that fucking RICO, all ya gotta do is get with a coupla people, have a sitdown—hell, about anything at all, right? Like your kid's communion, or your daughter's wedding, right? And wham, they slam ya on RICO, right? That the way it works?"

When Nick didn't respond, Richie picked up tempo. "I know we was all frisked. Hey, you think them chinks knew what they were doing? I don't think they were very comfortable about it, do you? Hell, my chink, he hardly skimmed me. How about yours? They make all kindsa mikes now. Like your ring, for instance. I hope ya didn't mind I checked it out. Christ, we can't be too careful. You might have, *anybody* might have, ya know, come up with somethin' and have it all on tape and . . ."

Without answering, Nick abruptly pulled across two lanes of traffic, the cars he cut off slamming on brakes, barely missing running into other vehicles. Tires were screeching, drivers yelling. Nick brought the car to a neck-wrenching stop on the grassy median along the parkway. Only his seat belt saved Richie from a header through the windshield. Before he could utter a word of complaint, Nick was out of the car, around to the passenger's side. He flung the door open and yanked at Richie, who fumbled at the seat-belt lock.

"Get the fuck outta the car. Now. Right now."

Richie stood open-mouthed and watched as Nick pulled his jacket off, tossed it to the ground. He loosened his tie, then, annoyed, pulled it over his head. Nick was going nuts; Richie didn't know what to do. As he continued to undress, bringing his foot up, hopping as he pried his shoes off, then his socks, cars were slowing down in all three traffic lanes, nearly coming to a halt in the slow lane. Passengers slid windows down in disbelief to watch the tall, well-built, obviously agitated man pulling off his shirt, popping buttons in the process, then ripping off his T-shirt.

A carload of young women, delighted, began to chant: "Take it off! Take it off!"

Richie yelled, "Nicky, what the fuck ya doin'? Nicky, for Christ's sake, holy God, whatsa matter with you?"

Nick undid his belt, hooked his thumbs in the waistband.

"Ya think the Chinese guys didn't do a good search? Okay. Fine. Get over here. Get over here, *you* do a good search."

He pulled the fountain pen from one pocket of his pants, the ballpoint from the other. Aimed them, one at a time, directly at Richie.

"There, see? A little inky, but I gotcha, Richie. How about this one?" *Click-click-click.* He turned the ballpoint toward the traffic and yelled, "Say cheese! Smile!"

Then he tossed the pens at Richie, who recoiled, but not in time to escape a smear from the fountain pen.

He flung his pants at Richie, who fended them off with a raised arm. As Nick grabbed the waistband of his briefs and began to slide them down, Richie rushed over to him. Nick grabbed his cousin's wrist.

"Ya wanna get inside, Richie, huh? That what ya wanna do? Get inside my pants? Now's your chance, you moron."

Richie pulled his hand away, turned his back to Nick, tried to shield him from being seen by passers-by, who were now starting to make whooping, encouraging noises as they passed.

Over his shoulder, he said, "Christ, Nick, the cops'll be here. Somma these people, they got cellular phones. Shit, we don't wanna get picked up by cops. Not now. Not for this stupid thing here."

Richie's face had gone gray and his stiff hair stood up in all the wrong places. He darted around, picking up Nick's clothing, his pens, tossing them to his cousin.

Nick caught the clothes and to the regret of his audience, put his shirt on, then his trousers. He shook Richie's hand off his arm, shoved him toward the car.

"You drive. I just might crack us up in the next mile or so. *Capisci? You* understand me?"

Cars waited respectfully as Richie steered into the faster lane, which began to pick up speed. They ignored the honking horns, thumbs up and grins from some cars. A carful of girls came alongside, windows down, and they shouted in unison, "Nice bod!"

Richie muttered, "Stupid bitches."

Nick stared straight ahead for nearly a half hour, then, when most of the cars had turned off, his voice cold and deadly, he said, "If you ever—*ever*, for the rest of your life—accuse me of something like that, it'll be the last time you ever accuse anyone of anything. You got that, Richie?"

Richie's voice was higher than usual. "Hey, Nicky, c'mon, kid. Ya know, everybody's uptight just now. A lot is riding on this, ya know. So, okay, I got a little crazy. I mean, ya gotta admit, you went real nuts." A quick look at Nick's face and Richie shut up.

He caught sight of himself in the rearview mirror and began pawing at his hair, trying to force it back into its preordained alignment.

"All right, all right, Nick. Okay, okay. I'm sorry, all right? You and me, we never been together on nothing. Now, all of a sudden—look, if Papa wants you in, who the hell am I to say anything against his decision, right? But ya gotta understand, Nick—"

"I don't have to understand anything."

Against his will, not wanting to, unable not to, Richie, in a soft, pleading voice, said, "Hey, Nick. Look. There's no reason, I mean, we don't hafta tell Papa anything about this, right?" Silence. Then he thought of another approach. "I mean, what would Papa think, you goin' nuts right on Grand Central Parkway in fronta all them gawkers and all? Jeez, those commuters got a lot to talk about tonight, don'tcha think?"

"He'd be more interested in *why* I did it. Don'tcha think?"

"Well, so okay, neither of us comes out lookin' too good. So, deal, right?"

He took his right hand off the steering wheel, offered it. Nick looked at the hand, then at his cousin's pleading expression. He smiled. He took Richie's hand and gave it a very weak handshake, and said softly, "Maybe ya missed your chance, cuz?"

At the house in Massapequa, all the downstairs lights were shining; the master of the house was awaited. Richie offered his cousin a cuppa, maybe something stronger. Nick didn't answer. He got out, walked around, found his own car, and drove toward Forest Hills. 1010 WINS repetitiously reviewed all the news— all the time.

CHAPTER 47

Back in Forest Hills, Nick stopped in front of the building, slipped the doorman a ten-dollar bill, asked him to put the Caddie in the underground garage. He carried his socks, undershirt, and tie in a bundle against his chest. Fingered the pens in his pants pocket. His hand felt damp as he dug out his keys. Until the moment he had stopped the car on the parkway, he didn't know what he was going to do. He closed his eyes for a moment and pictured the scene and tried not to laugh out loud. He'd become hysterical. Now he needed to stay very calm. He was drained of all the anger he'd had to contain for so long. It was one helluva performance, even if he couldn't tell anyone about it.

Coleman, coming from the kitchen with a glass of mineral water, was dressed in his customary beige, not a suit this time but slacks, sweater with pale shirt collar lining his neck.

Tom Caruso stood up quietly, gestured with his chin, then poured Nick a cup of coffee. Nick dropped his clothing on a chair, then moved to the round dining table and sat down. He rubbed his eyes for a moment.

"There was a meeting." Coleman didn't make it sound like a question.

"Oh, there definitely was a meeting. Dennis Chen was absent. Seems he got his leg broken by some impatient guy rushing for a plane." He nodded as Coleman and Caruso exchanged glances. "There was documentation: doctors' reports, police reports, the works. Even copies of his X-rays. Modern technology . . ."

"Speaking of which . . ."

Nick ignored Coleman. Gestured toward Tom Caruso. "I gotta take a quick shower. I am somewhat ripe from the night's activity."

He went into the bathroom, adjusted the shower; stripped off his clothing. Back standing before Caruso and Coleman, he wound a towel around his waist, reached up and pulled off his briefs. Carefully, he inserted his index finger and thumb into the crotch of the underpants and carefully extracted a small disc no bigger than his thumbnail. He rubbed his testicles under the towel and grimaced.

"Got a little rough around the edges."

Expressionless, Caruso said, "A little chafe cream will help."

"Listen, are you *sure*—positive, *court positive*—that this little gizmo works?"

Caruso held the device in the palm of his hand. "It works. I'm betting my career on it. Coleman and I have work to do. Take your shower. You earned it."

Nick dug into his trouser pocket, extracted his two pens. Coleman stood in the doorway, pale eyebrows raised.

Nick tossed the fountain pen to Coleman, who leaped to avoid a splash of ink. Almost successfully. "Legitimate fountain pen. A good one. Worth over a hundred bucks. Won it in a crap game, long time ago. Maybe worth a lot more now. I prefer the good modern *click-click* ballpoint." He turned first toward Tom: *click;*

then at Coleman, *click*. Then at himself, in the mirror: *Click*.

"Where the hell did that come from?"

Nick shrugged. "Oh, I got my sources. You should be able to extract some fairly good shots of the participants. The light wasn't great, but what the hell. The last buncha shots—they will look kinda strange. My cousin Richie in various stages of hysteria. And a coupla shots of cars. Just ignore those, they were just play shots, okay? Don't mean a thing."

He wondered what his "runners" would think if they'd seen his performance. And the risk he took, actually tossing the pen camera to his cousin. What the hell, all undercovers keep certain things to themselves.

"We're headed for my office where we'll start a transcription of this tape, and the pictures too. If this pen is working," Coleman said.

"It's working."

"Good."

For the first time, he saw Coleman smile. It was an odd, almost painful grimace, but accompanied by the glow in his normally blank dull eyes it absolutely was a smile. He dug inside his jacket, then tossed a videotape to Nick.

"No copies, Nick. Caruso here will vouch for that, in case you don't take me at my word. Although, I can't imagine why you shouldn't. Tom's had the tape since day one. But I wanted to be the one to return it to you."

"Jesus, Tom, you had it all the time? You could have . . ."

Caruso said, "Hey, I gave you an A on your course, what more do you want from me? Ya do nice work, kid."

Nick turned the water up as hot as he could bear, soaped himself, turned his face up, felt the heat, then slowly, very slowly introduced more and more cold water into the flow, at the same time reducing the hot. By the time it was almost pure ice, his body was numb and unfeeling.

Just as his brain was.

CHAPTER 48

Laura Santalvo telephoned him the next afternoon. While Nicholas Ventura was being placed under arrest two hours ago, at his home in Westwoods, Westbury, Long Island, he had suffered a heart attack.

"I'm downstairs, Nick. On my way to Long Island Jewish Hospital. Can I drive you?"

They rode in total silence. Her face was expressionless. Her hands on the steering wheel were virtually motionless, moving only slightly as she kept in the fast lane. She followed the turnoff signs, and when they entered the vast hospital parking lot, she quickly pulled into the first available spot. It was a long walk to the hospital.

Neither of them spoke a word.

Nick went to the information desk, then Laura followed him down a long corridor. Follow the red line, he had been told; take elevator two; then follow the red line again. Follow the yellow brick road. We're off to see the wizard.

There was a uniformed policeman stationed outside his grandfather's room—a partitioned section of the intensive care unit. Nick spoke to him and was allowed to enter. Laura followed, but kept a discreet distance.

There was the pulsating sound of various monitoring devices. The very walls seemed to throb with their persistent rhythm. There were tubes in and out of his grandfather's body.

Nicholas Ventura seemed to take up hardly any space in the bed. He was a nearly flat presence. The only definition in the top sheet was the two raised points where his feet rested. He seemed diminished, arms thinner—or had they always been that thin, hidden by expensive tailoring? His hands were bony and trembling; no rings, no watch. Anything would probably slide right off. Tubes were stuck into his arms; fluids flowing and draining. His usually well-groomed hair was rumpled. Old man's hair, dry, flaky.

The bones were clearly visible under his stretched skin, which was taut and waxy. There was a light gray, sparse stubble along his chin and cheeks. His nose seemed longer, sharper. His lips were parted and dry, and a hissing sound came periodically from his mouth, which was sunken. For the first time, Nick realized that his grandfather had had false teeth, removed for his own safety, lest he swallow or choke on them.

This anonymous, skeletal, barely moving body without recognizable facial definition was, in fact, his grandfather. The lids rolled back, revealing the bright blue eyes, which focused and, finally, confronted him. There was a working of the bony jaws; a dry tongue flicked the stretched dry lips. Nick found a glass of water with a bent straw, which he inserted into the toothless mouth. There was a gurgling sound; some water was swallowed, some dribbled down the stubby chin.

In a barely audible whisper he asked Nick, "Why? Please, Nick. Just tell me why?"

A pathetic, shrunken, dying old man who had done most terrible things; issued horrific orders. Nothing but a shell now, stripped of all power, all affect. All responsibility.

Yet still demanding something of him. Through the large, bright and steady sky-colored eyes. Yes. He *was* still there, inside that pathetic shell. Demanding: *Answer to me. Right now.*

Nick leaned closer and without even realizing it, he pointed a finger. "No. *You* tell *me.*" When the expression before him went blank with bewilderment, Nick leaned closer. "Why did you order my father killed? He wasn't even thirty years old, Papa. His death broke my mother's heart. I was left an orphan, Papa. *Because of you.*"

The old man shook his head from side to side, but Nick persisted. No pity.

"No one takes that kind of action without the okay from you. And you gave Vincent the okay. For him to kill my father."

"No." The voice suddenly became strong, familiar. He motioned for some water, gulped. "No, that is not true!"

"Papa. I know the truth. He called you; you gave the order. Vincent wouldn't have given the okay without your permission."

"I told Vincent no." His voice, despite the slurping toothlessness, was fierce. "I told him to bring Danny to me. He was my daughter's husband; my grandson's father ... I would have worked things out. I loved Danny. I loved him." He closed his eyes for moment, then, the blue blazing with determination and sudden wisdom, he continued. "Ah, yes. I see now. I understand. Your uncle, your Irish cop of an uncle, told you this. So that you would hate me. Even your mother, my angel, she believed that bastard. Wouldn't listen to me, wouldn't talk to me." He gestured emphatically and nearly pulled one of the needles from his arm.

"God never forgave me, that I loved my daughter more than God Himself. Do you think I could hurt her like that? Never. *Never*. I sent Vincent away. He was outside the family forever for disobeying my order to him. And the two men with him, they didn't live to see the sun come up again. Vincent tried to blame these two men—they misunderstood what he intended. But they did what Vincent told them to do. This—this mick, this Frank O'Hara. He lied to you so that you would betray me. Let *him* answer for your dishonor."

He was exhausted. He reached for Nick's hand, clutched it with surprising strength, motioned him closer. The smell of death emanated from every part of him, encompassed him and the air around his failing body. "Nicholas, my namesake, you are my daughter's only legacy. I forgive you for this betrayal. Please remember: I forgive you. I understand. I am grateful God gave me this moment to tell you these things. That you know the truth. On my deathbed, as I will see God face to face, I swear: I never ordered your father's death."

When Laura touched his shoulder, Nick had to pry his hand from his grandfather's grasp. She leaned to kiss the dying man's forehead; her voice was soft and melodious. "I'm here, Papa. Laura's here."

Nick walked down the corridor and stood staring vacantly out the window, which was smeary, greasy, dirty.

He thought about the many faces of his grandfather. He had seen him joyous among his family during celebrations. A gracious host; a considerate guest. He had been a fearsome taskmaster to those who served him: kind and compassionate to those who performed well; ruthless to those who violated his commands or trust.

He had seen this man soften with love toward himself, toward Peter, toward Laura. He had undertaken to make himself a scholar. Was self-taught in vast portions of history and art and music. He was a connoisseur of beauty and harmony. He had sought oneness with nature and peace through meditation: through time spent in his unique brick garden. He solved problems for everyone around him who sincerely asked for his help.

And he ordered people killed.

Nick thought about his grandfather's determined rationalization over his involvement in the drug trade. He had no interest whatever in the China White trade. All he wanted was the money; his share of the multimillions generated from its sale. He only used, handled, dealt with *money*. Laundered it; invested in legitimate trade; put it to good use. He created jobs; funded schools for disabled children; had hospital wings named for him. Founded the Peter O'Hara Foundation for Animal Welfare.

And ordered a hit on Salvy Grosso and his stupid nephew. Just like that. Snap of the fingers.

Nick hadn't realized he was crying until he looked up, saw Laura through his tears. He wiped his eyes roughly with the back of his hand.

Her voice was steady and cool. "There's a room down the hall for patients' families. I checked it out. It's empty and there's coffee available."

She closed the door behind them; handed him a cup of coffee, opened a can of plain soda for herself.

"There are a few things I want to tell you, Nick. Papa said I should."

"Say whatever you want to say. I'm listening. If Papa said . . ."

"First, probably this isn't really important now. But it is to me. Papa said I should have told you right away, that night. But you know me. No excuses, no explanations, no apologies. So—this is just for your *infor-mation*, okay?"

No. She hadn't been intimate with Richie. Ever. And he never had a key to her apartment. Ever.

"I figured that out myself, Laura. And you were right. I shouldn't have questioned you."

Her smile was sad. "But you *didn't* question me, re-member?"

He smiled, too. "In my heart, I did. And you read me. *Remember?*"

Laura drank some soda, put the can down. She be-came very serious; looked out the window, then turned and faced him squarely.

"I have something else to tell you."

"Papa said you should?"

Her smoky gray eyes caught glints of ice from the cloudy sky. "He doesn't know this. I'm leaving for Lon-don tomorrow night."

He stood up, looked down at her. "Wadda ya gonna do, buy some more diamonds from your friend, Mr. Chen? Or did you hear about his broken leg, and you're gonna nurse him. What?"

"I'm going to visit my son, Anthony." She spoke quickly, not breaking the pattern of her speech, or she might not be able to continue. "Dennis's and my son, Anthony Chen. He is nearly thirteen years old. He's enrolled in a good school in England. A little sooner than expected. I want to help him settle in."

"Jesus Christ, Laura. Do you know what kind of a man Dennis Chen is? Do you know that he had one of his own sons killed because of the street drug deal when Peter got killed? *His own son!*"

She placed her forefinger over his lips and shook her head. Her tone softened. "Oh, Nick. My God, Nick, are you still so gullible? That wasn't *his* son. Anthony is his only son. He has two daughters who live with his wife in Taiwan. I don't know anything about any boy being killed."

Everybody lied to him. Everybody. "How do you know so much, Laura? How involved are you in all of this?"

"Not at all. Dennis has been my lover, for many years. We see each other from time to time, but when we are apart, we ask nothing, demand nothing from each other. That's how it is."

"*You* warned Chen not to come." It was obvious to him now. "Why? How did you know about the meeting? About the drug dealings, if you're not involved, Laura? Tell me the truth."

"*I always tell the truth*. I knew about the China White as sort of a peripheral reality. I know nothing, want to know nothing about any of your grandfather's ... dealings. Or Dennis Chen's. Neither of them ever brought me into anything. Each man has a special place in my life. I knew about a meeting because I've learned through the years to pick up signs. I didn't know when, or even why, or *who* would be gathering. Just that it was big. And very risky."

"What made you call Dennis? What made you suspect that ... ?"

"*You* did, Nick. Don't look so surprised. I told you, I pick things up peripherally. Through my skin, my bones, my lifelong way of knowing. It was obvious to me in this case. I came by your apartment one night and watched you and your redheaded friend, Eddie, walk from the building to his car. Your *partner*, Eddie. I came to apologize, maybe, to explain about Richie. The two of you held my attention. There was a closeness between you; a trust renewed. You've told me how good it had been working with him, the 'Sicilian Irish poster boy,' you called him. I tried to think: why would you be seeing him? For what purpose? None except that you were still a cop, Nick."

"So you decided to warn your . . . lover?"

"I warned Dennis because if I let him walk into a trap, I would lose Anthony forever. He is my only link to my son. He would disappear from my life and I would never be able to find him. Not ever."

"That was why you warned him?"

She turned away for a moment, then held him with a challenging stare. "One of the reasons."

He felt his breath catch. There was a knock on the door. He wrenched it open, then stepped back apologetically, nodding to an obviously distressed elderly couple. Nick walked back to the window at the end of the hall.

When she came to him, he asked, insistently, "If you suspected it might be a trap, why didn't you warn Papa? I thought you were so close to him—like a grandfather—"

"Oh, much closer than that, Nick." Quickly, she modified her tone. She didn't want to insinuate anything deeply private. It wasn't necessary. "I went straight to Papa that night. The night of the 'redhead.' We talked—about my not explaining to you about Richie. He said I should clear it up. Well, I just did." She narrowed her eyes and studied him closely. "He *knew*, Nick. He knew there was something else. He's known me since I was a child. I never lie. He asked me if there was anything else I *wanted* to tell him. Not that I *should* tell him. When I said no, nothing I wanted to tell him, Nick, he knew. It was in his eyes, in his expression, in his posture. He read me, clearly. He had a decision to make then. His own choice. I warned him in my own way. Message delivered, message received."

"You expect me to believe he walked into that meeting, knowing it might be a trap?"

"I don't expect you to believe anything but what you want to believe. If you want to know why he made this choice, I can make an educated guess. He was tired, Nick. Of all of it. Just as you've obviously been living a double life, so has he. Maybe he loved one part of his life and hated the other. Maybe that's why he made his choice."

She had so much information, so much knowledge of how things worked, how men's minds worked.

"If anyone else, *anyone*, told me what you've just told me, I wouldn't believe one single word. I'd be positive that person was up to her neck in all of it—the money laundering, drug distribution. Right in the middle of everything."

She held her wrists up in front of him, surrendering. He clutched them in his hands. Shook his head. "Laura, Christ, Laura, I'll never understand you."

"That's part of my charm, isn't it? We had fun with each other. And by the way, your grandfather—I know you haven't asked, but remember, I can read you— never asked me to get close to you. When he realized it, he just said that I should be very careful with you. That you are very vulnerable. I hope I haven't hurt you, Nick."

"I don't know what the hell you've done to me." He sighed deeply, ran his hand through his thick dark hair. "At least I had a chance to talk to my grandfather. I'm going to see how he's doing."

She blocked his way. "Too late, Nick. He's gone. I was holding his hand and he smiled at me and just let go. Just like that. He had a long life. I know he was very pleased that you came to see him."

Nick turned away. He paced back and forth, leaned against the window frame. His voice was husky. "God.

I'm glad I came. It would have haunted me all my life if I hadn't. I'd never have learned the truth. About my father's death. I finally got to ask him about what happened that day. Up on the structure."

"And what did he tell you?"

It was the way she said it. Softly. Almost sadly. The same tone of voice she had used when she said to him, "My God, Nick, are you still so gullible?"

She took his hand. "Don't say a word for a minute, okay? Listen. And think. *Why* would Vincent—not the brightest guy in the world, or the bravest—why would he go against an order from Papa? *Why?* Nick, Vincent Ventura wouldn't go up and down a staircase without his father's permission."

She nudged his shoulder lightly. "The only person your mother loved as much as you and your father was Papa. He was her personal god. He showed her only wonderful things in life; protected her; cherished her. But your mother was bright, smart, knew how to listen and to read people. After your father's death, she had one ten-minute conversation with Papa. And then she knew. *To the depths of her soul, she knew.* There was no way she would accept his lie. She had so many losses all at once: her husband, her father. Her heart was fragile, but what happened and how it happened, the terrible, unforgivable betrayal by her father, all contributed to her early death."

Nick dug his hand into his trouser pockets; he clenched and opened his fists, could feel his fingernails digging into his flesh.

"Your grandfather died a happy man, Nick. He knew you'd consider a deathbed statement practically sacred. That's a cop thing, isn't it?"

Of course, she was right. Everything she said made sense. His original motivation in all of this, his double-triple life, all these months living practically on the edge of paranoia, all his actions to avenge the long-ago murder of his father, the loss of his mother, and the painfully recent death of his son—they hadn't been misdirected.

Why in God's name, Nick thought, wouldn't a murderer also be a deathbed liar?

CHAPTER 49

Nick stopped at his grandfather's bedside for a moment, stared at the empty dead face, said a prayer, and left. He planned to go back to his apartment to sleep for a while.

Tom Caruso intercepted Nick in the parking lot. "Let's get in the car and talk. We've got a slight problem."

One look at Caruso's face convinced Nick the problem wasn't slight. It was major. The first part of Nick's tape was loud and clear: names of those attending, carefully articulated by Nicholas Ventura, were the highlight. Then the tape became garbled. Statements were disconnected to anything said before or after.

"When we tried to enhance it, all we came up with were sounds like clicking, chair-scraping, paper rattling, a humming sound. They could have been guys at a meeting anywhere, any time. At the end, we got you saying goodnight to your grandfather, I assume by the car. The pictures were excellent, Nick. We've had DEA experts ID almost everybody. But we are in the Dumpster with the rest of it." He stopped speaking and looked closely at Nick, who seemed to have blanked out. "Hey, you with me or what? You hear what I'm saying?"

Nick held his hand up. "Wait. Just wait a minute." He stared at Caruso, then asked, "Where've you got Joe Menucci? My grandfather's driver?"

Menucci, held as a material witness, was at Papa Ventura's home, trying to keep the old woman, Aunt Ursula, out of the way. Agents had come with an assortment of search warrants and were ripping through the house, room by room. Papa's sister was under the impression that they were dinner guests and she was upset: No one was in the kitchen cooking.

She didn't really recognize Nick, but he told her quietly that her brother Nicholas had sent him to tell her to get some rest. She seemed relieved, nodded, and disappeared.

Nick led Joe Menucci by the arm into the hallway. Through open doors, he could see men methodically going through all the papers, file cabinets, shaking books, dumping them on the floor. They were filling large corrugated cartons they had brought with them.

Joe the Brain stared hard at Nick, who leaned forward and rested a hand on the man's shoulder. "Joe, I gotta talk to you."

"How come you're here? Everybody else got picked up. I'm being held—material witness or some shit like that."

Nick said, "Me, I'm just the grandson that worked in the real estate office, *capisci?* So far. I helped them go through the files at the office. They closed it down for now. I'm nothing to them. Yet."

"Is it true, Nick? Is . . . is Papa dead? I heard it but . . ."

"That's why I'm here, Joey. To pick out a suit and clothes for him. Help me, you know what he liked best."

The intelligent black eyes blinked rapidly. Joe the Brain smeared the tears from his cheeks with the back of his hand. Nick knew how much pain the man was holding. Papa Ventura had been his world.

One of the DEA agents called them into the office. "How come there's nothing on this computer? Not a damn thing."

"Papa Ventura never used it. He kept it here for when kids came to visit. They liked to play games with it."

"Yeah? Well, somebody knew what to do. It's been swept absolutely clean. I don't think kids did that."

Menucci shrugged. He told the agent why he and Nick had to go upstairs. The agent consulted his immediate boss. It was okay; there were agents in Ventura's bedroom.

They stopped at the top of the sweeping staircase and Nick drew close. "I've gotta ask you something, Joey. You never had a chance to go back to Ingram Street last night, right?"

Joe raised his chin; his eyes narrowed. "What for?"

"Look, Joe. I know all about the bug you put in for Papa. See, when they find that, they got everybody real tight. Including me." It was obvious that Joe was suspicious. The bugging had been strictly between Papa and himself. Nick needed to convince him. "Look, I know Papa had you bug Chen's house . . ."

"He never trusted them chinks."

"I know that. And I know he wanted to have a tape of the meeting, to make sure, later, that all commitments were met by everyone. Christ, tell me where it is before these gloms get an idea and rip the place apart. Or Augie the Butcher's kid finds it and—"

"The kid wouldn't do nothing."

"But the feds would."

Joey leaned close, looked around, and whispered the

details, and they entered Papa Ventura's bedroom.

Joe the Brain swept the wide bed free of various items the feds had tossed haphazardly. Stoically, he selected from Papa's wardrobe a handsome midnight blue suit, shirt, tie, socks, pocket handkerchief, shining black shoes. They pulled down one of Papa's smooth calfskin suitcases. The agent checked it out carefully, then let them pack up the clothes. Joe folded, caressed each item, his large hands smoothing wrinkles, fingertips lingering for a moment.

"You talk to a lawyer?" Nick asked him, as they went downstairs.

"Not to worry. Taken care of; they can hold me a while, then I'm gone." His eyes filled with tears and his voice was husky. "Nicky, tell them to get Georgie the barber to fix Papa's hair, okay?"

CHAPTER 50

Joe the Brain had installed two state-of-the-art bugging devices in the basement of the Ingram Street house: one directly under the flimsy table around which the meeting was held, and one in the ceiling. Both tapes were perfect. Recorded on hair-thin filaments, the sound was loud and clean. Carefully, experts deleted Nick O'Hara's name during Papa's introduction. From both tapes.

Each voice had its own definition. Once identified by the DEA men, voice was matched to photograph.

Everyone breathed a little easier.

CHAPTER 51

It was nearly a year between the indictments and the various trials. During that time, five men from the Ventura and other families associated with them were killed in what appeared to be unfortunate accidents. Three others were left in luxury cars, motors running, with bullet holes to the head in the classic style. These events more than justified the no-bail policy for most of the top people and their close associates. Including and especially Richie Ventura.

From the Chen Triad, people "disappeared" in alarming numbers. Presumably legitimate businessmen, conducting presumably legitimate businesses, from Queens, New York, to Hong Kong, via Chicago, Detroit, Miami, Las Vegas, San Francisco, L.A., and other cities around the world, simply went missing. Along with records, bank accounts, the voluminous data that outlined and detailed the relationship of one company to another. No one knew where they went. They were just gone.

Dennis Chen reportedly went to a sanitarium in Switzerland to recuperate from his difficult leg surgery. He was reportedly seen in France, Italy, the Bahamas, Hong Kong, and London. There was no hard evidence of his participation in the China White deal, but he moved around. Just in case. His many legitimate businesses ran smoothly without him, just as he had always planned.

Joe Menucci was dropped as a material witness and retired to New Jersey.

The law of *omertà*—the vow of silence—depends on two things: The honor of the man taking the vow. And his understanding of the word "honor." The idea of self-sacrifice for the benefit of abiding by some words spoken at a ceremony, where small pieces of paper are burned in the palm of one's hand, kisses and hugs exchanged, promises asked and given: All that by now has changed drastically. When one man tries to live by his solemn vow only to find out his best friend plans to betray him, a reevaluation usually follows. When faced with life in prison, no chance of parole, many factors have to be considered. There were many deals made during the windup of the China White case.

Because of Menucci's tape, Nick's photographs, and tremendous amounts of other evidence, Nick never had to testify. He turned down a promotion to first grade detective. He banked the salary he had earned but never collected for all the months he worked on the case, and retired with a good pension. His uncle Frank O'Hara also retired to spend his years playing golf down in Florida.

Kathy called Nick one night. The old dog, Woof, Peter's favorite, had died. Would Nick meet her at Peter's grave? Together they scattered the ashes so that boy and dog would be reunited. Though somber, of course, Kathy looked radiant as she introduced Nick to the man she was to marry.

Nick stayed on for a while, communing with Peter, remembering their open, trusting, hopeful, loving boy.

He knew the kid would have been proud that his father had received a scholarship to Berkeley for graduate study. He wished to God it had been Peter who was going west to find a new life.

Despite the fact that billions of dollars' worth of China White was confiscated, and billions seized in money and merchandise, many more billions of heroin were held back by other dealers until things calmed down. Holding it back would only make the product that much more valuable. New resources for distribution, laundering, investment, and profit were on the horizon.

The Ventura-Chen connection was over, of course. Richie Ventura and many of his closest cohorts were convicted of a series of felony crimes and sent to Marion, Illinois, home of the toughest federal prison in the country. Numbers of other "family" members entered the Witness Protection Program and found themselves, after their usefulness was over, condemned to a life of lower-middle-class anonymity, boredom, and loneliness. Not to mention the terror of possibly being discovered by some very angry and ruthless former colleagues.

Members of families up and down the coast, headed by aging, not-quite-with-the-times old men, were convicted of further crimes. Younger family members began restlessly looking around for new leadership. They would find it, after a period of time.

Some law enforcement personnel in various agencies were promoted; shifted; retired; wrote books; joined private firms.

The word "honor" rarely crossed anyone's lips.

EPILOGUE

Nick O'Hara paced across his hotel room, glancing at his notes, biting into a large peach. He had never tasted fruit this marvelous. It was brought in daily from outlying farms some twenty miles from Rome. He had asked room service for a light breakfast: coffee, a little fresh fruit. The waiter brought him a platter of grapes, peaches, apricots, cantaloupe slices, honeydew melon wedges, and he just kept eating.

The thesis for Nick's master's degree from Berkeley had been "America's Late Introduction to Worldwide Terrorism." As a graduate student, he had taught some basic courses in criminology and police science. He brought something to the classroom that most instructors could never acquire: street experience. And that teaching experience was good preparation for his current employment with a government agency convened to combat the growth of international terrorism.

One of the things that unnerved him when he first delivered a paper in a foreign country was the time delay for translation. When he made a remark meant to be amusing, he felt sweat on his upper lip as a response to the stony silence that came back at him. After a delay, laughter exploded and he could relax.

Nick was winding up a three-week tour of participation in a series of international seminars. Rome was
his last stop, then home. To Berkeley. He took a quick
shower, put on a fresh white shirt, lightweight beige
garbardine suit, comfortable but handsome shoes, a
good silk tie. He had come to enjoy fine clothing, and
discovered at the same time that he had excellent taste.
He carried himself differently now.

Nick brushed his dark hair quickly; ran fingers over
his smooth face; splashed a little very-low-key after-
shave on his cheeks. He glanced at his watch, picked
up his thin leather case and checked that his notes were
in place. Not that he needed them; he had become very
good at speaking and thinking on his feet.

As he started for the door, his telephone rang that
strange, loud, double European ring. Probably someone he'd see at the seminar. He opened the door, then
stopped. He always found it hard to ignore a ringing
phone.

Nick picked up the receiver and said, "Hello?"

The voice in his ear, unheard for a few years, was
whispery, playful, challenging, and as familiar as his
own reflection in the mirror.

"Hi, Nick. Guess who's in Rome?"